THE
Quarryman's
BRIDE

Books by Tracie Peterson

www.traciepeterson.com

House of Secrets
A Slender Thread
Where My Heart Belongs

LAND OF THE LONE STAR
Chasing the Sun
Touching the Sky
Taming the Wind

BRIDAL VEIL ISLAND*
To Have and To Hold
To Love and Cherish
To Honor and Trust

SONG OF ALASKA
Dawn's Prelude
Morning's Refrain
Twilight's Serenade

STRIKING A MATCH
Embers of Love
Hearts Aglow
Hope Rekindled

ALASKAN QUEST
Summer of the Midnight Sun
Under the Northern Lights
Whispers of Winter
Alaskan Quest (3 in 1)

BRIDES OF GALLATIN COUNTY
A Promise to Believe In
A Love to Last Forever
A Dream to Call My Own

THE BROADMOOR LEGACY*
A Daughter's Inheritance
An Unexpected Love
A Surrendered Heart

BELLS OF LOWELL*
Daughter of the Loom
A Fragile Design
These Tangled Threads

LIGHTS OF LOWELL*
A Tapestry of Hope
A Love Woven True
The Pattern of Her Heart

DESERT ROSES
Shadows of the Canyon
Across the Years
Beneath a Harvest Sky

HEIRS OF MONTANA
Land of My Heart
The Coming Storm
To Dream Anew
The Hope Within

LADIES OF LIBERTY
A Lady of High Regard
A Lady of Hidden Intent
A Lady of Secret Devotion

RIBBONS OF STEEL**
Distant Dreams
A Hope Beyond
A Promise for Tomorrow

RIBBONS WEST**
Westward the Dream
Separate Roads
Ties That Bind

WESTWARD CHRONICLES
A Shelter of Hope
Hidden in a Whisper
A Veiled Reflection

YUKON QUEST
Treasures of the North
Ashes and Ice
Rivers of Gold

LAND OF SHINING WATER
The Icecutter's Daughter
The Quarryman's Bride

*with Judith Miller   **with Judith Pella

THE
Quarryman's
BRIDE

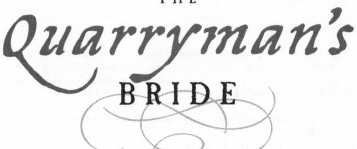

TRACIE
PETERSON

BETHANYHOUSE

a division of Baker Publishing Group
Minneapolis, Minnesota

© 2013 by Tracie Peterson

Published by Bethany House Publishers
11400 Hampshire Avenue South
Bloomington, Minnesota 55438
www.bethanyhouse.com

Bethany House Publishers is a division of
Baker Publishing Group, Grand Rapids, Michigan

Printed in the United States of America

Library of Congress Cataloging-in-Publication Data
Peterson, Tracie.
    The quarryman's bride / Tracie Peterson.
        pages cm. — (Land of Shining Water)
    Summary: "Historical romance series Land of Shining Water is set in 1890s
    Minnesota; Emmalyne and Tavin are separated by duty yet bonded by love,
    daring to dream that God could change the hearts of those keeping them
    apart"—Provided by publisher.
    ISBN 978-0-7642-1115-7 (cloth : alk. paper)
    ISBN 978-0-7642-0620-7 (pbk.)
    ISBN 978-0-7642-1116-4 (large-print pbk.)
    1. Families—Minnesota—Fiction. 2. Minnesota—History—19th century—
Fiction. 3. Christian fiction. 4. Love stories. I. Title.
PS3566.E7717Q37 2013
813'.54—dc23   2013002242

Scripture quotations are from the King James Version of the Bible.

The internet addresses, email addresses, and phone numbers in this book are accurate
at the time of publication. They are provided as a resource. Baker Publishing Group
does not endorse them or vouch for their content or permanence.

Cover design by Brand Navigation

13   14   15   16   17   18   19   7   6   5   4   3   2   1

Chapter 1

ST. CLOUD, MINNESOTA
APRIL 1886

Seventeen-year-old Emmalyne Knox tried to suck in air but found it impossible to breathe. Her throat constricted, and air couldn't seem to get past her mouth and into her lungs. Blackness edged her vision.

She reached out and gripped Tavin MacLachlan's hand, not caring if anyone thought it inappropriate. They were, after all, engaged to be married in less than two months. His presence strengthened her, and at last she found she could draw in a shuddering breath.

"Let us pray," Reverend Campbell announced in sober tones. "Father, we commit these bodies to the ground and these spirits to you. May your comfort be upon those who have suffered these losses. Amen."

"Amen," Emmalyne whispered along with the rest. She looked up to meet Tavin's sorrowful expression.

"Are you all right?" he asked softly.

"As well as I can be." She looked to her left, where her mother, clad in black, stood pale-faced and rigid. Rowena Knox's eyes were dry at the moment but swollen from long hours of weeping. Emmalyne's young brother, Angus, stood on the other side of their mother. Barely twelve years old, he favored his mother in appearance with his dark brown hair and green eyes. Their mother's Scottish and Welsh ancestry made her a handsome, albeit petite woman, while Angus already stood inches taller than Emmalyne. He would surely soon surpass even his father.

Luthias Knox might have been short of stature, but there was no doubt that he was a man of strength. Even now, Emmalyne's father showed no emotion. His ancestry, beginning with his origins in the highlands of Scotland, was proven in his red hair and fierce blue eyes. His brogue and hesitancy to spare a coin for anything even remotely frivolous left no doubt.

"I'm so sorry for your loss," Emmalyne heard Tavin's mother say softly, coming up to them with her hand outstretched. Emmalyne nodded, seeing Tavin's younger brother, Gillam, and sister, Fenella, standing just behind their mother. Fenella and Emmalyne were the best of friends.

Emmalyne looked into the warm gaze of the woman she would soon call mother-in-law. "I can scarcely believe they're gone." She let her glance return to the two open graves where her younger sisters, Doreen and Lorna, had just been laid to rest.

"The tornado took so many lives," Morna MacLachlan said, nodding her sympathy.

It hadn't yet been a week since a massive storm ripped through St. Cloud and Sauk Rapids. The devastation had taken lives in both cities, but Sauk Rapids had borne far more of its destruction. Emmalyne's family was just one of hundreds that had suffered the tornado's wrath. The house they had lived in was now merely a pile of wood.

"God's wrath," her father had said with an angry fist raised to the heavens. The memory made Emmalyne shudder even now.

"Dory was just fourteen," Emmalyne murmured, forcing her thoughts away from her father's near blasphemous anger. "Lorna only ten. How can they be . . . gone forever?" Her eyes welled with new tears.

Morna embraced Emmalyne. "'Tis a hard truth to bear. I dinnae see your older sisters. Were they unable to come?"

Emmalyne nodded, returning the embrace. "They live too far away and couldn't afford the trip. They have their own families to worry about now, so Mother didn't really expect they would come."

"Still, they would have offered her comfort," Morna replied.

Fenella stepped closer to join in the hug. "Oh, Emmy, I'm so very sorry. You know I loved them so." She, too, began to cry.

"I know you loved them," Emmalyne whispered. "They loved you, too." She relaxed in the warmth of the three-way embrace, relishing their comfort and support.

"At least I needn't bear this pain alone," Emmalyne said, finally pulling back. "You have been so good to my family. Mother said she would never have made it through those first few nights without your kind intercession and invitation into your home."

"Letting you stay with us was the least we could do," Morna replied. "You're soon to be family in every way, and there was no need to delay welcoming you into our numbers."

"And I have always wanted a sister," Fenella assured her. "Soon that very wish shall come true." She smiled, but the sorrow of the occasion kept it from lasting too long.

"Yes, but I know that our presence in your home hasn't

been easy. My father . . ." Emmalyne let the words trail off as she cast a quick glance to see if he'd overheard. But he was busy scowling at something the pastor was telling him.

"He can be most difficult." Emmalyne let out a long breath, as if the truth had been pent up inside her for quite a while.

"He's grieving the loss of his children, Emmalyne. You'll need to be patient with him. Come, Fenella. We must offer our condolences to Mr. and Mrs. Knox."

Morna's excuse for Emmalyne's father was gracious, but Emmalyne knew there was no good reason for her father's unyielding temper and harsh words. She'd never witnessed or received gentleness or kindness from her father, and she seriously doubted he was capable of either. Emmalyne had grown up to fear and venerate him, to never question his decisions or commands. Perhaps that was why she always cherished Tavin's tenderness toward her.

Emmalyne felt a gentle squeeze on her shoulder and turned to find Tavin there, his green eyes showing concern. She felt a rush of comfort from the love she found there. "I'd best speak my condolences, as well," he told her. "I wouldn't want your father to think me rude."

"Father won't think anything," Emmalyne muttered, "except how much this is costing him." She was glad Morna had already moved away to speak with her mother.

"Try not to fret, love," Tavin said close to her ear. "'Tis but a few short weeks, and you'll no longer have to worry about what he thinks." He drew her along with him and walked over to her father and mother.

Extending his hand, Tavin met Mr. Knox's hard-fixed stare. "May the peace of God be upon you. I'm heartily sorry for your loss, sir."

Father refused to take Tavin's hand, and Emmalyne's heart sunk at the sight. Her father could at least receive the sympathies of others without being uncivil. Tavin appeared unconcerned, however, and moved to give Emmalyne's mother a hug.

"Mother Knox, you have my deepest sympathy. I was very fond of Doreen and Lorna."

Mother nodded, her expression one of disbelief and shock. She had cried herself out in the previous days and now seemed at a loss as to what she should say or do. She looked down and shook her head. "I . . . I . . ." There were no words.

Tavin patted her arm, then turned to speak to his own mother. "I'm going to walk Emmalyne back to the house."

"Nay." Emmalyne's father suddenly interrupted the conversation. "Ye'll not be doin' that."

Shocked expressions fixed upon Luthias Knox. Emmalyne couldn't imagine what had gotten into him, but from the look on his face, she knew it didn't bode well for any of them.

"If you need us to stay, Father . . ." she began, but her words quickly trailed off.

By now the few attendees of the funeral were making their way back to their carriages, as the grave diggers began shoveling dirt atop the small caskets they'd recently lowered into the ground. Emmalyne hated the sound of the dirt hitting the wooden lids.

"Ye and Rabbie have been most good to us," Father finally said, looking with a grim nod to Robert MacLachlan, Tavin's father. "I'm sorry to say I cannae stay and repay ye just now."

"There's nothing to repay," Robert MacLachlan declared. "You would've done the same for me and mine."

Father nodded once, and Emmalyne thought she saw just

a hint of softening in his expression. He fixed her with a gaze just then that almost seemed regretful, something she'd never witnessed in her father's countenance before.

"We're movin' to Minneapolis," Father declared in his abrupt manner.

"But surely nae until after the wedding," Morna interjected. "'Tis but a few weeks away—"

"There will be no weddin'."

Emmalyne's heart began to pound, and her jaw dropped open. She held her breath and thought to do the unthinkable and contradict her father.

Tavin spoke up. "What are you saying, sir?"

"I'm sayin' the weddin' is off. Emmalyne has a responsibility to her own family. With her younger sisters dead and her older sisters married, it falls to her to remain and care for her mother and me."

An icy chill settled over Emmalyne. *The tradition!* She'd forgotten all about it. Having been the third oldest and far from the last daughter in the Knox family line, she had seldom given the tradition much thought. Now, however, she was the youngest daughter, and in the Knox family lineage that made her responsible to give up a life of her own to care for her aging parents. It had been done that way for generations.

"You gave your blessing. The wedding has been planned," Tavin protested.

Emmalyne looked at her father. His ire was up, and there was fire in his eyes. "Ye'd do well not to question me, boy. The wedding is nae gonna take place, and that's ma final word."

"But, Luthias—"

Father waved Robert off. "We have our way of doin' things, Rabbie. You know that as well as any man."

"For sure I do, but—"

"There's nothing more to discuss. I've just buried two of ma daughters, and we have a long trip ahead of us."

"Surely you can stay one more day," Morna argued.

"Please, Luthias. I don't feel at all well," Mother inserted, seeming to wilt before their eyes.

Emmalyne watched her father wrestle with the moment. He finally took hold of his wife's arm. "I suppose ye'll just be faintin' on the way if I try to see ma plans through. We'll stay one more night, but on the morrow we take our leave."

Emmalyne fought back a wave of nausea as everything she'd planned for crumbled to dust around her. The tornado had not only taken the lives of her sisters and destroyed their home; it had cost Emmalyne her future.

Sleep refused to come that night. Tavin's sister, Fenella, tossed just as restlessly as Emmalyne, and given the narrow bed, when one moved, they both did.

"I can't sleep," Fenella finally declared, turning over once more, this time onto her back. "I can't believe your father is doing this, Emmalyne. You must not allow it."

Emmalyne stared into the darkness. "What choice do I have, Fenella? I must respect his wishes. The Bible makes clear that I owe him honor and obedience."

"But you love Tavin."

"Aye. I do love him."

Fenella leaned up on one elbow. "And he loves you. You cannot go and leave him like this."

Emmalyne wished with all her heart there might be another way. "I don't *want* to leave him. You know I don't."

"Then don't. Go to him. Elope tonight." Fenella got up from the bed. "I'll go get him right now. You two can leave before anyone wakes up."

"I know you mean well," Emmalyne whispered through trembling lips. "But, no. I cannot. It would be a dishonor, and my father and mother would never speak to me again."

Fenella was already pulling on her robe. "Just talk to Tavin about it. Maybe he'll have some idea of how to make it all work. Your mother and father won't reject you. You'll see." She hurried to the door, pulled it open, and gave a little shriek.

Emmalyne sat straight up in bed. "What's wrong?"

"It's Tavin," Fenella said, stepping back. "He must've had the same idea."

Tavin stepped into the room and stopped at the foot of the bed. "I won't lose you, Emmalyne. You're to be my wife."

"Tavin, you can't ask me to go against my father and mother," she said, clutching the blankets around her. "It wouldn't be right. I love you, but we must give them time. Perhaps Father will see the pain he's causing and change his mind. I plan to speak with him in the morning."

"Let's just leave tonight and be married," he begged. "Once it's done . . ."

"That's what I suggested," Fenella put in as she lit a candle.

The warm glow barely punctured the darkness of the small room, but it was still enough to see the desperation on Tavin's face. Emmalyne wished she could offer him some comfort, but she needed it herself. She knew her father's mind was set, and she had never known him to back down once he had determined his course of action.

"Once we're married, they won't be able to undo it," Tavin said, trying again. "We can show them that we still intend to see to their well-being. I want your parents to be assured that they would have care in their old age."

Emmalyne shook her head miserably. "Father says that marriage divides the heart and mind. He doesn't think a woman can be both answerable to her husband and to her parents. He believes the tradition—"

"Curse the tradition," Tavin spat out. "It's ridiculous to put such a demand on someone's offspring. Your parents are being totally unreasonable in their expectations."

"But they're still my parents, Tavin." Tears were filling her eyes, and she blinked them away. "We both believe in the one God and that the Bible is His Holy Word. The Bible says that I am to honor my mother and father, that my days may be long. Don't ask me to defy the Word of God."

"I'm not asking you to defy God. I just don't want you to throw away our happiness together. The Bible also talks about a man and woman leaving their parents and cleaving to one another."

"Tavin, don't you see? We could never be happy . . . not with my father's curse upon us, and that's what it would be. He would never forgive me."

Tavin's expression changed from one of loving desperation to an expression Emmalyne had never seen in him before. "And that's your final word? You choose to worry more about your father's forgiveness than my love?" His implied accusation made her stomach clench.

"I choose to honor God, Tavin, as best I know how," she finally said, "and do as He would have me do."

"Right. So that your 'days may be long.' Well, have it your way. Your days will be long . . . and no doubt very lonely." He stormed out without another word.

Emmalyne felt a single tear trickle down her cheek. *So that's the way it is to be*, she mourned, pulling her knees up and leaning her head on them while a new flood of grief escaped.

Her father's anger and God's judgment . . . or her beloved's wrath and deep disappointment.

Somewhere in the midst of it all were the shattered remains of her heart.

Chapter 2

Emmalyne had just finished brushing her mother's long dark hair as her father entered the hotel room. He cast a quick glance in their direction, then motioned to Angus.

"Go bring the wagon around," he ordered his son.

At twenty-three, Angus was a little taller than their father and just as muscular. He finished securing his boots and stood to stretch. "Aye, I'll see to it." He left without further comment, and Emmalyne quickly turned her attention back to her task.

She twisted her mother's dark brown hair into a service-able knot at the nape of her neck. Rowena Knox was still a fine-looking woman, though the hardships she'd endured had taken their toll. Her spirit seemed broken, and she no longer showed any interest in what was happening around her. Emmalyne feared that her mother's melancholy had robbed her of any pleasure, for nothing seemed to please the woman.

"So we'll be going to inspect the house MacLachlan secured for us," Father announced. "There will nae doubt be a fair amount of cleanin' to do."

"I haven't the strength," Mother protested, her voice weak

15

and lifeless. She lifted her eyes in supplication to Emmalyne. "I'm afraid you'll have to see to it without me." Her voice was missing the heavy Scottish brogue revealing her early upbringing in the south of Wales.

"'Tis all right, Mother. I can tend to it."

For Emmalyne, the last decade was consumed by a routine that did not vary. Her mother's sadness left her with little energy or will, and hence the bulk of responsibility, as expected, fell to Emmalyne. Emmalyne, now twenty-eight, accepted her lot in life with as good an attitude as she could muster. Yet her broken heart had never really healed, no matter the amount of time she spent in prayer or reading God's Word. She kept searching for some sort of sign that would indicate God's blessing was upon her for her obedience. But misery and suffering were her only companions.

"We'll take a broom and mop. Soap and towels, too," her father said. "At the price we're payin', I'm sure we can borrow from the hotel. If we have need of more, I'll return to town. Rabbie said there's a good-sized pot out there for heating water outdoors and a working well."

Emmalyne finished assisting her mother and went immediately to her trunk. They had left Minneapolis only days before, and she hadn't wanted to return to St. Cloud for fear of running across Tavin again. But she couldn't help but wonder how he was and if he'd married yet. Eleven long years had passed . . . and for eleven years that unanswered question had whirled through her mind.

She'd exchanged a few letters with Fenella after their move to Minneapolis, but even those had stopped after a time. Fenella was no doubt married with wee ones, and taking time to write to an old friend was probably difficult to spare.

Pulling a heavy work apron from the trunk, Emmalyne nodded to her father. "I'm ready."

"Oh, I wish you wouldn't leave me alone," Mother begged, taking hold of Emmalyne's hand as she passed. "A doctor is supposed to come today, and I would rather not be here by myself."

"Hush, woman," Father demanded. "There's no need for Emmalyne to remain. She'll have work to do to set the house right. I'm not gonna spend a single dollar more on a hotel room than I have to."

Mother looked properly chastised and bowed her head. "Aye, Luthias, of course you are right. I pray you won't be long."

Emmalyne saw her father give a brief nod, but in no other way did he acknowledge his wife. It seemed sad that two people who had shared so much should be so distant. Emmalyne couldn't help but wonder if her father had ever shown love to his wife. If so, Emmalyne had certainly never witnessed it, and her mother was unwilling to speak on such matters.

Making their way downstairs, Emmalyne longed for a cup of strong tea and something to eat. She glanced toward the dining room. "Father, might I have a bit of breakfast first? The day will no doubt be long."

He looked at her with a scowl and gave an exasperated sigh. "Bring along something ye can eat in the wagon."

"What of you and Angus?" she asked, trying her best to sound sweet.

"We were up long before ye and ate at a decent hour."

Emmalyne nodded. "I won't be but a minute." She hurried into the hotel dining room and motioned to one of the serving girls.

"Yes, ma'am. How may I help you?" The waitress didn't

look that much younger than Emmalyne, and it seemed strange to be called "ma'am."

"I find myself in need of breakfast that I can take with me. I wonder if you have some biscuits and cheese, perhaps?"

"Let me see what I can find for you. I'm sure we can prepare something."

Emmalyne nodded and added, "Please hurry. My father is waiting."

The waitress scurried from the room, ignoring one man waving his cup for more coffee. Emmalyne glanced toward the door, where her father waited. He would no doubt be angry that she had delayed their departure; however, she'd been up quite late with Mother. When Rowena had one of her spells of sadness, it was best that she keep company with someone—and that someone was most generally Emmalyne.

When the waitress returned with a small wrapped bundle, Emmalyne put aside thoughts of the night. "Thank you so much."

"I put in an apple, as well," the girl said. "Should I charge this to your room or will you pay now?"

Emmalyne dug out a few coins and handed them to the girl. "Will this cover it?"

"Yes," the girl replied. "If you wait here, I'll bring you your change."

"That's all right," Emmalyne said, taking the food. "You keep it. I appreciate your quick help."

She made her way to where her father stood. "I'm ready. They were quite kind to prepare this in a hurry."

"I'm thinkin' the cost will be outrageous," Father grunted.

"I paid for it with my own money, Father." She hoped that might put an end to his grumbling, but of course it did not.

"The sooner we are out of this hotel, the better. Everything costs so much. Why, they charge more'n any man has a right to."

"But we have a clean room, and you and Mother a good bed," Emmalyne offered. She didn't bother to remind him that at least he had slept in one—she and Angus made do with the floor. "With Mother feeling so poorly, it's best for her to be close to a physician, Father. Didn't you say that this house we'll live in is outside of town?"

"Aye. MacLachlan said it was the best he could get us for the price I could afford. I'm sure ye can make it suitable. Your mother will just need to get better."

Emmalyne tried not to grimace at another reminder that the MacLachlans were once again going to be an intricate part of their lives. Why her father had decided to uproot his family and move back to St. Cloud was beyond her. Father trusted only a few people, and among those was Robert MacLachlan. But given the past between them, Emmalyne thought it strange they would return to the very place where they'd known such pain. Mr. MacLachlan must surely have offered Father a most lucrative deal, because as far as Emmalyne knew, money was the only thing capable of enticing her father these days.

She climbed into the back of the wagon and sat on the edge, dangling her legs as she ate her biscuit and cheese. Beside her were the various cleaning items her father had somehow secured. The bulk of their household goods were due to arrive by train that afternoon.

Biting into a biscuit, Emmalyne again thought of Tavin. Fenella had told her in a letter that Tavin had packed a few belongings and left shortly after the Knoxes' departure. What little communication she'd had from Fenella after that only mentioned Tavin briefly, stating that he had gone east in search of quarry work. He had planned to make his way to Maine, where he had heard the work was plentiful. His anger was all that seemed to guide him, and Fenella had been quite worried about him.

Are you still in Maine, Tavin? Her mind churned with questions, finally ending with the one that haunted her constantly: *Do you think about me as much as I think about you?*

St. Cloud had grown considerably since Emmalyne had left. When they had previously lived in the area, they had resided in a small house located between the city and Sauk Rapids, just to the north and east. Now, however, her father informed them they were to live southwest of St. Cloud, closer to the MacLachlans' home and quarry. Emmalyne prayed fervently that Tavin would stay away. She feared she'd never be able to put him from her thoughts otherwise.

She tried her best not to be bitter. God had command of her life, didn't He? At least that's what she had always been told and believed. Even after her father abandoned his faith, she had continued to trust God for wisdom and guidance. But her father had little tolerance for attending Sunday services, and that extended to his wife and children. Emmalyne knew her mother missed attending services; she missed them, as well, though as the years passed, Emmalyne had found occasion to slip away to church. Sometimes she'd even convinced Angus to escort her. He never complained, but neither did he seem overly interested. Emmalyne sometimes wondered about her brother's beliefs. He said little, most likely because he knew Father wouldn't tolerate such talk around the table. There was very little occasion for conversation at other times.

Trying a taste of the cheese from her perch at the end of the wagon, Emmalyne glanced around at the town of St. Cloud. There were banks, churches, and a bevy of storefronts that offered nearly anything a person could think of—jewelers, clockmakers, dress designers, stores selling ready-made clothing, barbers, and grocers. The town was nowhere near the size of Minneapolis, but it certainly had increased its offerings since Emmalyne had last been there.

"Looks like they've had fair weather," Angus said from the wagon seat beside Father.

"Yes," Emmalyne agreed. "Everything is so green and pretty." The sun had already warmed the morning and felt good against Emmalyne's face.

"Hope there's still time to get in a gairden," Father commented. "Rabbie said there are plum trees on the property."

Emmalyne finished one of the biscuits and put the other aside for later. "We can make jelly and jam. That will be good." She noted the busy streets were less congested as they made their way west. Here residences began to dot the landscape and businesses were fewer. A church rose up before them, and Emmalyne noted well-tended flower gardens gracing the property. Maybe it wouldn't be so bad living here. After all, she'd simply go on caring for her mother and father—Angus, too. At least until Angus found a wife and married. The thought brought a pang to her heart. That wasn't to be for her. She gave her head a small shake and went back to her inspection of the town.

She saw more trees as the wagon lumbered along away from the city proper. Emmalyne noted elms, maples, black walnut, and cottonwood among their numbers. She recalled that her father had mentioned there being a small stream on the property—a burn, her father called it—and a pond, if she remembered correctly. It gave her hope that there might also be willows, her favorite tree. As a child she had loved to hide beneath their sweeping branches and imagine herself in a castle.

The town eventually gave way to farmland and fewer houses. Emmalyne found herself enjoying the ride, imagining a simple outing to see the countryside with no work awaiting her. The sounds of birds and the rustling of the grass complemented her daydreams. How wonderful it would be to merely lie upon a blanket and stare up at the sky. Emmalyne smiled to herself and drew in a deep breath. The scents of the country filled her. Perhaps she had missed it more than she'd realized.

Several miles from town, Father turned onto a much narrower dirt road. The farmlands were now edged with forest and rocky outcroppings that bespoke the wealth of granite available to those who cared to try their hand at the difficult labor of quarrying it. Emmalyne's family had always been involved in quarry endeavors. Her father had at one time worked with the stone itself, but over the last twenty years he had contented himself with managerial tasks in the business. He was good with figures, and this made him an asset for invoicing and keeping accounts in order. In Minneapolis he had worked for a small factory doing just such work.

"How much further?" she asked, hoping her question wouldn't upset her father.

"Jest a ways," he replied, seeming to be deep in thought.

After years of living in the large city of Minneapolis, Emmalyne now could only wonder at life in the country. She was used to having things readily available to her. If there was a need, she could simply walk a short distance to obtain whatever was desired. It would be more than a short walk to St. Cloud, and since they had no extra horses or wagons, Emmalyne knew those trips would be few and far between. There would also be no electricity or indoor plumbing, both of which she would miss dearly.

Father turned the wagon down yet another even narrower road that dipped in and out of thickly treed grounds. Emmalyne looked upward at their shade and hoped their property might also be filled with such beautiful foliage. It might make for some very pleasant evenings outdoors, if the flies and mosquitoes would leave them be.

She tried to imagine their home. Father had said it was a wood-frame structure that had two large bedrooms on the first floor and a third upstairs. Emmalyne had already chosen the upper floor for her room—not that she'd really been given a choice. She imagined the privacy and ability to get away from the arguments her father was bound to have with Mother. It seemed the two were always quarreling over one thing or another—usually related to expenses.

Perhaps she would be allowed to paper her room. She would, of course, have to buy the materials herself. Her father would never pay for such a frivolous thing. Emmalyne still had some money of her own she'd received from sewing, but it was dwindling fast. She couldn't help but wonder if she might be able to take in some sewing here. Of course, with their home so far removed from town, it would probably be difficult to find customers.

The wagon slowed, and Emmalyne craned around to see if they had arrived. Her father urged the horses right. Emmalyne gasped, unable to silence her shock. The driveway was little more than a grass-grown path with ruts, but it served to bring them alongside a well-weathered house—if the place could even be called that. Signs of neglect were everywhere. Thick, high weeds had taken over what might have once been an attractive little yard. The walkway that led to the broken-down porch was obscured by an overgrowth of vegetation and debris.

"What hath God wrought?" she finally murmured.

Chapter 3

Alighting from the wagon, Emmalyne stared at the sight. Were they really to live here? The porch roof sagged at an odd angle and clearly needed support. The wooden steps to the porch were . . . well, missing, with the exception of a partial frame showing where they once had been. The structure itself was in great need of paint and repair. Two of the windows were broken, and the tail of a tattered curtain blew out of one as if shooing them away from the abomination.

"Well, donnae stand around like a stookie," her father declared, his Scottish brogue thick with irritation.

A stookie, an idle person, would not be a correct description of Emmalyne. There would be no rest for her in the weeks to come.

"Ye be a-cleanin' the bedrooms and kitchen first," her father ordered. "We'll be stayin' here on the morrow."

"But this place will take weeks to put in order," Emmalyne protested. "Unless, of course, you want to hire someone to help me."

"Wheesht! Be quiet! Ye know I donnae have the coin to spare. Ye can manage jest fine. Yer mither can help ye."

"But Mother has been sick," Emmalyne countered. "This wouldn't be a good place to bring her. She should be close to a doctor."

Her father turned a fierce scowl on her. "Ye need to be mindin' yer mouth, lass. Now leave us go in and see to matters there."

Emmalyne felt herself grow red at the rebuke, but she nodded, knowing that inside would probably be no better. It turned out she was right. The former owners had abandoned the place, it seemed, without thought to putting anything to rights. Several broken chairs were overturned atop a tattered rug. Beneath that, very worn boards made up the floor. They were so scarred and damaged, Emmalyne wondered if they could ever be properly sanded and stained.

She moved as if in a daze through the downstairs. The front room where the curtain flapped from the window was mostly empty. A thick layer of dust covered everything, and the fireplace looked like it hadn't ever been cleaned. Animal tracks and their droppings were easy to spot, and there was a strange collection of leaves in one corner.

"The frame seems solid enough," Angus offered hopefully.

Emmalyne looked at him in disbelief. "If it is, then I'm Queen Victoria."

He grinned at his sister and gave her a wink. "Well, Ye Olde Vic, you'd best not let our father hear you say so."

"Where is Father?" she asked, looking around in surprise. "He was right here a minute ago."

"Said he wanted to see the rest of the property. There's supposed to be a barn in the back for the horses."

"I can't believe the state of this place." Emmalyne wouldn't have dared to grumble so in her father's presence. "I suppose there's nothing to be done about it." She grabbed the scarf she'd tied around her neck and arranged it on her head to keep her hair protected from the dirt and dust.

"I'll fetch the mop and bucket."

"I'd rather you find the big wash pot Father said was here. I'll need that carted outside."

Angus nodded. "I can manage that well enough. Anything else?"

"A fire. I'll need a fire to heat the water."

Again he nodded. "Would you like me to chop some wood, as well? I doubt you'll get by with just one pot of hot water for this place."

"Aye." Emmalyne headed for the door. "We'll need plenty of wood, water, and soap to make this house livable."

She heard a scratching noise and looked over in time to see a large mouse scurry across the floor toward the kitchen stove. If mice were the only current residents, she'd count herself lucky.

"Angus, we need to be on our way," her father called as she stepped out onto the porch.

"Where are you going? I thought you were going to help me." Knowing she'd once more overstepped her bounds, Emmalyne tried to soften her voice. "I mean, I thought we could get more done together."

"I cannae. We're to meet with Rabbie and his men," Father said, surprising her with an actual explanation. "Ye get to work, and we'll be back by and by."

Angus came around the side of the house. "Your kettle is out back, Emmy. There's gonna be no moving it. I'll bet it weighs three hundred pounds. It's well positioned for a fire. I'll get you some wood."

"Nae." Her father shook his head. "We must be on our way. Yer sister knows well enough how to set a fire and chop wood."

He made his way to the wagon and took out the supplies from the back. He placed everything on the ground and then motioned to Angus. "Come along." Looking back at Emmalyne, he nodded toward the house. "Set it to rights, lass. We'll be back in a few hours to see what ye've managed."

With no further comment, he climbed into the wagon and waited only long enough for Angus to join him before flicking the reins. In all her twenty-eight years, Emmalyne had never known her father to show the slightest concern for her welfare. It never seemed to cross his mind that it might be dangerous to leave his daughter alone or that the work might be beyond her strength to accomplish alone.

Emmalyne sighed, gathered as many of the cleaning supplies as she could carry, and made her way into the house. She was glad she'd tucked her apron and remaining food into the bucket. At least she'd have something to eat if her father delayed in returning.

Inside, she pulled on the apron. Getting the water heating was of primary importance. She walked through the sad little kitchen and found an even sadder back door hanging from a single hinge. Though rickety, the stairs were still in place here and led to a nice clearing. The dirt was so hard-packed that it very nearly made a smooth surface on which to work. Not far from the caldron a rusty-looking pump gave her hope of easily accessible water.

Emmalyne inspected the caldron and found it to be serviceable. It would have to be scoured before it would provide an adequate receptacle for clean water, however. She quickly went to work gathering downed limbs and branches for kindling. She was happy to uncover a small collection of logs near the side of the house. A growth of new weeds among the old, along with dried vegetation from a previous summer, had hidden the wood from cursory glances. Fearing the possibility of snakes, Emmalyne gingerly gathered the pieces and looked around for an axe. To her dismay, there didn't appear to be one anywhere. She did, however, find an old handmade hammer. That and a wedge served her well enough, and soon the wood was split and a fire burned bright.

Next she turned her attention to the pump. Priming it, she prayed that God would let the water flow. Her prayers were answered. Water began to sputter through the pipe and fall onto the hard-packed dirt. Taking up a bucket, she put just enough water into the caldron to clean it.

Using water, shaved soap, and her mop, Emmalyne managed to scrub the iron pot. It wasn't perfect, but she felt satisfied for today. She knew it would take a great many cleanings before things were in the kind of order they would need. They would just have to abide the situation.

With the caldron finally in acceptable shape, Emmalyne filled it with bucket after bucket of water. She surmised from her trips back and forth that the kettle held about forty gallons. It was a good amount of water to get her started. Hopefully by the time she needed more, her father would have returned, and she could tell him of their need for an axe and maybe a saw.

With the water heating, Emmalyne went back into the house to figure out what to do first. Her father had said the bedrooms and kitchen were to be her priority, and she had to agree. However, Emmalyne had been cleaning house long enough to know that it was always best to assess the entire situation before actually starting.

On her way upstairs, she noted the steep and uneven steps. Near the top, Emmalyne tripped on the lip of one step and nearly fell headlong onto the floor. Righting herself, she frowned. "A ladder might have been easier . . . and safer."

In her room, sunlight filtered in not only from the single dirty window, but from a hole in the roof. The room wasn't large by any means, but it would be big enough for her. There was space for a bed and a dresser, but not much else. She would have to see if Angus could climb atop the roof to patch the hole—especially before the next rain.

Going back downstairs was just as perilous as it had been going up. This time, however, Emmalyne was more cautious, and she reached the bottom without further problems. She immediately inspected the other two bedrooms. They weren't much larger than the one upstairs. She determined that the bedroom on the front of the house was a tad smaller and figured that would be Angus's room. With this in mind, she started in on the other bedroom, knowing her mother and father would expect to take residence there. The room held a collection of odds and ends discarded from the previous tenants. Emmalyne took the castoffs outside and sorted them into stacks. There was always a chance she might find some useful items. Then she checked the water and found it still too cool. It didn't matter; there was plenty to do before she'd have a chance to wash anything.

If there had been a single bad thing about being left alone, it was that it gave Emmalyne too much time to think. As always, her thoughts drifted to Tavin and the life they might have known together had she not acquiesced to her father.

Fenella had written, begging Emmalyne to change her mind, certain that if Emmalyne gave the word, Tavin would come to the city and rescue her. But Emmalyne had given no such instruction. Then it wasn't long before Fenella had told her that Tavin had left. No one knew exactly where he was bound or when he might return.

A part of Emmalyne had been relieved. With Tavin's location unknown to her, she could better fight the urge to give up her promise to her parents. If no one knew where he was, there was no sense in her setting out to find him. At least that's what Emmalyne told herself. She also tried to convince herself that it was foolish to go on thinking of him—that he was forever out of her life. Unfortunately, her heart told her otherwise.

Looking about, Emmalyne couldn't help but wonder how close they were to the MacLachlans' property. She went on to reason that they must surely be within a short walk. Maybe once she'd arranged the house and Mother had adjusted to her new quarters, Emmalyne could make a visit and reestablish her acquaintance with Morna MacLachlan. That is, if Tavin was still gone from the area.

Emmalyne frowned and wrestled with her thoughts. It would be a blessing to see Tavin's mother again. Maybe Fenella lived nearby, as well. Renewing her friendship with Fenella might make the move back to St. Cloud bearable. The two girls had once been the best of friends, and Emmalyne missed their closeness. But as she imagined the two of them chatting about the years gone by and all they had experienced, Emmalyne suddenly felt less inclined to see her friend again. As little more than a glorified maid to her parents, her life had been dismal and boring at best. She could tell Fenella about books she'd read and a musical performance or two that she'd once attended with Mother, but life in Minneapolis had not left her with a wealth of pleasant memories. And what if Tavin decided to come home for a visit? Or for good? She shuddered. That would be sheer misery.

Emmalyne turned her focus back on the work to be done. By late afternoon, she was filthy and exhausted. She had eaten the last of her breakfast and had cleared out the two main-floor bedrooms and the front room, as well. The walls cried out for paint and paper, but she doubted Father would spare the coins required for either. A little whitewash would go a long way toward cheering up the little place, however. Perhaps she could spend some of her own precious money for that.

She had just started work in the kitchen when she heard the wagon pull into the yard. Rushing to the door, she was surprised to see the conveyance full of furniture and trunks. Her father appeared from around the side and began to untie a rope.

"Our things came in early," he explained.

Emmalyne nodded, pleased. "We can just put everything in the front room. I have it cleared out, and that would make a good place to organize it."

Her father glanced at her. "And what of the bedrooms?"

"Yours and Angus's are clean. I didn't worry about mine just yet. There's a hole in the roof, and I figure Angus will need to climb atop to patch it up."

"You figured that, did you, sister?" Angus teased from his side of the wagon. "I suppose for some of your good shepherd's pie, I might be persuaded."

"And I suppose I might be willing to make that for your supper tomorrow," she said with a smile. Emmalyne cherished her brother's good nature, especially in light of her father's harsh spirit.

Her father grunted and lowered a huge trunk from the back of the wagon. Hoisting it onto his back as though it weighed very little, he trudged toward the house. Angus picked up a couple of chairs and handed them to Emmalyne.

"I'll see to the roof momentarily," he told her.

"And the steps to the porch, perhaps?" she asked hesitantly, her voice low. "It's quite difficult climbing up and down without them."

He glanced that way, hand shading his eyes. "Aye. I'll see to it. I spied a couple of good-sized stones, large and flat, near the barn that might suffice for now. Most likely cut for some similar purpose. I'll see what I can do about bringing them around."

"Thank you." She trudged to the porch and settled the chairs on the rough floor before hiking her skirts to make the high step up. Her father burst out the front door, nearly knocking her aside, and without so much as a "by your leave," made his way to the wagon for more goods.

Back at the hotel that evening, they found their mother asleep. Emmalyne wanted nothing so much as a hot bath and something to eat. She was famished, but she knew she could never settle down to enjoy a meal in her current condition.

"I'm going to have a bath," she announced.

"There'll be a charge for that," her father said, frowning.

"Aye, but I cannot go to supper in this condition," she said, looking down at herself. "Please don't feel you have to wait on me. I can eat alone."

"We can bring your food to you," Angus offered.

Emmalyne thought on the offer momentarily. "That would be good. That way you can go and enjoy your meal without delay."

"And ye won't be needin' to spend good money on a bath," her father declared.

"Father, please." Emmalyne pointed to her filthy attire. "I must have a bath."

"Ye'll only get jest as dirty on the morrow."

"It's but a wee expense," Mother offered quietly from her place on the bed.

Father glared. "And a wee expense here and a wee expense there is takin' ma coin much more quickly than ye'd know."

"I'll pay for it myself," Emmalyne said under her breath, knowing better than to prolong the argument. She gathered clean clothing and her hairbrush without another word.

On the way down the hall to the bathroom, she couldn't wait to lock the bathroom door and isolate herself from the rest of the world. Especially from her father.

Chapter 4

Emmalyne sat in the back of the wagon beside her mother. The rest of their things, including newly purchased groceries, were stacked around them. While Father squared the bill with the hotel proprietor, Mother questioned Emmalyne about the new house.

"Is it very big?"

"No," Emmalyne said slowly, scrambling to find positive things to say. "But it has some lovely grounds. Of course, there's weeding and planting to be done. There's been no one on the property for some time."

"But the house is in good condition?" Mother looked so hopeful, but Emmalyne knew she couldn't lie.

"It was very dirty. Parts of it still are. There are repairs to make, but I think we can set it to good order in the days to come. I'm hoping perhaps to purchase some whitewash so we can at least freshen up the inside walls."

"And what of our things?"

"Father and Angus brought everything by yesterday. We stored it all in the front room, and today as I get more of the house in order, I will see to helping you arrange them."

"Oh, I'm hardly well enough for that." Her mother put a hand to her forehead and sighed. "I'm quite weak. I shall need to go straightway to bed." She sighed again and slumped against the side of the wagon. "I feel so tired."

"Well, Angus and I will need to set up your bed before you can rest properly," Emmalyne told her. She wasn't at all sure where she'd get stuffing for the mattress. Seeing her father approaching from the hotel, she figured it would be best to question him now, before they left town.

"Father, what are we to use for mattress stuffing?"

He looked at her and narrowed his eyes. "What do ye suppose?"

"Well, some fresh straw would work well enough for a time. I thought it might do us well to purchase some bales before heading too far from town."

"Always somethin' to spend more of ma hard-earned dollars on."

"I was hoping, too, that we might purchase some white-wash for the walls. They're in very poor shape, and painting would help—"

Her father's sputtered oath stopped her comment. He shook his head. "Mebbe ye'd like to be buyin' eiderdown instead of straw, as well." He climbed into the wagon seat and grabbed up the reins. "I swear, wimen cannae leave a man his coin." He continued to mutter after putting the horses in motion.

Emmalyne said nothing further. It was best to let him rant and vent his anger. For whatever reason, her father was of the mind that the entire world had one purpose: to rob him of his cash.

They drove away from the heart of St. Cloud, and Emmalyne tried her best not to worry about the matter. Her father would relent on the straw; after all, he would have to sleep somewhere, too, and she knew he wasn't about to make his bed on the floor. He might even give in on the whitewash, because she knew he expected a tidy and well-managed house.

Lord, she finally prayed, *you know our needs. It does little good for me to fret over them. Please provide for us.* She caught sight of her mother dabbing a handkerchief to her face. *And please help Mother to feel better. Amen.*

They were well to the west side of town before Father slowed the wagon and stopped in front of a hardware and feed store. He motioned to Angus and came around to the back of the wagon.

"Ye'll need to arrange things here to make room for the straw," he told Emmalyne.

"Aye, Father. I'll see to it now."

She wasted no time as her father and brother disappeared into the store, almost fearful that if she delayed, Father might change his mind. The wagon now held only the things they'd traveled with from Minneapolis and some crates of food items her father had purchased earlier. Emmalyne quickly stacked the three small trunks atop each other and pushed the crates together toward the front of the wagon.

It wasn't long before her father and brother reappeared. "We're to drive around back," her father announced abruptly.

Emmalyne didn't dare to ask about the whitewash, but she continued to pray that God would influence her father's choices. Her father might be of a mind to ignore God, but Emmalyne was quite certain that God wasn't likely to ignore Luthias Knox.

Her father parked the wagon near an open barn behind

the store and climbed down once again. Angus went with him to where two men were standing. Emmalyne saw her father produce the bill of sale, and the men sauntered off to retrieve the goods.

To her surprise, her father had purchased ten bales of straw. It was most generous, given his earlier comments, and Emmalyne felt very fortunate. Ten bales would go a long way to making their beds comfortable.

As they continued to bring bale after bale, Emmalyne had to assist Mother from her perch on the wagon bed and exchange it for a seat on one of the bales.

"This should prove more comfortable, anyway," she told her mother with a grin. "You can lean back against the trunks."

Once the bales were loaded, Father stepped toward the front of the wagon. Angus, however, turned and went back to the barn. In a moment, one of the workers appeared with four tins of whitewash, two in each hand. Emmalyne watched in silence as Angus took the cans and hoisted them into the back of the wagon. He threw Emmalyne a wink, then lifted her into the back, as well. Before he left her there, he pulled a broad paintbrush from his back pocket and handed it to her.

God had heard her prayers.

Once Father had the horses move out, Mother began to again question Emmalyne.

"Is there a good fireplace?" Her voice was low.

"I believe it will be suitable. I did a bit of cleaning on it, but of course we'll need to check the chimney. As long as it has sat idle, there are bound to be nesting birds within."

Her mother frowned. "Is it still terribly dirty?"

Emmalyne couldn't very well lie to her mother. After all, she would see for herself the extent of the situation soon enough.

"It is, but I'll be hard at work to set it right. Your bedroom is clean enough, and Angus will set the bed up while I find the ticks and stuff them. That way you can rest right away."

"Is there a fireplace in the bedroom?"

"No."

"What of a stove?" Mother asked.

"No, but I'm sure if the bedroom doors are left open the warmth from the kitchen and fireplace will provide enough heat."

"But what of the winter?"

Emmalyne shrugged. "Maybe Father will buy a stove before then." She didn't believe he would, but it was better than telling her mother they'd simply have to pile on additional quilts.

Mother seemed uncertain. "Perhaps we should have stayed in town," she murmured as she looked around. Their journey was taking them farther and farther into the less populated countryside.

"I would have liked that, too," Emmalyne admitted, "but Father felt it necessary to leave the hotel and save money. At least we have the whitewash and other supplies. I'm sure we can make a nice home. There are repairs that will need to be made, of course, but you mustn't let that cause you worry. Angus and I will see to it."

Her mother gave a heavy sigh and lowered her voice even more. "This place reminds me of . . . your sisters." She wiped a tear from her eye. "When I think on them, I can't help but wonder what kind of women they might have become."

"I know, Mother. I think about that sometimes, as well." She patted her mother's hand.

"And ye think of him."

The matter-of-fact statement surprised Emmalyne. She

didn't have time to mask her emotions as an image of Tavin filled her mind. "Aye. I do now and then."

Her mother nodded. "I sometimes think on him, as well. I wonder what kind of life you might have had with . . . Tavin." She barely breathed the name.

They said little else for the remainder of the trip. Emmalyne felt a growing sense of sorrow deep within . . . the loss of her sisters, the loss of her friendship with Fenella, the loss of Tavin. She fought against the feelings, however. They would serve her no good purpose. If she allowed herself to become melancholy like her mother, neither of them would be of any use. It wasn't easy to hold back her sadness, but Emmalyne had learned over the years that if she forced it down long enough, it would retreat, rather like an admonished pup.

When they finally arrived at the house, Emmalyne waited for her mother's reaction. The older woman looked at the house and then at Emmalyne. She seemed to want Emmalyne to confirm—or more likely, deny—that this was indeed to be their home.

"Father and Angus are going to shore up the porch roof, and then you'll have a nice place to sit in the evenings," she offered, scooting from the straw bale and off the wagon. "The kitchen isn't ready, but I plan to tackle that while you rest. I have the rocking chair set aside for you so you can sit there while Angus and I see to your bed."

She continued chattering on, knowing her mother's fears were great and many. "Of course, now that we have the nice whitewash, we won't want to place too many things before we have a chance to dress up the walls. Oh, and I think the rugs we brought from Minneapolis will work well in the front room."

Angus lifted his mother from the wagon while their father

stepped down and considered the house for a moment. "As soon as we unload," he told Angus, "we'll be headin' over to the MacLachlans."

Emmalyne frowned. Once again her father intended to leave her to see to all the things that must be done in the house. She decided to risk his ire. "Father, there are a great many repairs to be made. If you want to sit down to a meal this evening, I will have to have Angus's help."

Her father said nothing for a moment, but then nodded. "As ye say." He went to the back of the wagon. "Where do ye want the straw?"

Emmalyne was surprised he even bothered to ask. "The porch would be good." Despite the sagging roof, she felt it was the most convenient place to stuff the mattresses.

It took little time until the wagon was emptied of its contents. Meanwhile, Emmalyne helped Mother into the house. She could see her mother's immediate dismay, so decided to direct her attention elsewhere.

"If you sit here, you can see what's going on." Emmalyne helped her mother to the rocker in the front room. "Maybe if you feel up to it, you could peel some potatoes for me."

"This place is worse than I imagined," her mother said in a whisper.

"Aye, it has many problems, and a great deal of work is yet to be done." She tried to make the statement sound casual and unimportant, but Emmalyne knew exactly how her mother felt.

"Oh, this is terrible." Mother buried her face in her hands.

"It will be better soon," Emmalyne assured her, trying to hide her own dismay.

She left her mother sitting in the rocker and went to search for the mattress ticks. She found them quickly and immediately went to work. Stuffing mattresses was a tedious task; having rolled up her sleeves for the hot work, Emmalyne suffered countless scratches to her skin by the prickly pieces of straw. But there really wasn't an alternative. If she put her sleeves down, the straw would merely work its way through, and then she would have the added task of later picking it out of her clothing.

Once she had her parents' tick stuffed, Emmalyne and Angus carried it to the bed.

"I have the sheets and quilts ready," she told him. "I'll get the bed made, and you can help Mother. She's taking this rather hard."

"I know," Angus said, nodding. "City living was easier for her."

"Aye. More convenient and orderly," Emmalyne said.

Their mother hadn't wanted to make this move, but she had known it would happen with or without her approval. She had instructed Emmalyne in the packing and because of that, items that were necessary to everyday life were arranged at the top of the crate, while others used less often were settled below. The bedding, which had been freshly washed and ironed, had been carefully secured in cloth sacks before being put in the crates. Mother had hoped this would protect them from dirt and soot during the trip

Emmalyne unfolded her mother's quilts and sheets and smiled. It looked like the trick had worked. "They seem to have fared quite well." To her surprise, Angus helped her make the bed, and the process went faster with the two of them working together.

"As soon as Mother is in bed, I'm going to go upstairs and

see about that hole in the roof," Angus told Emmalyne as they returned to the front room.

"There's a hole in the roof?" their mother asked, shaking her head in disbelief. "Is there nothing good in this place?"

"There will be only good once we set it to rights, Mother," Emmalyne declared. "As you've often said, sometimes the only good to be had is what you bring with you." She smiled. "Now we have your bed ready, and you can have a little rest."

She was glad to get her mother settled in the back bedroom before turning to the massive endeavor of cleaning the kitchen. She'd managed a portion of the work the day before, but the room was nowhere near ready to prepare a meal. No doubt her mother would fret and fuss if she were to see the true state of that most essential room.

Emmalyne lost track of the time as she prepared hot water for cleaning. From time to time she heard hammering and smiled to herself. Angus would see that she had a solid roof overhead before nightfall.

For now she tore through the cabinets in the kitchen and scoured them thoroughly. She wasn't about to unpack her mother's good dishes until she could be assured that they would be safely stored.

Goodness, but what was Father thinking? This is no house in which to bring a sick woman.

The heat of the day was well upon them, and sweat trickled down Emmalyne's face and neck. She pulled the scarf from her head and wiped at the dampness, then got back to work. She was battling cobwebs near the corner of the room where the cabinets ended when the sound of an approaching wagon filled her with dread. Had Father returned already? She wasn't nearly finished. . . .

Climbing down from her perch on an overturned box, Emmalyne went to the door. To her surprise and horror, however, she saw a smartly dressed man climbing down from a small buggy. He was tall and lean, with brown hair that looked kissed by the sun. Emmalyne thought him quite handsome, and when he turned and smiled, she couldn't help but react the same way.

"Welcome, sir."

"Thank you. Is this the Knox home?"

Emmalyne couldn't contain her chuckle. "Such as it is. I'm afraid we've a great deal to do in order to make it a home."

"I'm Dr. Jason Williams. I saw your mother at the hotel yesterday and promised to check in on her today. When I arrived at the hotel, they told me where you'd gone. Since I had to see a few other patients out this way, I thought I'd stop by."

"That was very kind," Emmalyne said, fervently wishing she weren't so dirty. "Please come in. I've been working, as you can see, but my mother is resting in her room. I'll show you the way."

Dr. Williams entered the house behind her and followed her to the bedroom. Emmalyne opened the door a crack. "Mother? Dr. Williams is here to see you."

"Let him in," her mother replied, her voice sounding frail.

Emmalyne pushed the door open and stepped back. "I'll be getting back to work now," she said, excusing herself. "Let me know if you need me for anything." Dr. Williams nodded and smiled, and Emmalyne found herself wishing she didn't have to return to her task. He was such a nice-looking man. Tall too. She wondered what it might be like to dance with him, then chided herself for being silly. She had no time for dancing! Besides, there would be no man for her. Not with the tradition in place. That wasn't going to change.

She climbed back onto the box and busied herself with the cobwebs. Minutes ticked by, and Emmalyne couldn't help but wonder what the doctor might conclude about her mother's condition. For the last eleven years her mother had seen a bevy of physicians, druggists, and healers, and they always left her with bottles of medicines that seemed to only make her more disinterested in life and her family.

Emmalyne moved onto a chair in order to reach the very tops of the cabinets and considered what she would do if Dr. Williams recommended the same treatments as previous doctors. It had been difficult to convince her mother that laudanum and the like were bad for her, but such drugs had Rowena all but incapable of minimal functions. If yet another person of authority suggested this treatment, Emmalyne feared Mother would once again succumb to the addictive grip of such medicines.

Perhaps if I spoke to the doctor and explained the situation, he wouldn't be inclined to give her such things, Emmalyne thought. The man seemed quite nice, and perhaps he would agree that such medications did more harm than good.

"I hoped you would be nearby," Dr. Williams said, coming up behind her.

Startled, Emmalyne turned much too quickly and lost her balance. She caught her heel on the edge of the chair and began to fall. She let out a little squeal, trying to maintain her grip on the cabinet door, but the piece broke off in her hand.

The good doctor stood ready to assist, however. He caught her easily and gave a laugh as the chair fell over.

"You needn't throw yourself at me, for I must admit I've already found you to be quite fetching."

Emmalyne's face burned with embarrassment. "I . . . I'm so . . . so sorry. You startled me, and I lost my balance."

Their faces were barely inches apart. He grinned. "I know. I was here."

"Of course," she said, shaking her head. "Thank you."

Emmalyne grew uncomfortable as he continued to support her. "Uh, you can put me down now."

"I suppose I should." He flashed her a smile. "But it seems such a shame." He chuckled as he let her feet touch the floor, waiting to release her until she appeared stable.

Emmalyne brushed back her hair that had escaped its protective scarf and tried to regain her dignity. "How is Mother?"

"I think she'll be just fine. I recommended she get outdoors more. The fresh air and sunshine will do her more good than anything. You might consider setting up a place for her outside. She could rest there and read, watch the birds."

"I think I could arrange that," Emmalyne said, relieved that he wasn't offering yet another drug. "Do you have any idea of what's wrong with her?"

"Not in full. At this moment I don't feel I know her well enough to make a complete diagnosis. She seems exhausted. Perhaps the move has been harder on her than anyone realizes."

Emmalyne nodded. "Maybe. She has been quite tired for a very long time, however."

"Well, I shall return tomorrow to check on her again. Maybe I'll have a better chance to discuss her condition with her. Or with you."

Emmalyne couldn't think of anything to say. Dr. Williams's presence made her most . . . uneasy. It wouldn't be hard at all to lose herself in those blue eyes and deep voice.

"I suppose until tomorrow . . ." he said, letting the words trail off.

"Hopefully I'll have things in better order when you come again," Emmalyne said, feeling silly about her girlish thoughts. "Perhaps then I can offer you some tea."

"Maybe you should stay off the chairs. Unless, of course, someone is around to catch you." He smiled and walked from the room, leaving Emmalyne fighting the urge to follow him.

Chapter 5

Dr. Jason Williams was whistling a tune by the time he returned to St. Cloud. He strolled into Dr. John Schultz's office with a smile on his face and plans in his heart. Plans to once again see Emmalyne Knox.

"You seem mighty chipper," the older doctor said, looking up from his desk.

"I am. I just might be in love," Jason said, feeling sheepish but also exhilarated.

Dr. Schultz shook his head. "I thought you were tending patients. Seemed to me it was mostly older folks. How is it that you found time to fall in love on the way?"

Jason laughed and sank down into the leather chair opposite Dr. Schultz's desk. "I went to tend to Mrs. Knox and found she has a beautiful cinnamon-haired, blue-eyed daughter . . . Emmalyne."

Schultz chuckled, leaned back, and folded his hands. "And you found her condition to be much more interesting than that of her mother's, I take it?"

Shrugging, Jason picked lint from his trouser leg. "I suppose I was taken by surprise. In more ways than one. The young lady fell into my arms, you might say."

"And how did that happen, may I ask?"

Jason related the story and ended with a devilish grin. "I must say, I didn't mind the imposition at all."

The older German man laughed. "*Ja*, I can see that. So tell me how you found the patient."

"Mrs. Knox? I believe her to be suffering nothing more than melancholia. I'll know more after additional visits, but her vital signs were good and she had no complaint of pain. She spoke of feeling tired, and after listening to her I believe it's more a weariness of the soul and mind."

"That kind of weariness can lead to physical ailments, as you must know," Dr. Schultz countered.

"I do. My work in Kansas City included many such cases, especially in older women."

"And our other patients?"

Jason smiled. "They were quite welcoming to me. You've done a good job of preparing folks for your retirement. They are sorry to see you go, however. Mrs. Bushburn told me she would never trust another doctor as much as she trusted you."

"In time she'll realize that she can feel the same way about you." Dr. Schultz pulled glasses from his face and rubbed his eyes. "It will simply take time for folks to get to know you. I knew that when I advertised for someone to take over my practice."

Jason had answered that ad some three months earlier and now felt that St. Cloud was as much home to him as Kansas City had ever been. Having been born and raised in Kansas, Jason found Minnesota to be similar in many ways. Vast farmland bore rich crops, and the people were warm and welcoming. Country folk seemed more than willing to lend aid to their neighbor, where city dwellers were more reclusive. Jason found he much preferred the former to the latter.

"How are you feeling today, John?" Jason asked, seeing the man grimace as he replaced his glasses.

"The pain is increasing. I would imagine we're due a storm."

Dr. Schultz suffered an increasingly debilitating form of arthritis that left him less and less capable of dealing with even simple daily tasks. Much to his disappointment, it had begun to interfere with his medical work, and so he had decided to resign and move east to live with his daughter and son-in-law.

"It was clouding up to the south and west," Jason told him. "No doubt we'll see rain by nightfall."

"No doubt."

"Did you manage to make it over to the MacLachlans'?" Dr. Schultz asked, looking relieved to put aside any further talk of his own condition.

"I did. I met most of the family. Mr. MacLachlan was even present. He's fully recovered from his back injury and said to give you his appreciation."

Dr. Schultz smiled. "I've known Robert and his family for a long while. They're good people. It's a shame so much sorrow has visited them of late."

"Didn't you also say something about knowing the Knox family?"

"I didn't really know them," the older man replied. "I knew of them. They were in this area when the tornado of '86 came through. They left right after that. I don't know much else. I believe perhaps they lost their home to that storm." Gazing upward, he rubbed his chin. "Seems maybe there was even a death in the family." He shook his head. "That was a long while back."

"Maybe returning to this area is one of the reasons for Mrs. Knox's sadness. I shall question her more about it when I see her next. Or maybe it would be better for me to talk with her daughter." He got to his feet. "After all, she might be able to give me some details that her mother would be unwilling to tell."

"Perhaps," Dr. Schultz replied, shaking his head. "Just try to keep in mind who the patient is and where your attention needs to be."

Emmalyne continued to think about Dr. Jason Williams days after his departure. He had not made it back the next day as he'd indicated, and she couldn't help but wonder if somehow her actions had offended him. He hadn't seemed offended, truth be told. In fact, he'd seemed more than happy to have assisted her. Emmalyne gave a little shiver of delight at the thought of his arms about her.

"Dr. Williams said the sunshine and fresh air would do you good, Mother," she said. "I'm going to make you a nice little arbor retreat where you can relax and read a book."

Her mother limply waved a handkerchief. "I'm not up to that today. I'm much too tired. Just bring some tea and toast to my bed."

"Dr. Williams seems to really care about your well-being, Mother. I think he's probably a very wise doctor. He didn't suggest any of the silly remedies that some of your physicians have given you in the past. I think he may truly be able to help you get your strength back."

Her mother sighed and looked toward the single window in the bedroom. "I don't know that I'll ever have my strength again. Your father . . . well, he knows how hard it is for me to come back to this place. Even if my health were better, it would be difficult for my heart to bear." Her eyes filled with tears.

"I know it is hard to be here," Emmalyne soothed, gently cradling her mother's hand in her own. "But maybe in a few days you'll feel better, and we can make a journey to the . . . cemetery. Perhaps it would comfort you to see the nice stones that the MacLachlans arranged for Doreen and Lorna."

Her mother continued to gaze toward the window. There was nothing to see, however. Emmalyne knew the glass was coated with grime since she'd not yet had time to clean it. Besides that, the view was limited to the rickety old building they called a barn. Even so, the glass did allow for some light to enter the room. Perhaps cleaning and opening it would introduce Mother to the doctor's suggestion of fresh air and sunshine.

"A mother never recovers from the loss of a child," Rowena said in a hoarse whisper. "A mother never intends to dress a child for burial or touch her cold, lifeless face. The pain in my heart is only made stronger by returning to this place. It would be better for me to have died."

Emmalyne felt her heart constrict. "Now, Mother, you know such talk gains you nothing," she said. "Obviously God had a reason for you remaining here with Father and Angus and me. The tornado could have just as easily taken any of us." She gripped her mother's hand.

"But if I hadn't sent the girls to town that day, they might still be alive. Your father has oft said as much."

She murmured something, but Emmalyne couldn't make out the words. In times of deepest sorrow her mother would often revert to the Welsh language of her youth.

"Mother, you had no way of knowing there was to be a storm." Emmalyne reached for her mother's robe. "Why don't you sit here in the rocker while I straighten your bed?"

Her mother seemed oblivious to the question. "They were so close to home when the storm hit. If I'd sent them earlier, they might have returned in time to take cover in the cellar."

Emmalyne knew it was useless to attempt to halt her mother's regretful memories. They would simply have to play themselves out.

"Mother, you have often told me that only God has the power of life and death. Doreen and Lorna loved God just as you taught us. We mourn their passing, but they are in a better place now."

"It was such a bad storm." Mother slowly shook her head. "So much damage. So much death."

"Aye, many lives were lost," Emmalyne agreed. "Ours was not the only family to have faced death that day."

Her mother looked at her for a moment, then nodded. "Of course you're right." She looked at the robe Emmalyne held. "Is that for me? I'm not chilled."

"I didn't think you were, Mother. I need to straighten your bed, however. You will be much more comfortable with nice smooth sheets."

"Aye. 'Tis true." She allowed Emmalyne to help her up.

With her mother settled in the rocker, Emmalyne went quickly to work to remake the bed. "We have some very nice trees on the property, Mother," she said, hoping to engage her mother in more pleasant conversation. "Aspens, mulberry, juneberry, oak, maple . . . Oh, and there are several pines, although I'm not certain of their type. There are plum trees, just as Father told me. It looks like there will be a nice crop of fruit this year." Emmalyne tucked in the sheet and smiled. "There's a nice stream that runs behind the barn and a clearing in the shade nearby that might be a good place to set up a lounge for you."

"We had a lovely burn that ran along our property in Scotland," her mother murmured, her voice sounding far away. "My brothers oft fished those banks, and we girls liked to wade there in the warmth of summer."

With the bed made and the pillows fluffed, Emmalyne said, her voice light and encouraging, "Wouldn't you like to stay up for a while? You could keep me company while I do the kitchen walls."

"I suppose I could sit up for a short time," her mother said, sounding less than enthusiastic about the idea.

"Good." Emmalyne gave her no time to change her mind. "Come along, then. You can sit at the table. Angus put it together this morning before he left." She helped Mother to her feet. "I can make you some tea if you'd like."

"That might be nice."

Once she had made her mother comfortable, Emmalyne went to the stove. "I've managed to get things fairly well arranged. It was very dirty in here, but not as bad as I'd originally thought. Only two of the cabinets were in need of repair." She didn't bother to add that one of those had suffered only because of her grip on it when she fell . . . into the doctor's arms.

Checking the stove's fuel, Emmalyne added a few pieces of wood. The day would be much too warm to keep the stove heating at full capacity. She'd already put together a nice hash for their dinner and baked it during the cooler hours of the morning.

"The water will heat shortly. I made some scones this morning. Would you like one? You hardly ate any breakfast, and it's already well past lunch."

"I suppose I must. Do we have any jam?"

"Of course," Emmalyne said with a smile. "Remember all the preserves we put up in Minneapolis?" Mother hadn't participated all that much in their preparation, but Emmalyne knew she would remember the steaming jars lined up to cool. "I have some plum, blackberry, or apple jelly."

"Plum sounds fine."

Emmalyne prepared her mother a small scone with butter and the plum jam and brought it to the table. After the water heated and the tea was prepared, Emmalyne finally pulled on one of her brother's old shirts and went back to her brush and the whitewash.

"Don't you think the white color brightens things up considerably?" she asked over her shoulder as she retouched areas where the wash seemed thin.

"I suppose so." Mother nibbled at the scone, and Emmalyne gave her a smile.

"Perhaps one day you will feel like making some curtains for the window. I had to throw the old ones away. You always make such nice curtains, Mother. I especially like it when you sew them with smocking and lace. They make a kitchen look so inviting."

"I haven't the energy to even think about such things."

Emmalyne continued to wield her brush. "Well, I think in another few days you'll start to feel better." She was going to say something more, but the sounds out in the front yard drew her attention. "Sounds like someone is here. Maybe Dr. Williams has come to check up on you."

She put the brush down and went to the front door. "Oh, it's Father and . . ." She fell silent at the sight of Mr. Mac-Lachlan. Tavin had always favored him, and even now the resemblance was enough to silence her. Emmalyne swallowed hard. "It's Mr. MacLachlan."

"Oh dear. You must help me back to bed. I can't be welcoming people in my condition." Mother was already struggling to her feet.

Emmalyne returned to assist her mother, but found she was nearly to the bedroom. Rowena could move quickly enough when she needed to; perhaps her condition wasn't quite as serious as they'd thought. Emmalyne decided she would allow her mother to get herself back to bed while she saw to the matter of welcoming their guest.

Her father halted the wagon and met Emmalyne's curious gaze as she stepped out onto the porch.

"We've brought a few needed items," he said, motioning to the back of the wagon.

Emmalyne saw several crates, and upon closer inspection found they held laying hens. She looked beyond that and saw that her father had procured an icebox. It was quite unlike him to even concern himself with such things, much less spend money on such a luxury.

"Well, if it isn't little Emmalyne," Robert MacLachlan said, stepping down from his horse. "Lass, ye do me heart good. Yer the very picture of springtime."

Emmalyne couldn't help but smile. "More like autumn with my red hair."

"Perhaps," he said, grinning. "'Sakes, Luthias, but ye ought nae keep such a beauty hidden away. She's a right bonny lass."

Emmalyne blushed. "And how are you, Mr. MacLachlan?"

"I've fared well enough. Morna too. Ye'll come to visit?"

"Aye," she replied.

"Visitin' will have to wait," her father interjected. "There'll be more than enough work to keep her hand to."

"Aye," Emmalyne said again. She looked to her father's stern face. "I see you've brought us an icebox."

"We had an extra," MacLachlan said before her father could respond. "Chickens too. And yer guid faither bought a milk cow."

Emmalyne was more than surprised by this news. Just then the cow bellowed mournfully as if in greeting, and Emmalyne stretched on tiptoe to find it tied at the back of the wagon. It certainly would be nice to have a milk cow, but with no one but herself to care for such a beast, she knew her workload had just been significantly altered.

"She's missin' her wee one," MacLachlan offered. "Sold the little fella only last week."

"Well, I'm sure she'll make a fine addition to our family. It's been a long time since I've had to milk a cow myself, but I'm sure it will all come back to me."

Mr. MacLachlan laughed. "Ye ne're forget such useful things. I'll untie her and put her in the barn. The hens, as well. Ye can do with 'em as ye like."

What she would like would be to go back to having no chickens and no cow, but since they lived a good distance from town, it was probably best that they keep both.

The two men made short order of the work, and by the time they brought the icebox into the house, Emmalyne was ready for them. She had a substantial area of the kitchen walls already whitewashed and a nice little spot for the icebox.

"I put some ice in it afore we came," MacLachlan said as he patted the top. "Ought to be guid and cold."

Emmalyne nodded. "Thank you." She saw Mr. MacLachlan give her a glance and then look away, muttering something about it being a pity. She wasn't sure exactly what he meant, but it made her feel sad.

"It was guid of ye to help me," Emmalyne's father told his friend. "I'm sure we'll be better for it."

Feeling a bit uncomfortable with Mr. MacLachlan's expression as he watched her, Emmalyne hurried to interject, "Would you like some tea or perhaps a scone? I baked them fresh this morning."

Emmalyne waited for Mr. MacLachlan to respond, but he said nothing. He now was busy surveying the walls she had completed.

"I feel bad that we could nae make this place ready for ye. I knew it would need a good bit of work. We did get the pump runnin' well. Water ought nae be a problem."

"It's not," she assured him.

"'Tis no matter, Rabbie," her father declared. "The lass is quite capable."

"Aye, that she is." Tavin's father turned his gaze back to her. His eyes looked so like Tavin's.

Without even thinking, Emmalyne asked, "Do you ever hear from Tavin?"

Her father frowned and grunted something about the wagon. He left the room before Robert MacLachlan had a chance to speak. Emmalyne was just as glad he did. She was embarrassed at having blurted out such a question.

"We get a letter from time to time, but Tavin ne're seems to stay put for long. He was well the last time I heard."

She nodded, realizing that to ask anything more would be unseemly. "And Fenella? Is she doing well?"

The man's countenance changed, and a frown crossed his face. "I'm afraid she's been quite unwell."

"Oh no!" Emmalyne searched his face. He seemed unwilling to discuss the matter further, so Emmalyne didn't pry. "I am sorry to hear that. I hope to make a visit to see her and Mrs. MacLachlan soon."

"I'm sure Morna will be lookin' forward to that."

Without another word he turned to go. At the door he gave her a smile and looked as if he were going to say something, then must have thought better of it and departed. Emmalyne couldn't help but wonder what he had wanted to add. Maybe he wanted to say something more about Tavin but knew her father would be displeased. Emmalyne frowned and turned back to the new icebox. She touched it rather tenderly, idly wondering if perhaps Tavin had used it at one time.

Her mind was filled with images of the dark-haired young man with his thick brown-black brows and green eyes. She was sure those eyes had been able to look straight through to her soul. How she missed him. Seeing his father only deepened her longing. How could it be that a woman could love a man so fiercely? Had she ever seen such love between her mother and father?

Years of longing and separation had toyed with her heart. Emmalyne hurried to busy her hands. Stop thinking about the past.

Stop thinking of what might have been.

Stop thinking of . . . Tavin.

Chapter 6

Tavin MacLachlan sat quietly contemplating a now-tepid cup of coffee. All around him boisterous, rowdy men guzzled ale and told tales of hard times at sea. The ancient dockside tavern was no stranger to these men. If the walls could speak they would no doubt retell tales from a half-century ago. Tales of lives lost to rogue waves and acts of bravery that would rival Greek myths.

"You want somethin' to put in that coffee?" the barkeep asked, looking hard at Tavin and awaiting his response.

"No. I'm just waitin' to board the *Liza Jane*. Shouldn't be much longer." Tavin knew the man was concerned that little money would be made by Tavin's patronage, but he didn't really care.

The bartender shrugged and moved to the other end of the bar. Tavin downed the cooled coffee and slammed the mug down harder than he'd intended. His heart was torn between seeing this thing through and running as fast as he could in the opposite direction.

Going home to St. Cloud wasn't something he'd planned to ever do again. The place was filled with memories that haunted him and refused to leave him at peace. It didn't matter that his parents had moved to a new house situated on the quarry land his father had purchased only a year ago—or was it two now? Why his father had given up the freedom of working for whomever he chose to manage his own business was beyond Tavin. Sure, working for yourself had its advantages, but disadvantages were many. There was no getting away from the greater responsibility that came with being in charge. It was something Tavin had learned more than once. He neither enjoyed being the boss nor sought it, but his natural leadership skills seemed to always put him in that role.

A brief scuffle across the room drew Tavin's attention. Two large men seemed bent on pummeling each other, but then just as quickly as it had begun, it ended. The men laughed heartily, slapped each other's backs, and returned their attention to their drinks.

"So where are you bound on the *Liza Jane*?"

Tavin looked up to find the barkeep had returned. "Heading west."

"A lot of folks answer that call. You goin' out to the Wild West to start a ranch?" the man asked with a cocky grin.

"No. I'm Minnesota bound."

The man considered the answer a moment. "Never been. What's it like?"

Tavin had no desire to continue the conversation. He put down a coin for the coffee and got to his feet. "Quiet," he said, reaching for his bag.

Outside, the bright sunlight made a sharp contrast to the darkness of the tavern. Tavin had to blink several times in order for his eyes to adjust. He walked to where the *Liza Jane* was berthed and noted that the crew had finished loading her.

There's still time to change your mind, a voice seemed to whisper in his ear.

He shook his head. He'd deserted his family before when times weren't nearly so bad. Now with his sister gravely ill and his father injured, they needed him. His brother, Gillam, wasn't able to manage the business alone. Of course, the last letter he'd had was some months earlier. Could be things were much better now.

Or they could be much worse. Again the nagging voice pierced his thoughts.

Guilt washed over him. Tavin knew he'd not been a good son to his parents. He hadn't bothered to keep in touch very often to let his poor mother know that he was still alive and well. He was lucky to get a letter off to them twice a year, and usually it was from a different location, which he did not explain. The fact that this latest letter from them had caught up to him had been something of a miracle. Months old, the letter had found its way to him through some associates who happened to locate Tavin quite by accident. By the time they forwarded the letter, even more time had passed.

He had thought about trying to telephone someone in the St. Cloud area or sending his mother a telegram to learn more about his father's condition, but it seemed an unnecessary expense. Besides, his parents lived far beyond the city limits and wouldn't have a telephone. Who would he call? He didn't know much of anyone in St. Cloud. After all, he'd been gone for nearly eleven years. He brushed away his concern for his father. Worrying wouldn't change a thing.

"We're ready to board our passengers," a ship's steward announced through a megaphone. "Please make your way forward and have your ticket in hand."

Tavin slung his bag over his shoulder and reached into his pocket. He presented the ticket and waited for the man to look it over. The steward raised a brow at the lack of cabin assignment but said nothing. He no doubt knew that the captain of this steamer was more than happy to make a few extra dollars selling tickets to those who were willing to sleep on deck. So long as the Great Lakes and the weather cooperated with them, Tavin figured it would be an easy enough journey even without a room of his own.

The man directed Tavin to the appropriate deck and turned to the next passenger. Without another word, Tavin boarded the ship and went in search of a comfortable place to bide his time. He glanced down at the deck and pondered the days to come. Not looking where he was going, he ran headlong into a young woman.

"Oh my!" the redhead declared. Her bonnet slid to one side, and she quickly put up her hand to secure it.

"I apologize, ma'am," Tavin said, tipping his own hat. He was startled for a moment at the woman's brilliant blue eyes. They were so like Emmalyne's that he nearly reached out to touch the young woman's face.

"It's all right," she assured him. "I'm no worse for the wear." She smiled and made her way past him to the rail.

Tavin couldn't help but look after her for a moment. The color of the stranger's hair was several shades lighter than Emmalyne's and she was clearly younger. Nevertheless, the woman brought back a flood of memories that Tavin would have just as soon left alone.

He remembered every detail of the last time he'd gazed into Emmalyne's eyes. It had been the night he'd asked her to elope. He'd been so angry that her father had put an end to their engagement he could barely think straight. Luthias Knox had no right to put such a demand on his daughter, denying the couple their plans to start a life together.

"And she had no right to break my heart," he muttered, not willing to even speak her name.

Emmalyne was reaching up to set a clothespin in place when Dr. Williams made his presence known. This time she managed to keep her composure.

"I hope you have a moment to speak to me," he said with a smile and a tip of his hat.

"Of course," Emmalyne replied, looking down at the nearly empty basket. "Let me finish here, and then we can return to the house if you'd like."

"It might serve us just as well to stay here. What I have to say is better said without your mother present."

Emmalyne's hand went to her throat. "Is she that ill?"

He shook his head. "No. Not at all. I'm sorry if I frightened you."

"I suppose you did." Emmalyne drew a deep breath and picked up one of her brother's shirts. She spoke over her shoulder as she pinned it to the line. "Mother has been unwell for so long now, I suppose I feared the worst."

"I can understand. I spoke to your mother about the past, and I thought maybe you could offer me more insight. She didn't want to speak much on the matter."

"On what matter?" Emmalyne asked. She secured the shirt and turned to face him.

"Mostly the past and what happened to cause her such sadness."

"That's easy enough," Emmalyne replied, but she hesitated a moment, unsure of how much she should say. "My sisters died eleven years ago in a terrible storm that destroyed much of St. Cloud and Sauk Rapids. Many people were killed."

"I've heard about that storm," he said, nodding sympathetically.

"My two youngest sisters were among the victims. My father blamed my mother because she had sent them to town on errands. They didn't get home in time and were killed by debris."

"I am truly sorry. It's easy to see why your mother bears such sorrow."

Emmalyne picked up another shirt and hung it up before turning to the doctor. "That's not the only sadness she's faced. I suppose it isn't for me to say, but I think she feels a sense of loss . . . well, in her marriage, too. My father is a very hard man. He shows little kindness or love. I know this wounds her."

"I can well imagine. Has it always been so?"

"Not to hear her tell it. But apparently my father blames her not only for my sisters' deaths, but for him not being able to save his own family. Mother had talked him into eloping and marrying against the wishes of his family. Soon after, a fire took the lives of my grandparents and several others. Father felt it was his punishment from God for having married Mother. Mother has borne this burden of guilt all of her life."

"Hardly right to put such a thing on another person. She couldn't have known a fire would start, much less take lives."

"I know. I tell her that whenever the topic arises, but Mother can't be comforted. You have to understand, my father is harsh and ill-tempered most of the time. He might not speak on the matter to me, but I know he still brings it up to Mother from time to time. When my sisters were killed, Father was convinced it was more punishment from God. Now he hates God just as much as I think he hates Mother."

Dr. Williams shook his head. "Such hatred could easily cause the kind of melancholia that I see in your mother."

"Is that all that's wrong?" Emmalyne asked.

"You make it sound trivial, but we're learning more each day on the powerful effects of such sadness. We don't yet know how best to treat it, but we see the degrading and devastating way it wears at the body. Some people have even willed themselves to die."

Emmalyne wasn't surprised by this, and she nodded. "I often worry that Mother would do exactly that . . . if she could."

"She may well be on her way there," the doctor said soberly. "I'm hopeful, however, that together we can help her to regain her health—to care about life again."

"What do you suggest?"

"It's important to get her involved again in daily activities."

"But she's always so tired."

"Exhaustion goes hand in hand with the sorrow. You'll most likely have to encourage her to do more. At first she will probably fight against it, but in time, I believe you'll see a change."

Emmalyne thought for a moment. "So I should give her small tasks to do?"

"To start that would be good. I would also get her outdoors, as I mentioned before. The sunlight and fresh air will do her a world of good. This is a lovely setting—she could enjoy the sun for a time, then perhaps retire to the shade.

You could arrange for her to sew or take up some reading. Anything to busy her mind. And if you could get your father to have a change of heart . . . that might help, as well."

Emmalyne's short laugh sounded harsh to her own ears. "If I could have done that, it would already be accomplished. Father makes life quite unpleasant for all of us."

Dr. Williams frowned. "I am very sorry to hear that. Perhaps your father is unable to deal with his own guilt and grief. Perhaps his anger is the only way he knows to face it."

Emmalyne didn't want to hear anything that would reasonably explain her father's attitude toward them. She found it much easier to simply consider him a heartless tyrant. "I don't think it would be possible to ever know for sure, and even less possible for him to change."

"The Bible says all things are possible with God."

She took a deep breath and finally nodded. "Indeed. And for the most part, I have always believed that."

"But not when it comes to your father?"

Emmalyne picked up the wicker clothes basket and shrugged. "I suppose a person has to be willing first." She decided enough had been said about the subject. "Would you care to have a cup of tea before you go?"

The doctor smiled. "I would very much enjoy that, but I'm sorry I can't this time. I'm expected back in town. Dr. Schultz has some business matters for me to attend to."

"Maybe another time."

"I would hope so," he said. "It's not often I get to enjoy the company of such a lovely young woman."

"I'm not that young." She gave a brief chuckle. "Not young at all."

"You cannot be that old, either."

"I'm twenty and eight."

"And I'm thirty-three. We're both still quite young."

She looked at him oddly. "Most people would say otherwise."

"And they'd be wrong," he declared. "I firmly believe that age is all about the mind and the heart. If the mind sets out to think in youthful ways and the heart feels young and carefree, it could beat inside an eighty-year-old, and that person would still be young."

Emmalyne frowned and let out a heavy sigh. "Then I'm even older than my years. My heart feels neither young nor carefree."

Dr. Williams reached out and placed his hand over hers. Emmalyne gripped the basket beneath his hold.

"Perhaps you're in need of a doctor's attention," he said with a smile.

Emmalyne shook her head. "The cost would be too great." She broke away. She had nearly reached the back door of the house when the doctor took hold of her arm.

"I'm sorry if I offended you."

She turned and locked her gaze with his. Emmalyne felt sorry for him. He looked so confused—so worried. "I apologize," she finally said. "I'm afraid the duress of all that has happened and all that is required of me has made me testy. Please forgive me."

"There's nothing to forgive," he said, his smile returning.

"Good." She squared her shoulders. "Then if you'll excuse me, I need to see to supper. My father and brother will soon return from a hard day's work at the quarry and need to be fed." She went inside without another word.

Jason stared after the feisty redhead for several moments after she'd disappeared into the house. He wasn't sure why his comments had upset her so much, but it was clear they had. Perhaps she was simply tired and overworked. But he really had a feeling the problem went much deeper.

He returned to the front yard, climbed into the buggy, and took up the reins. This was a most curious situation, he thought. He'd finally found an intriguing, witty, and intelligent young woman, and she appeared uninterested in his attention.

"Well, as I said, all things are possible with God, Miss Knox." He glanced at the house once more, then snapped the reins with a shrug and a smile. Maybe it was time to focus on what God had in mind, rather than what Emmalyne Knox did not.

Chapter 7

"I cannae believe you're really here!" Morna MacLachlan exclaimed, embracing her eldest.

Tavin felt her warmth and breathed in the scent of her hair. She smelled of lavender soap and freshly baked bread. It stirred his heart as nothing had in the last eleven years. It was good to be home—good to be in his mother's arms. Did a man ever truly move far enough away that those arms could no longer reach him?

She pulled back and looked at him again, tears rolling down her cheeks. "You've grown. I thought you were done with that afore you left, but now look at yourself. You must be at least another two inches taller."

He smiled and patted her head like he might a small child. "Or maybe you've shrunk, Ma. I seem to remember you being taller."

Morna laughed and waggled a finger at him. "I'm still big enough to put you o'er my knee, and don't be forgettin' it."

Laughing along with her, Tavin glanced around the room. It was a well-kept house with beautifully papered walls and painted trim. The paper had a floral and striped print that made the room decidedly feminine and bright. Curtains at the sparkling windows were handmade by his mother. Their blue color matched the ribbons of blue in the paper.

"Tell me where you've been and what you've been doing," Mother ordered him, leading him over to chairs on either side of the fireplace.

Tavin shook his head. "This and that. But honestly, I'd rather know what's happening here. Father, for instance. Is he worse?"

"Oh no. He's completely recovered," his mother replied. She tucked a strand of graying brown hair behind one ear. She'd aged considerably since he'd last seen her, and Tavin wondered if he had been the cause of such a change. Eyes that matched his own shade studied him carefully. "He's off to the quarry even now."

"Whatever possessed him to buy a quarry? I thought he liked the idea of his freedom."

She shrugged. "He had the opportunity to purchase a quarry that was already established. A good friend of his was injured, and your father had been working for him. The man needed to sell, and your father thought it would be a smart investment. Everything fell into place quite naturally, and your father declared it the work of God."

Tavin thought it more likely his father's ingenuity. "And how many men work for him?"

"Well, your brother, of course, and about twenty or so other men. Some are drillers, others handle the derrick and horses. They've mainly been working with getting the rock out of the ground and nae so much with high polishing and finish. There are plenty of other shops that will take the stone off their hands."

Tavin nodded. "And Gillam is well?"

His mother broke into a smile. "More than well. He's married now, and they're expecting a wee one in November."

"Married?" Tavin asked in disbelief. "Who would have him?" He grinned, remembering the scrawny kid brother who always seemed to be in motion. He'd been only thirteen when Tavin had left.

"He married a local Swedish lass named Irene. She's salt of the earth and all that a mother could hope for her bairn."

"And Fenella? You wrote to tell me that she lost her husband. I think it was a year or so ago."

"Aye." His mother looked up at the fireplace mantel. "There's a photograph of them when they wed a few years back."

Tavin stood and picked up the small portrait. A long-legged man sat in a chair with a rather stern expression. His hair was parted in the middle and seemed to be as light in color as Fenella's was dark. His sister stood slightly behind her seated husband, looking for all the world the picture of a model bride. Dressed in white with a veil and flowers in her hair, Fenella appeared quite happy.

"He died in an explosion at the quarry," Morna said quietly. "He was skilled in working with black powder and dynamite, so it came as a shock to everyone. His death . . . well . . . it changed Fenella. She's not recovered."

"And didn't you also say that they have children?"

"Aye. Two wee bairns. Gunnar is four and Lethan just a little over a year. They're sleeping just now, but you'll meet them when they wake. They're precious lads."

"And where is Fenella?"

His mother glanced toward the staircase. "In her room. She is seldom anywhere else. I'll take you up in a while. She might be glad to see you, but it's hard to say."

Tavin saw his mother's worried expression and sat down again near her. "Is she all that bad?"

"Aye. I wish I had something braw to say."

"Good things to say don't change the bad that's going on," Tavin said, reaching out to put his hand on hers.

"'Tis true. The loss of her husband has caused her such grief. She's not been able to care for the wee ones, so I've found myself watchin' over her and the boys. Poor little Lethan thinks I'm his mother." She wiped tears from her eyes once again. "I fear Fenella will never recover."

"Is that what the doctor says?"

"He doesn't know what to say or think. None of them do. She's seen several, and they all say the same thing. They think she's become tetched from the loss. Fenella may well be lost to us forever."

Her sorrowful words left Tavin wondering what he might do for her. "So," he began in an effort to change the subject, "do you have a room for me in this new house? I thought I might stay on for a while."

"Oh, but 'tis joy to my soul," she said, looking over at him with an expression of great happiness. "And of course we have room for you. There's a nice empty room at the top of the stairs. It used to be Gillam's, but now it can be yours. I'll show you if you'd like."

"In a while. There's no rush. Why don't you show me around down here, Ma?"

She nodded, and they both stood. His mother looked at him with such love and rejoicing that Tavin felt a pang in his heart that he had not returned sooner. She gave him another hug, then led him through an arched entryway into the dining room. "We can seat twelve if need be," she told him.

Running a hand along the highly polished surface of the oak table, Morna MacLachlan seemed thoughtful. "Although we seldom have company these days."

"It's a lovely room, Mother."

"Your father gave me the furnishings as a gift for my fortieth birthday. Of course, that was some long years ago, and we could barely squeeze the table into our other place. Here it fits quite nicely." She gave a little chuckle. "I told him I'd be expectin' even better things when I reached fifty."

Tavin smiled. "And what did he say?"

"He told me he was already hard at work to figure out exactly what that might be. He threatens to get me one of those newfangled horseless carriages. Said he could just imagine me driving it around the countryside." She chuckled once more, then paused and looked at her son again. "He'll be so happy to see you, Tavin. He's missed you and worried about you for as long as you've been gone."

"I'm sorry to have caused you all to worry after me," he said, his voice low.

"'Tis no matter now. You're home, and that will warm his heart. I wish I could get word to him at the quarry. 'Twould be good for Gillam, too. He and Irene could join us for supper."

"Perhaps another evening, Ma. I'm fairly spent from the journey."

She looked at him as though seeing him for the first time. "But of course you are! Here I stand, bletherin' on like you've just risen from a sleep. Let me get you settled upstairs, and you can take a rest. Your father winnae be done for another two hours at best."

"I think I'd like that," Tavin replied. He'd not slept much

in the last seventy-two hours, and the thought of stretching
out in a real bed sounded most inviting.

His father's expression was more than enough to make
Tavin certain he'd done the·right thing in coming home.
Robert MacLachlan had aged as much or more than his wife.
Tavin didn't like to think of his parents getting old. Though
still quite capable of taking care of themselves, their graying
hair and wrinkles were reminders that their youth was long
behind them.

"Son, I cannae think of a better answer to prayer," his father
declared, shaking his head. "Ye've made my heart glad. I've a
new large contract, and I sure can use yer help at the quarry."

"Grandpa, can I help, too?" four-year-old Gunnar asked.
"I want to cut the rock like my papa did."

"Yer a tad too wee for such ventures. Give yerself some
time to grow tall like yer uncle." He nodded toward Tavin.
"See how big his hands are?"

The boy looked at his own hands and then at Tavin's.
"When my hands are that big, Grandpa, will you let me cut
the rock?"

"Aye. I'll be right proud to have ye by ma side." The boy
beamed with pride and jumped up to do a little jig while his
little brother pounded the flats of his hands on his high-chair
tray, as if approving.

"Gunnar, sit back down and eat your supper," his grandmother told him. The boy did so quickly.

Tavin laughed at the antics of his nephews, which did his
heart good. Maybe coming home wasn't going to be so bad
after all.

"I can't say that I like quarry work any better than I used to," Tavin told his father, picking up his fork, "but I do want to be useful to you."

"And what is it ye have yer heart set for?"

"I continue to enjoy working with the stone to set images and script," Tavin admitted. "I find it much to my liking, in fact."

"And have ye done much of this since ye left us?" Father questioned.

"When I could. I've worked at quite a few jobs, as I mentioned in my letters. I wanted to experience different trades to see what suited me best. Of course, that isn't always easy. Some tradesmen are less inclined to train strangers than others. Even so, I worked for a good long time at my last job, helping to carve gravestones."

"And this is what you desire?" his mother asked.

"Aye. I find the tools to be a part of me, and the rock comes alive under my hand. It fills me with wonder at times."

"Rocks can't be alive," Gunnar said, looking at Tavin with a frown.

"Oh, but you're wrong," Tavin said, rubbing the boy's head. "And one day I'll show you, if you'd like."

Gunnar nodded warily. "Can they talk?"

"In a way." Tavin grinned. The boy seemed positively mesmerized by the idea.

Before anything more was said, however, Tavin's father spoke up. "I'll be makin' ye a deal, son. Ye come and help me fill this contract, and I'll see ye set up in a business of carvin'. Much of the stone around here is well suited to that, and I'm thinkin' there is many a need for grave markers and statuary. We could build ye a room off the quarry office or maybe make a separate shed. What do ye think?"

Tavin hadn't expected his father's interest and enthusiasm. "I think it sounds good. Do you really believe there would be enough of a market in this area to keep me in business?"

"Aye. And don't be forgettin' that Minneapolis and St. Paul are only a few hours from here. Those big cities are always needin' something from the stone. Ye might well find yerself with more orders than ye can handle."

"That would be wonderful," Tavin said. He dug into the meat pie his mother had served him. "But not nearly as guid as this bridie," he said, pouring on a bit of Scottish brogue for effect.

"There's more if you'd like," his mother replied, beaming with pleasure at his praise.

"Aye. I'm sure I will." Tavin had all but forgotten his mother's good cooking. The life he'd known in the past decade had been strewn with few pleasures and a great many poor meals.

"So ye'll commit to help me?" his father asked.

He sounded rather hesitant, but Tavin figured it was nothing to be concerned about. No doubt his father was still surprised to find his eldest child back in the nest. "I will. You have my word. I'll help you to meet your contract, and then we'll discuss my future business." His father seemed pleased and went back to his meal.

After supper was over, Tavin went outside with his father, enjoying the warmth of the quiet evening. "It seems different here than the place we had before. I know our old house was to the north of the city, but it wasn't all that far away. Yet this place has a different feel. I can't really say why."

"Mebbe because ye're older," his father offered, pulling a pipe from his pocket. "The years have a way of changin' a man." They both seated themselves on a bench situated by a small plot of flowers.

"Aye. They do."

The sound of a wagon approaching caused Tavin to crane his neck in the direction of the road. "Are you expecting company?"

His father shook his head. "I cannae say I am."

As the wagon drew nearer, however, Tavin felt the blood drain from his face. He recognized the older man in the driver's seat as Luthias Knox. "What is he doing here?"

"He works for me," his father answered casually, continuing to pack tobacco into the bowl of his pipe.

Tavin bristled. "I didn't realize." He felt his heart pounding as Mr. Knox caught sight of him and frowned. The older man halted the horses and just stared across the yard at Tavin, as if seeing a ghost.

"Remember yer promise to me, son," his father reminded him quietly. "Yer gonna help me quarry the granite."

"But that was before I knew he would be here. Does that mean . . . are they . . . is she . . . ?" He couldn't even ask the question. Getting to his feet, Tavin looked at his father. "I can't stay." He stormed back to the house, not bothering to explain whether his words were meant only for the moment . . . or for the future.

Chapter 8

"We've a fine porch now," Emmalyne told her brother. "I appreciate all the fixing you've done." The two were sitting on the back of the wagon, legs swinging, as they enjoyed a few minutes together after the evening meal.

Angus shrugged. "I suppose it's not so bad." He smiled and motioned toward the house. "You've managed to make the house fit to live in, so I think of the two of us, you're more to be thanked."

"The whitewash made all the difference. It really brightened up the walls. Maybe one day we can splurge and get some real paint and some wallpaper, but for now I'm content. At least things are clean."

"Aye." Angus frowned as he cast a glance around the yard. "There's still much work to be done out here. I suppose there's time to benefit from the plum trees and the berries."

"I've been keeping an eye on them, to be sure," Emmalyne replied. "I wish I'd had more time for a garden. Seems a shame to have good ground and do nothing with it."

"I don't know when you would have had the time for that," Angus said with a shake of his head. "Father expects too much of you."

"No more than he expects of you." She gave him a tired smile. "Father sees it as our duty."

"Like you forsaking marriage to care for him in his old age. I think the notion is admirable enough, but there's no reason a woman can't be married and care for her parents, too."

"It's all water under the bridge now." She tried to keep the regret from her tone. Angus already knew how much her father's decision had hurt her. There was no sense dwelling on it.

"I've tried to talk to him," Angus said, fixing Emmalyne with a sympathetic look. "I've told him that you've been more than faithful to help them. I reminded him that it's nearly 1900, that to keep such old-fashioned notions is out of line. He said I was the one out of line."

Emmalyne laughed. "I can well imagine. But really, Angus, you needn't worry about me. I've accepted my lot in life. I have my regrets, but I've also moved forward. God has always given me great comfort in my obedience to Father."

Angus seemed less than convinced. "I know in those early days there were a great many tears. I find it hard to believe there are none now."

"I didn't say that," she admitted. She had tried to keep her emotions hidden away, knowing her father and mother would be less than receptive should she break into tears. However, there were still times when her heart got the better of her. "I simply said that God has always given me great comfort. He's faithful to heal my wounds."

"Wounds that should never have been made. Honestly, I think you should have eloped with Tavin and been done with it."

Emmalyne winced at the sound of his name being spoken aloud. Sometimes it flowed over her like a gentle, haunting breeze, but other times it was like a knife to the heart. "So, have you managed to meet any fetching young ladies?" she asked, trying for a change in the conversation.

He looked at her oddly for a moment. "Just when would I have done that? Father keeps me so busy, I've scarcely had time to draw a deep breath."

"Are you going to start working with the other men soon? Father said something about that a few nights ago."

"Aye. I've been mostly helping him get his office in order and learning how to handle the horses. It's been decided I can best help with the transportation. I fill in for a couple of the other men, and soon I'll be responsible for my own team."

"So you aren't going to actually quarry the stone?"

"No, not just yet. Perhaps in time. There's a big contract that has to be filled and apparently plenty of men are available to help at this point. It might be different later on, but for now I'm just as happy to do this. At least I won't be breathin' in all that rock dust."

She nodded. "I suppose you'll get enough of that just being at the quarry." The sound of the front door opening caused them both to turn toward the house.

At the sight of their mother coming outside, Emmalyne and Angus couldn't help but exchange a brief glance.

"How are you feeling, Mother?" Angus asked, sliding off the wagon and walking to where she was taking a seat on the porch.

"I'm feelin' a bit done in," she said, settling into the rocker. "Supper was good, Emmalyne. I almost forgot to tell you."

Emmalyne smiled. "Thank you. I'm glad you've come outside to enjoy the evening."

"Your faither said he was going to bring me a post from

my sister. He forgot it in the barn when he got back from town, and he went to fetch it."

"A letter from Edinburgh or Glasgow?" Emmalyne asked.

"Edinburgh. He said it was from Eileen."

"It will be wonderful to hear what she has to say," Emmalyne said, sitting down on the porch step. "Do you suppose you can read it to us all?"

"I will," Mother promised. "It's so nice to get news from home."

Emmalyne couldn't hold back her smile. It was the happiest she'd seen her mother in weeks. Father came around the corner of the house just then, the envelope in his hand. Seeing them all gathered on the porch, he slowed his pace and frowned.

"Ye ken there's work to do."

"We do know," Emmalyne said with a nod. "But Mother says there's a letter from Scotland. We wanted to hear the news before we get back to our tasks."

Her father scratched his cheek and handed the letter over to his wife. "The hens look settled," he said, looking to Angus. "Ye made them right cozy."

"They should be safe from the foxes and anything else that might bother them," Angus agreed.

Mother had opened the letter and was scanning it quickly. She looked up suddenly, and Emmalyne thought she'd never seen such joy in her mother's expression.

"What is it, Mother? Good news?"

"Eileen wants us to visit. She said they have more than enough room." Mother looked to Father, as if awaiting his approval. "Just think of it—Emmalyne and I could go for a wee trip home."

"Hardly a wee trip," Father argued. "Yer sister's daft if she thinks I can afford to be sendin' ye."

Mother frowned. "We could make the trip worth our time. Think on it, husband. You were jest sayin' the other day that there werenae any decent wools to be had. I can bring some fine pieces home with me."

"It's nae gonna be that way," Father said, starting to sound angry. "Everyone wants to be spendin' ma money. They act like it jes grows in the ground around here. Tell yer sister that ye cannae be affordin' to come for a visit. Tell her there's too much work to do here."

Mother's eyes clouded, then filled with tears, and Emmalyne feared she would soon be sobbing uncontrollably. Speaking up seemed the only way to forestall it. "Mother has a good thought, Father. We could bring back all the things you've said you missed from home."

Father's face reddened. "I won't hear anythin' more on it. Angus, I need yer help in the barn."

"Aye, Father."

Emmalyne waited until they'd gone to address her mother. "Perhaps Father will change his mind in time."

"No, he won't." Mother let the tears slide down her cheeks. "Oh, Emmy, my life here is a misery, for sure."

It was the most her mother had voiced about their move, and Emmalyne longed to comfort her. "Mother, you must not let this defeat you. The doctor believes your sorrows are getting the best of you. I pray you will fight against the sadness."

Mother looked at her for a moment, then got to her feet. "I can't. It consumes me." Her voice broke as she reached for the door. "It will be the death of me."

Emmalyne stared at the house for several moments after her mother's departure. What could she do? What could she say? She thought to pray, but it seemed so feeble, so insignificant. How could a few pleading words to the God of the universe resolve this situation? Surely God had matters of greater importance to handle.

The burden of it all suddenly felt heavier than it had in years. Where was God in moments like this? Emmalyne had been raised to believe that obedience to God would protect a soul from the devil's torments. But that hardly seemed to be the case now.

Realizing her ponderings were getting her nowhere, Emmalyne went into the house and lit a couple of lamps. She had mending to do and knew there would be little time on the morrow for such things. Tomorrow she would need to bake and wash clothes. If there was time, she would see to some of her other projects, as well—a bevy of things needed her attention. Despite suggesting her mother make curtains, Emmalyne knew the chances of it happening were slim. So there was another task she would need to add to her list of duties, along with making a few new rag rugs.

She thought of the years they'd spent in Minneapolis and how much simpler her life had been there. She could sew and earn a bit of money on the side—at least enough to buy some of the little things she enjoyed—things her father would not agree to pay for. Here in the more remote area of Minnesota's quarry and farmland, she found provisions still available, but extra money would be much more difficult to come by. Not only was she far too busy to take on anyone else's sewing, she was too isolated to come in contact with possible customers.

Picking up one of her father's work shirts, Emmalyne tried hard not to think of how different her life might have been had she married Tavin. Angus said she should have eloped, and God knew that Emmalyne had often wondered if she'd made the right choice in staying.

The Bible was clear that she was to honor her mother and father. There was no way around that statement, and yet Emmalyne couldn't help but wonder exactly how far that command went. Were honor and obedience the same thing? Her father's anger at God kept them from attending worship. He made it clear he wanted no part in church attendance for himself or his family. How was obedience to that command biblical? Didn't the Bible also state that they should not forsake gathering together with God's people?

She had so many questions and few answers. How her heart ached. Emmalyne thought for a moment of Dr. Williams and how kind he'd been to her. He seemed genuinely interested in her, but Emmalyne knew it was to no avail; she would have to keep her distance or explain the matter of her circumstances. Neither choice made her very comfortable. Then she thought of the MacLachlans. They weren't that far away, and yet Emmalyne still had not had a chance to visit. Nor had their old friends made any attempt to come to the Knox house.

"Perhaps Morna and Fenella have no desire to see me again," she murmured, pushing the needle through to mend a tear under the arm.

"What was that?"

She looked up to find her brother watching her from the doorway.

She forced a smile. "It was nothing. If you have any other

mending for me, you'd do well to bring it now. I'm nearly done with this shirt and only have a few more things to tend to."

"No. I've nothing more," he said. "I'm going to head to bed afore long. Father said we'll be up before first light. As if I didn't know that," he added wryly.

Emmalyne stopped her needle momentarily. "I won't be up much longer myself. I'll see to it that you have a good hot breakfast in the morning. Oatmeal and berries, cream, and perhaps some smoked pork."

Angus's expression grew thoughtful. "It won't always be this way, Em."

She was startled at his words. "What do you mean?"

He shrugged as if not truly understanding his own state-ment. "I can't say for sure, but I just feel a certainty that you won't always be here like this. I've taken to praying for answers—for clarity."

She'd never heard her brother speak of prayer before. "I'm glad you pray, Angus, but I'm not sure what can be done about any of this. Mother in her misery needs so much more prayer than I do. She is so grieved." Emmalyne drew a deep breath and let it go. "The doctor says her sadness could damage her health, and I fear I see that happening. She's growing more frail . . . and just when something comes along that seems helpful, Father inevitably finds a way to put an end to it."

"A trip to Scotland would do her well," Angus said, "but I'm sure Father will never let it happen. You know how he is with money, and this move has set him back quite a bit. He complains about it all day long, despite the fact that I know Mr. MacLachlan reimbursed him for a good portion of the expense." Her brother shook his head. "I don't think Father knows what it is to be happy."

Emmalyne cast a glance back to her sewing. "I'm not sure any of us do."

Tavin stared at the ceiling in the dim light of morning. He could smell the aroma of coffee from downstairs and smiled. He hadn't known the simple pleasure of such a morning fragrance in so very long. In the past he had usually found a place to stay with other workmen, usually amounting to little more than a rickety building with beds or bunks squeezed into a common room. The smells there were of sweat, liquor, and other unpleasant odors. How wondrous to enjoy clean sheets and the earthy scent of coffee brewing.

Pushing back the blanket, Tavin sat on the edge of the bed and stretched. He rubbed his chin and knew that a thorough shave was in order. He must have looked quite a sight to his family in his travel-weary condition.

The memory of Luthias Knox interrupted his otherwise peaceful thoughts. He frowned and gripped the mattress until his hands ached. Knox was the last person in the world he had wanted to see. Especially on his first day back. Well, the second to the last. An image of Emmalyne Knox came to mind, but Tavin quickly pushed it aside in anger.

"I never should have come home," he all but growled. Letting go of the mattress, Tavin got to his feet. "I should have stayed as far away from here as possible. I must be a glutton for punishment."

He pulled his anger around him like a protective shield.

The Knox family had made his life most unpleasant, and he had no desire to subject himself to more of the same.

"But you made a promise," he muttered to himself, taking up his work shirt. His father had reminded him of that promise just before they'd retired last evening. Tavin could still hear the man's words. In the MacLachlan family, giving one's word meant everything. Even when the matter was something small. Tavin remembered his father speaking to him about such issues when he was very young.

"A man is no better than his word, lad. A man must always be true to his pledges, even when they seem trivial. So, my boy, dinnae give yer word unless ye intend to keep it." The memory made him uncomfortable. Surely his father could understand the difficulty Tavin faced in keeping his word this time.

I'll just tell him that it won't work. I'll explain how much I hate that man and how much he obviously hates me.

But even as he buttoned his shirt, Tavin could hear his father's statements from the night before. "I'm trusting ye to make guid on yer word. I know the presence of Luthias and Angus Knox might make ye feel uncomfortable, but I'm not askin' ye to work side by side. Luthias will be keepin' the books, and Angus is workin' with the horses. Ye need nae see each other."

Of course, that didn't mean they wouldn't see each other at all. Mr. Knox now knew that Tavin had returned. He no doubt was just as uncomfortable in that knowledge as Tavin had been in learning about him. Had they unwittingly let loose a box of snakes?

"They know I'm here, and I know they're here. Maybe that is enough to keep us away from each other," he said into the silence of his room.

But knowing they were here—knowing that Emmalyne was just a few short miles away—tortured Tavin's heart like he'd never known. There would come a time, he knew, that he would have to see her again. A time when he would have to face up to the fact that as much as he had tried to hate her and the very memory of their time together . . . Tavin MacLachlan still loved Emmalyne Knox.

Chapter 9

In the weeks that followed, Emmalyne watched her mother slip deeper and deeper into her sorrow. What little progress had previously been made was easily eliminated by Father's harsh spirit and refusal to consider the trip to Scotland. Emmalyne had tried twice to broach the subject with him, but he had quickly and abruptly put an end to the discussion. He had no money for such frivolities, and she would do well to put such thoughts away. The expression on his face confirmed his unmovable intention.

But the mere suggestion of such a trip had given her mother real joy, and Emmalyne wished there might be some way she could earn the money herself. Even then, however, her father would no doubt declare the trip impossible. He expected his womenfolk to remain at home, working and tending to his needs. Luthias Knox was a tyrant ruling his family with an iron fist. He had no compassion for them. *No love.*

The idea that her father didn't love her was a rather new realization. As a child she had convinced herself that all fathers conducted themselves in similar fashion: Fathers were too busy for hugs and tenderness. They showed their love through hard work and provision. Even his frugal nature could be evidence of his love, she had told herself. But now Emmalyne knew otherwise. She had spent a lifetime convincing herself of a lie in hopes of easing her pain.

Having finished separating the milk and cream, Emmalyne knew she needed to get to the task of making butter. It would be difficult as the day grew warmer, so she needed to begin to work in the early morning hours. Mother wouldn't awaken until much later, and Father and Angus had already headed off to the quarry.

Kirning butter, as her mother called it, had never been a favorite job. Emmalyne found it tedious work to paddle the cream, drain the kirn milk—or buttermilk, as it was usually called in America—and wash the butter until it was ready to mold into shape. Her mother had inherited a Scottish superstition about the task and insisted Emmalyne throw salt in the fire prior to churning so the butter would form. Other times, when the churning seemed to take overlong, her mother would press a hot poker into the contents to drive away the faeries. Whether Mother really believed in fairies or not, the trick always seemed to work.

With the house quiet around her, Emmalyne gathered the cream she'd put aside and began her task. Father would be glad for the new buttermilk. They'd been without his favorite treat for some time, and he had mentioned only last night having his heart set on a bowl of foorach. Emmalyne didn't particularly care for the taste of buttermilk and oatmeal, but she made the dish with some regularity for her parents.

To pass the time, Emmalyne tried her best to pray and recite Scripture passages from memory. Often she would churn the butter with an open Bible at her side. It was a good way to get in some extra reading, and usually it lifted her spirits.

It was a great disappointment that they were now too far from town for a quick walk to church. She knew such outings would do Mother good, but there would be no broaching the subject with Father.

I don't know why these things have come to rest on our shoulders, Lord, but I do pray for strength to overcome, the wisdom to learn, and the faith to hear your voice. Show me how to love and forgive Father.

In time, the butter began to form, and Emmalyne quickly drained and washed the yellow mixture. She had just set aside the kirn milk when she heard the unmistakable sound of a horse's whinny. She went to investigate and found Dr. Williams descending from the back of his tall black horse.

"Good morning," he called. He quickly tied off the gelding and grabbed his bag. "I've come to see your mother."

"She's still sleeping," Emmalyne replied. "But if you'd like to come inside and wait, I'm sure she will awaken before long. I'm churning butter just now and must return to it, but you are welcome to keep me company."

A smile revealed straight white teeth. "I'd like that very much."

She nodded and opened the screen door in welcome. Dr. Williams bounded up the steps and made his way into the house. Emmalyne took his hat after he'd removed it. "If you'd like to take a seat, I can get you a cup of coffee or tea."

"Thank you. Either would be fine." He sat down on one of the chairs by the table.

She went to the counter, where she knew there was some

coffee left from the morning meal. She felt the pot. "It's tepid. Let me warm it for you."

"It's not important. I'm not really in need of refreshment as much as conversation."

She looked at him oddly and placed the pot on the stove. "Conversation. With me?"

He chuckled and ignored her question. "I must say you've done amazing things with this place." He gazed around the room in awe. "I can hardly believe it's the same house."

"Angus has been good to work on the outside," she said, returning to the churn. "And I've done what I could inside. Together we make a good team." She rinsed the butter once again, satisfied that it was finally ready to put into the wooden molds.

"I would imagine you'd be an asset to any man. You'll make a wonderful wife."

His words startled her, and she looked up in some shock. It seemed to be a rather personal comment to make, considering they hardly knew each other. Emmalyne thought to answer, then decided against it. She returned her attention to the butter without another word.

If her silence offended the good doctor, he made no sign of it. "How is your mother faring?" he asked.

"Poorly," she admitted. "She was a bit better, but then had a . . . well, a disappointment."

"What kind of disappointment?"

Emmalyne looked over to find him watching her quite intently. "There came a post from Scotland. Her sister wrote to invite us to visit. Mother thought it would be a wonderful trip to make, but my father was against it."

"But why? Such a trip might very well make a great change in her physical and emotional health."

"I know. But for Father, the money is of more import. He worries constantly about the cost of everything. In fact, if he knew you were here today, he would no doubt send you packing. Money for doctors and such is only to be spared in emergencies. He's done nothing but grumble about Mother's condition; that she's not getting better causes constant strife."

"Then I won't charge for the visit," Dr. Williams said with a shrug. "Your father surely can't protest that."

"One would like to think not," Emmalyne said in a barely audible voice, "but you do not know my father."

The doctor nodded and rubbed his chin. "Nevertheless, I feel it's my responsibility to check on the ailing and injured. Your mother is suffering, and I won't leave her unattended."

"That's most kind of you. I must say, I appreciate your concern, even if Father does not."

"That's quite all right." He grinned. "It gives me a chance to know you better."

Emmalyne didn't know how to reply to that. She had no desire to explain the details of her family's traditions and why getting to know her better would be a waste of Dr. Williams's time . . . unless he was simply looking for a friend.

Without another word, she went to the stove and checked the coffee. Finding it warm enough to serve, she poured the doctor a cup and handed it to him. "Would you like cream or sugar?"

"No, black is fine."

She went to where she had left a covered tray and lifted the towel. "Would you care for a scone? I made them just this morning."

He gave her a look of pure delight. Emmalyne turned her attention back to the tray. "They're cinnamon and nutmeg. I can put one on a plate for you and bring you some butter."

"That would be wonderful. You are an extremely talented woman, Miss Knox."

She tried to ignore this further compliment and placed a scone in front of him. Next she dished up a portion of the new butter and put that on the table beside the scone. Smiling, she turned back to her task. "I have to get the rest of this butter into the molds, so I hope you won't mind if I keep working while we talk."

"Not at all. I rather like watching you work. You're quite graceful in all you do—why, you made falling from the chair look almost elegant."

Emmalyne had to laugh. "Hardly. It was by far and away one of my less graceful moments, and I would hope you might forget about it."

"I can't—not that I want to." His voice had turned husky, and Emmalyne couldn't help but look his way. She could see something akin to yearning in Dr. Williams's expression. She'd seen that same look in Tavin's eyes long ago.

Emmalyne quickly changed the subject. "I'm afraid I'm not a very good hostess. I didn't even provide you with a knife." She hurried over to the counter. "As I was saying earlier," she continued, handing him a knife, "Mother did seem to benefit from your suggestion of getting outdoors more. I set up a place for her down by the stream and another on the porch. She had enjoyed both locations prior to getting her sister's letter. Now I'm afraid she's taken to her room again."

"No doubt even small disappointments appear as major hurdles to overcome," the doctor said quietly. "Her spirit seems almost broken."

"I agree." Emmalyne pressed the butter into molds. So long as she could keep her hands busy and her attention on something other than the handsome doctor, she felt less uncomfortable.

"Does she have any hobbies or interests in life? Anything that she used to do just for the pleasure of doing it?"

Emmalyne thought for a moment. "She taught all of us girls to make creel baskets for fishing. They were popular in Scotland, and Mother said she and her sisters used to make them all the time. They would sell them for extra money to buy fabric for dresses and such." Emmalyne smiled at the memory of learning to make the baskets. "She taught me when I was quite little. I have two older sisters, and they were already very good at the task. So when I started, Mother gave me her undivided attention. I cherish the memory. We would have so much fun talking and dreaming while we worked."

"Might she make baskets again if you were to ask her?"

The pleasant image faded from her thoughts. "I don't think so. You see, she taught my younger sisters to weave the baskets, as well. We would make them and sell them. Fishing is quite popular here in Minnesota, as you must know. The stores were happy to take as many as we could make. My younger sisters were even faster and better at making them than I was. When they died, my mother never set her hand to another piece again."

"Maybe it's time to suggest she rekindle that interest. Maybe you could encourage it as a memorial."

"What do you mean?" Emmalyne stopped and fixed him with a gaze.

His smile sent tingles up her spine, and she almost dropped the mold of butter on the floor. Recovering, she hurried to put the containers in the icebox and chided herself for such silliness.

"I think you could explain to your mother that it would be a positive way to remember your sisters. Since you all had such a pleasant time making the baskets, maybe you and your mother could set out to make a few and talk about your sisters and how much they loved the craft."

"I suppose I could try, but I have a feeling it would only cause Mother more pain. I've offered to read to her as she did for us so long ago, but even that moves her to tears." She returned from the icebox and began cleaning the paddle and churn.

"And making the baskets might do the same—at first. It also might allow her to feel close to your sisters again. Do you talk much about them?"

"They are rarely mentioned, and never around my father. He will not hear of us speaking their names. In fact, he forbids us to speak the names of any of the dead." Emmalyne placed the churn on the counter and took up a cloth to clean the table where she'd been working. "As I've mentioned before, Father blames Mother for their deaths. His heart is quite hard toward their memory . . . and toward God, I'm afraid."

Dr. Williams devoured the treat before him, his expression revealing his utmost approval. "By the way, this scone was absolutely delicious." He licked the crumbs from his fingers. "You also need to realize that your father is using anger to cope with his own grief."

"It's always been his way," Emmalyne replied, "but I don't think it's just grief that makes him act that way. I think it's just his nature."

"Men often shield their pain in fortitude and indifference— at least *seeming* indifference." He picked up his coffee cup and looked at it for a moment. "Men are taught from the cradle that to show emotions or pain makes them less than the strong, upright men they were meant to be. I remember my own father telling me that I should never let anyone see me cry." He shrugged and drank from the cup. Putting it back on the table, his expression changed to one of regret. "He died shortly after that."

"How old were you?"

"Eleven." He gave her a sad smile. "And I didn't cry, though I wanted to."

Tavin turned the chisel and raised the sledgehammer again to strike and drive the steel deeper into the granite. A splitting line of holes had been placed by the quarry master, the first steps in the long process to break the block of stone away from the larger mass. About six inches apart, the holes were drilled approximately three inches deep. Next, iron wedges would be used along with pieces called feathers—long narrow shims—to widen the hole and further encourage a break along the so-called cleavage plane. Granite was easy to process in this manner, and the breaks were usually quite clean.

"Make sure you get these chisels to Smithy," he told Jimmy, one of the younger men. The blond-haired youth looked up and nodded. Each of the quarries had a blacksmith on-site. The man was probably the most valuable of all the employees, since it was his job to keep the tools sharpened and in good repair.

Tavin finished and pulled the chisel out. He reached for a dust spoon and cleaned the rock bits from the hole. It was just deep enough. Jimmy was already positioning the shims, and Tavin would soon begin the process of driving the wedges.

"Here's the last of 'em," Tavin said, tossing the boy his chisel. "Bring up another set when you come back."

"Sure thing." The young man hurried to collect the chisels and darted off the rock and up a wooden ladder.

Tavin rubbed his hands and winced at the blisters that had formed. His hands were naturally calloused from hard work, but drilling the rock always brought about sore spots that he never experienced with other activities. He wiped them against his bare chest, dampening them from the sweat that had formed. The moisture seemed to ease the pain a bit.

The sun overhead bore down and heated the rock around him. Tavin remembered days long past when he would quarry along with his father for other owners. The work was always exhausting. Tavin had little satisfaction in quarry work—unlike stone carving. Carving designs and artistic script into stone gave Tavin a sense of accomplishment. It was akin to leaving a part of himself in the rock. Cutting stone from the ground, as he was doing just now, was not as creative. Who knew where this rock would end up? Who knew how it would be used?

"Gawking off like that won't get the stone cut."

Looking up, he found his younger brother, Gillam, standing on the ledge some ten feet above. Tavin crossed his arms and shrugged. "I'm playing foreman." He grinned at his brother. "Isn't that how it's done?"

Gillam laughed. "Nah, you aren't in the shade. Any foreman worth his salt knows to get out of the sun. That's how I do it."

Tavin laughed, too, and stretched his arms over his head. "Then you'd do well to get back to your shade and leave me be. I have real work to do."

"Aye. I can see that well enough. I did come with a purpose, however. Father wants to see you. He said to leave what you're doing."

Tavin relaxed and reached for his shirt. "Tell him I'll be right there."

Gillam nodded and disappeared from view. Tavin couldn't help but wonder what his father wanted from him. It wasn't like him to take a man from his job in the middle of the day.

"Maybe he's reconsidered my promise," Tavin muttered to himself. "Maybe he's come to realize how impossible this situation is."

Chapter 10

"As ye know, there's an outbreak of measles in the area," Tavin's father began. "Ye lads took the disease when ye were young."

Tavin exchanged a look with his brother, Gillam. "Aye, we did. So what is this about?"

"Yer mither fears the wee lads have taken the sickness. She's not quite sure, but her suspicions are usually correct." Robert MacLachlan dusted off his trousers and picked up a sheaf of papers. "Ne'ertheless, we must see to this granite. Yer mither thinks it might be well if we were to remain here at the quarry in case the doctor puts them in quarantine. I figure to have some cots put up here in the office. We can warm our meals on the stove."

"Won't Mother need some help?" Tavin asked.

His father shook his head. "She dinnae want to risk exposin' us in case it turns out to be somethin' other than measles. We'll know soon enough. We're already down a man here at the quarry—Harry Withers. Could be Harry has taken the measles or some other malady. I cannae be sure."

"We'll just have to make do," Gillam said, shoving back

an errant lock of hair. He looked very much like Tavin and their father with his dark hair and green eyes. The worry in his expression matched that of his father's. "I will stay here. I don't want to cause danger to Irene or the babe she carries."

Father nodded and Tavin did likewise. "I don't much care where I sleep," Tavin said with a shrug. "I've certainly had worse than this."

"There's somethin' else. A wee matter of the union officials and their desires to see all of the quarries belongin' to the Stonecutters."

Tavin shrugged. "Is that such a bad idea?"

"I dinnae ken," his father replied. "I've been on both sides of this, and I cannae say either one has all the answers. The man I bought this place from was of a mind that no man would tell him how to set his prices. The men aren't used to bein' a part of the union, but I cannae say they would be against it."

"I think it's something to consider," Tavin replied. "The unions have helped to get hours regulated and pay increases. Of course, in the past we've been on the side of the laborer, and now you're the owner. I suppose it could make a big difference."

"Aye," his father agreed, giving the papers in his hand a wave. "Of course, there could be trouble. We've already had some problems, and there's no way of knowin' for sure if the union was to blame or not, but it could be their way of scarin' us into sayin' yes."

Tavin considered his father's words a moment, but it was Gillam who spoke up. "I suppose we keep prayin' about the right way to go, Father. You said yourself that was the best way to gain wisdom."

"Aye, that I did."

That solution wasn't one Tavin wanted to dwell on. Since losing Emmalyne Knox, he'd given up on God answering his prayers. He picked up his cap and headed for the door. "You two figure out what's to be done about the unions. I'm going to get back to work."

Tavin opened the door and came face-to-face with Luthias Knox. The older man seemed surprised to find Tavin there and did nothing to hide it.

"What're ye doin' here?" Luthias asked with a scowl.

Nodding toward the office, Tavin said only one word before pushing past the older man. "Business."

Emmalyne tried hard to pique her mother's interest in basket weaving, but nothing she said seemed to raise her spirits. "There are plenty of lakes around here and fishing is quite popular, Mother. Just think of it. We might even be able to raise enough money for a trip to see Aunt Eileen." This sparked a hint of interest in her mother's expression, and while Emmalyne was heartened by her response, she was also fearful she might be encouraging her mother in a direction that would only mean another sorrow and disappointment.

"It would take a great many baskets to earn enough for such an endeavor." Mother frowned and shook her head. "Besides, your father would never be lettin' us go. You heard him—he thinks it a waste of money and time."

"But if we raised the funds ourselves, he couldn't complain about the cost," Emmalyne countered, hoping it was true.

"He could and he would. You know how he is."

Emmalyne couldn't deny that. She took a seat at the table

opposite her mother and leaned closer. "Why did you ever marry such a man? You have always been a loving and kind soul. It seems strange that you should marry someone so harsh and cold." The words were out of her mouth before she'd thought them through, and Emmalyne suddenly wished she could take them back.

Her mother gave a sad smile. "Weren't always so. Luthias was a good and loving lad in his youth. There wasn't a man around who could steal my heart away from him."

Imagining her father as a loving and kind youth was difficult for Emmalyne. "What happened to make him so heartless, then? I've never known a time when he wasn't this way. It's only gotten worse as the years go by."

"You know that your father blames me for the death of . . . of the girls." Her mother's thoughtful expression sobered. She looked Emmalyne in the eye. "He also blamed me for the death of his family. I'm the one who encouraged him to run away and for us to be wed. We were madly in love, and it wasn't hard to convince him."

"Were your parents against the wedding?"

"Not so much that, but I was just sixteen. They wanted me to wait another year or two, and I was unwilling to hear their arguments." Mother looked at her hands and the slender gold band she wore. "I loved Luthias with all of my heart, and he loved me. We didn't wish to wait for any reason."

"So you ran away together." Emmalyne had always known of her parents' elopement, but her mother had never offered many of the details.

"We did. Your father came for me just after midnight. I had packed a bag and left it near the privy. When he came, I slipped from bed and snuck out the window, wearing nothing but my nightdress." She smiled at this memory. "It was quite chilly and damp. The weather almost changed my mind."

"But it didn't," Emmalyne interjected.

Her mother looked up. "No. It didn't. Luthias promised me that his love would warm me and keep me safe. I told him I'd just as soon put on my dress and boots. He laughed at me and collected my bag. We were well away from the house, however, before I stopped to dress."

"It sounds as though Father was quite different then."

"He was. He was happier. He laughed and enjoyed life." She paused to gaze out the window. "But then the fire took his family."

"Tell me about it, Mother. What happened?"

"No one could say for certain, but the house caught fire in the night and took the lives of all within. Luthias was devastated at the news. We had just returned to announce our marriage and planned to tell his folks first. We knew they would assume that was what had happened, and they weren't nearly so against us marryin' as were my folks. We selfishly thought to have an easier time of it with them and maybe even get their help in explaining the matter to my family."

"But they were dead?"

"Aye. Luthias and I went out to his family's farm, where we were met by the neighbors who told us the sad tale. I stayed with them while Luthias rode on to survey the scene for himself. He came back a changed man. He hardly spoke two words to anyone. There was a funeral that week, and we buried his father and mother, two younger sisters, and a brother. He didn't speak a word during the entire service, and even afterward he remained silent as people paid their respects."

"Like he did when we buried Doreen and Lorna," Emmalyne whispered, remembering her father's stoic silence.

Mother fell silent for a moment, and just as Emmalyne
thought the story had concluded, she began to speak again.
"It wasn't until nearly two weeks later that he said to me
what had happened was my fault. He told me that if I hadn't
convinced him to elope, he would have been with his family
and could have gotten them to safety."

"But there was no way of knowing that," Emmalyne protested. "He might have been killed, as well."

"I said as much, but he wouldn't listen. Instead, he left
me with my parents and went to deal with his parents' farm.
My mother was beside herself. She feared I might be with
child and that Luthias would never return. But I wasn't expecting, nor would I be for a time. Your father wouldn't
even touch me."

Emmalyne could only imagine the heartache of a young
woman, deeply in love, who then was rejected for something
over which she had no control. Her mother's pain must have
been quite overwhelming.

"What happened to the farm?" Emmalyne asked.

"He had to sell it. Your father took a terrible loss on the
land, but he used the money to set us up in a little place near
a quarry. He used some of the money to buy tools and ap-
prenticed himself to learn the business of quarrying stone.
However, once the quarry master learned your father was an
educated man, he approached the owner about other possibilities for Luthias. Your father was soon taken from the
laborious work and put into the office, where he was taught
to keep the books. This was more to his liking. He didn't
have to work with the other men or even see them except

on paydays. He preferred it that way, and he seemed to grow even more stern and hard.

"I finally worked up my nerve to ask about his coldness," Mother continued. "He told me I was to keep the house and the wash, cook his meals, and tend to his needs . . . but above all, I was to do it in silence. He said he might have made the mistake of being caught in my spell, but he would right the matter in his own way." Her voice had dropped to a whisper.

"By taking away his love?"

Her mother nodded. "I cannot even tell you what he was thinkin'," she said, her lips trembling. "I suppose he thought the spirits of his family members might be appeased by his sacrifice of being miserable. All I could do was stand by and watch . . . and . . . endure his anger."

"As we've all had to do." Emmalyne reached out to touch her mother's hand. "I am sorry, Mother. I didn't ask about this to cause you more pain. I've just needed to understand why Father is the way he is. I've often seen other fathers show tenderness and affection, and I've wondered why I was denied it. I thought I had done something grievous to cause Father to act in such a manner."

"Nae, 'twas never you, Emmalyne. Oh, for sure he was disappointed when I gave him a third girl-child, but it wasn't so much about you as it was my failing. Always it's been about my failings." Mother bowed her head. "I oft wish I'd ne'er been born, or that the good Lord would take me now . . . or give me the strength to . . ." She fell silent.

Emmalyne winced and wondered if her mother was contemplating ending her life.

"You used to tell me that our being here on earth was proof that our work was not yet done," Emmalyne said carefully.

"That God was still using us to further His will. Obviously He has a plan in all of this for you, or you wouldn't be here, Mother."

She raised her gaze. "Unless this is my hell . . . my punishment."

"And is that how God would treat His children . . . His faithful? You have remained true to Him throughout all the agonies and losses. Surely God honors your love and faith, rather than punishes it."

"I would like to think so," Mother replied. "But no one knows the mind of God. We have no right to question why He allows such pain."

"Perhaps we have no right," Emmalyne said, "but surely He is a loving Father and allows for His children to seek answers and wisdom. Would He punish us for our questions? Our doubts? Did not even Jesus allow for doubts when Thomas demanded to touch the wounds in His hands and side? As I see it, Scripture is full of times when people questioned God and asked for understanding. God is a loving Father. You have told me so since I was a little child at your knee. How is it that He is less than so with you, Mother?"

She saw her mother's pain-filled expression soften. "Yes, He is a loving Faither. You are right to remind me of it. I suppose the sorrows of life have caused me to doubt that."

"Then we must do what we can to put those sorrows in their place," Emmalyne said, getting to her feet. "I wonder if you might take a walk with me. The doctor said that fresh air and exercise in the sunlight would do you good. I plan to walk to the MacLachlans. I thought by now they would have dropped in to see us, but since they have not, I believe it would be the right thing for us to do."

"Oh, I could never walk that distance," Mother replied. "But you go ahead. I'm just as surprised that Morna hasn't come to visit, but perhaps she's been too busy. Surely she still considers us friends."

"Of course she does." Emmalyne moved to the kitchen counter and took up a plate of shortbread. "We can walk slowly, Mother. We can rest along the way if need be."

"No, you go ahead. I'm feeling very tired. I think I'll just rest awhile." Mother got to her feet and plodded off toward the bedroom. Emmalyne watched until Mother had closed the door behind her. The house suddenly seemed too quiet.

Emmalyne wondered if remembering the past had caused her mother even further grief. Remorse washed over her. *Perhaps I should remain home. Mother might need me.*

She vacillated between visiting and staying home. If she left and something happened to her mother, Emmalyne might never be able to live with the consequences. On the other hand, Dr. Williams had encouraged Emmalyne to allow Mother to do more for herself. But Emmalyne couldn't help but wonder why Morna and Fenella had not been by to see them. Perhaps seeing her would only be a painful reminder of Tavin.

"But I might also be able to find out how he's doing." She looked at the plate of shortbread.

Indecision tore at her, and finally Emmalyne decided to just be done with it and go. If she met with a cool reception, she would at least know where she stood. She took a peek at her mother, who seemed to be asleep, whispered a prayer that this was the right choice, and headed down the lane.

The MacLachlan house and quarry were two and a half miles to the west, according to her father. She surmised she could make the walk in three-quarters of an hour if she put her mind to it. With the decision made, she picked up the plate of shortbread and set out at a brisk pace. She was only about half the distance when a horse and buggy approached from behind. She stepped to the side of the road, then turned to find Dr. Williams driving his horse quite fast. He pulled the animal to a slow walk just a short ways from Emmalyne.

"Whoa," he called, pulling back on the reins. He looked down at Emmalyne and smiled. "Good day. I'm glad I caught up with you."

"How did you know I'd be here?" she asked.

"Your mother told me. I arrived just after you left. She must have heard my knock from her bedroom, and she said you were on your way to the MacLachlans'."

"That's right. I wanted to take them some shortbread I made." She held up the plate.

"I can take it for you," he told her, "but I cannot allow you to visit them just yet. They're in quarantine. I thought your father might have told you."

"Quarantine? For what?"

"Measles," the doctor replied. "There's been an outbreak in the area. You'd do well to just stay home."

"Well, I've had the measles myself." Emmalyne frowned. "Who all is taken with the sickness?"

"The two young boys and their mother."

"Fenella?"

He nodded. "She was the last to come down with it. They've all been quite sick."

"And she has two boys?"

Again he nodded. "Yes. The oldest is four and the youngest is a little over a year. A dangerous age to have the measles."

"I'm sure any age would be a risk." Emmalyne shook her

head. "I can't imagine how awful this must be. Are you certain I couldn't go and see if they need anything?"

"I really would prefer you didn't. We need to keep the disease from spreading; there are already quite a few cases in the area. I'll see to it that they have everything they need," he assured her.

"I suppose then I will give you these—and please tell Morna how sorry I am not to be able to bring them myself," Emmalyne said, moving toward the buggy and handing him the plate.

"And, of course, I get to have a sample as my pay, right?" He threw her a big grin.

"Of course," she said. "The worker is worth his wage."

Jason laughed at this and took a sample. He closed his eyes and smiled in pleasure.

"I'm glad you are enjoying yourself, Doctor," Emmalyne said wryly. "Now, I suppose I shall make my way home and get back to my chores."

"Perhaps one of those chores," he said, looking at her with a twinkle in his eyes, "might be making shortbread for the doctor of the community. I happen to know that he will happily take baked goods in lieu of payment."

Emmalyne chuckled. "I suppose that could be arranged—after all, we do owe the doctor quite a debt."

He sobered and shrugged. "Perhaps we could discuss further payment sometime over . . . shortbread and coffee."

A shiver of delight rippled through Emmalyne. It had been so long since a man had paid court, and while she knew this must never amount to anything more than friendship, she found herself very much enjoying the attention.

"I shall be happy to discuss the matter with the doctor at his convenience," she said archly, turning to go.

"I'm sure he will waste little time in attending to the matter," Dr. Williams called after her.

Emmalyne smiled and began to hum.

Deep inside, however, a voice seemed to warn her against feeling too happy. *Nothing can ever come of this*, the voice told her. *Just as you had to deny yourself Tavin's affections, you'll have to deny Dr. Williams's interests, as well.*

Chapter 11

Tavin looked at his father in disbelief, then back at the young man before him. Angus Knox seemed no less stunned. Robert was unconcerned. "I ken ye both are surprised to find the other one here. I thought by now yer faither would have told ye Tavin was back, Angus."

"Well, he didn't." Emmalyne's brother turned a wary gaze on Tavin. "No one has said anything."

"For that I'm sorry," Tavin's father continued. "But I need the two of ye to fetch a load of supplies from town. It cannae wait, and 'tis too much for one man."

"I can handle it alone," Tavin said quickly.

"I wiltnae hear it. Ye go together. The horses know Angus and will work better for him."

Tavin realized his father wasn't going to change his mind. "Very well," he said, heading to the door. He blew out a long breath.

"Ye'll need this list," his father said behind him.

Stopping midstep, Tavin drew in another breath and turned back to get the list. Angus wiped his forehead with a handkerchief and looked to the floor. For just a moment Tavin thought the younger man might refuse.

"I'll bring the team around," Angus finally said.

He hurried from the room, leaving Tavin to question his father. "Why me? You know I wanted to stay as far away from the Knoxes as I could."

"And I did ma best to see it so," his father told him. "I'm sorry, son. This cannae be helped. I trust ye to get the things I need, and I trust Angus to handle the team. Sometimes a man has to do what is unpleasant."

"It would seem that is especially true of me."

His father's tone was stern, but his expression turned sympathetic. "I need ye to work together this once. Mebbe it won't be so bad."

List in hand, Tavin nodded, knowing there was nothing else to be said. He slammed the door behind him, then threw a brief glance toward the far end of the building where he knew Luthias Knox kept his office. A part of Tavin wanted to go confront the older man and demand answers to eleven years' worth of questions, while the other part simply wanted the Knox family to go as far away from St. Cloud as possible.

Within a few minutes Angus pulled up with a matched team of Belgian geldings. The large horses were needed for the heavy work of pulling the granite, and Tavin knew that in the wrong hands the beasts could be quite unmanageable. He supposed it only made sense to have Angus's help, but he sure didn't like it. Apparently Angus didn't like it any better. He looked for all the world as if he'd been sucking on sour grapes.

Once Tavin climbed into the wagon seat, Angus flicked the reins and guided the animals toward the town road. Tavin tried to relax, despite the fact that Angus sat stiffly with reins in hand and kept his focus straight ahead. For a good long time neither man said anything. Tavin was just as glad for the silence, but at the same time, he felt a nagging impulse to ask after Emmalyne.

"I didn't know you were back," Angus said, breaking the silence without warning. "Em doesn't either."

"It's just as well." Now that Angus had opened the subject of Emmalyne, Tavin felt it only fair to ask, "Is she . . . well?"

"She is. But when she hears this news, I can't say how she'll be."

"So the family tradition lives on, I take it?"

Angus threw Tavin a side glance. "If you mean is she still caring for our father and mother, then the answer is yes." Angus looked back to the road. "She's honored her word."

"I suppose that's all that matters," Tavin said, unable to hide his bitter tone.

They rode on in silence after that. Tavin wanted to say more, but Angus seemed content to keep his thoughts to himself. In fact, the younger man looked rather pale. Tavin couldn't help but wonder if it was from the shock of seeing him or from the worry that Emmalyne would get hurt all over again when she learned the truth.

Maybe she won't even care. Just because I still feel the pain doesn't mean that she does. It was probably just as well to let go of his memories and pretend she was still far away. After all, in matters of the heart, she was completely out of his reach.

In St. Cloud the hardware store had everything Robert MacLachlan had requested. Tavin was informed that the items could be loaded in less than an hour's time, and he and Angus could have lunch in the meanwhile. Since it was noon, Tavin saw no way around the suggestion.

Without a word, he and Angus walked to a small café two blocks away and took a table near the open door. The waiter brought them the daily special—thick slices of roast beef, fresh bread, and a large bowl of gravy. Tavin ordered coffee and was surprised when Angus asked for a glass of water instead of the stronger brew.

"Don't you like coffee?" Tavin asked, thinking it a safe enough subject.

"It's fine enough." Angus rubbed his eyes. "I'm feeling kind of parched and figured water might help. Fact is, I'm feeling a bit odd."

"Are you ill?" Angus looked up, and Tavin could see the man looked flushed, where earlier he had been a pasty white. Maybe it was the heat of the day. "You might have gotten too much sun. It's easy enough to get heat stroke in the summer. Water is the best thing for you."

The man returned with their drinks, and Angus immediately downed half a glass of water. Tavin was already eating his first bites of roast and gravy before Angus even managed to serve himself a single piece of the roast. He seemed indifferent toward the food.

Tavin suspected the poor fellow was probably much sicker than he was letting on. "You want some gravy on that?" Tavin asked, pushing the bowl toward Angus's side of the table.

Angus gave a short nod and spooned some of the dark brown gravy onto the meat. But after doing so, he barely picked at the food. Tavin ate his fill while Angus moved the meat around on his plate. By the time a half hour had passed, Tavin had consumed more than his share and Angus hadn't eaten more than a few bites.

Tavin paid for the meals, not waiting to see if Angus would offer. As they made their way back to the wagon, Tavin was almost certain Angus was fighting dizziness. He seemed to weave a bit in his walk, and his steps seemed less sure than normal.

They climbed up into the wagon, the items stacked behind them, and Angus took up the reins. He drew a deep breath and seemed to be all right, so Tavin said nothing. They were hardly past the edge of town, however, when Angus began to slump toward the side. Had Tavin not reached out to pull him back, the younger man would have fallen headlong from his seat.

"Angus, are you all right?"

Angus looked at Tavin with glassy eyes. "I don't know what's wrong. I think I'm gonna be sick." He no sooner said the words than he began to heave over the side of the wagon.

Tavin held on to him while Angus lost what little contents his stomach held. Through the thin material of Angus's shirt, Tavin could feel that the man was burning up.

"You have a fever. You need to get to bed."

"Can you get me home?" Angus asked, leaning back hard against Tavin. "I can't see so well."

Tavin took the reins from Angus. "Lean against me."

He put the team into motion, grateful that the animals didn't seem to notice the change in drivers. Tavin knew from what his mother had said that the Knox house was on the same road as their own, so rather than take the northerly road to the quarry, Tavin continued west.

His thoughts were in a whirl of torment. Would he see Emmalyne again? Could he somehow avoid it? He had no desire to come face-to-face with the only woman he'd ever loved, the one who had rejected his love. He'd spent eleven years trying to forget the details of her heart-shaped face and pert little nose. The memory of her cinnamon-colored hair and blue eyes caused his heart to pick up speed. Tavin felt his chest tighten.

I can't do this. Perhaps Angus would be all right if he were dropped off at the edge of the Knox property. But even as the thought crossed his mind, Tavin knew better.

He approached the Knox house much like a man heading to the battlefield. Dread and raw anxiety washed over him. Emmalyne would be in the house or in the yard. He would see her again, and his heart would be pierced. Tavin squared his shoulders and made a decision. He would see to it that Angus got to the porch, and then he'd leave. Hopefully the man wouldn't collapse as soon as Tavin walked away. With any luck he could get Angus to the door and make a run for it. Maybe the women wouldn't feel a need to come outside in greeting. Maybe they'd be hard at work in the back and not even hear the wagon.

His plan seemed to be going well enough when he brought the team to a stop. Angus straightened, looking a little better. He climbed down from the wagon, but sank to his knees. Tavin knew he had no choice but to help the man into the house. He secured the brake and reins, then climbed down to help Angus to his feet.

"Sorry," Angus whispered.

"No matter," Tavin told the barely conscious man. He glanced toward the open door, grateful that there was no one staring back at them. "Come on. I'll get you to the door."

"Em . . . Emmalyne . . . she doesn't . . ." Angus's words faded.

Tavin secured his arm around Angus's shoulders. "I know."

Emmalyne heard the wagon outside. It was far too early in the day for her father and brother to be returning from work. She also knew it didn't sound like the lightweight buggy Dr. Jason Williams drove. Curious, she opened the door a crack to find her brother staring at her.

"I'm . . . sorry . . . Em . . ." He sounded nearly incoherent.

"What's wrong, Angus?" she gasped. "Are you hurt?"

"I'm sick," he said, his eyes seeming not to even see her. "Gotta . . . tell you . . . something else."

His frame suddenly tilted, and just as Emmalyne reached for him, his knees buckled and he fell backward into the arms of another man. Before she even had time to wonder who it was, she reached out to grab her brother.

Emmalyne first noted her brother's pale face, then gently touched his cheek. He was burning up. She looked up and stared into a pair of dark green eyes. Eyes she knew as well as her own.

"Tavin," she whispered.

He said nothing. For a moment Emmalyne couldn't even move, but then she realized that Tavin was just standing there, holding her brother.

"Bring him this way." She led them to Angus's room and hurried over to pull back the covers on his bed.

Tavin carried him across the room and laid him down. Emmalyne lost no time in tending to her brother's feverish body. She struggled to pull his boots off, and without a word, Tavin stepped forward to free the boots from Angus's feet.

Seeing that done, Emmalyne ran to fetch a basin of water, then began wiping him with the wet cloth. "What happened?"

"I don't know. He got sick in town and asked me to bring him home."

"Would you fetch some more cool water, please?" Without waiting to hear Tavin's reply, she turned her attention again to Angus. He opened his eyes, looking blankly at her.

"Angus, I'm going to take off your shirt and pants. You've a high fever, and I must get you cooled down."

"Sorry." His voice was barely audible. "So sorry."

She didn't know if he was apologizing for being sick or for the fact that Tavin had brought him home. It didn't much matter. One thing was pretty much as bad as the other.

Unfastening the buttons on his shirt, Emmalyne pushed the front open and immediately noted the splotches of red that dotted his chest and stomach. "Oh, Angus, I think you've got the measles."

He moaned and closed his eyes. "My head is killing me. The light just seems to bore right through me."

Emmalyne put aside the cloth and hurried to pull the curtains. Once the room was darkened, Angus seemed to rest better. Emmalyne quickly rid him of his clothes and took the cloth up once again. She looked around for Tavin. Had he stayed? Was he waiting to speak to her? Her heart skipped a beat and a myriad of questions came to mind. When had he returned? Would he remain in the area? Was he happy to see her again? Or . . .

"Where do you want this?" Tavin asked from the doorway. He held out a bucket.

"Over here, please," Emmalyne instructed. She pulled Angus's quilt from the bed. "I'll be right back." She found the trunk where they kept clean bed linens. Taking up a sheet, she hurried back to her brother's bedroom.

She dipped the sheet in the pail of water and began to ring it out to place over her brother. When Tavin pulled the linen from her hands, she didn't protest. He was stronger and quicker. Once the excess water was squeezed away, he held the crumpled sheet out to her.

Emmalyne took it and snapped it open. "This will help bring your fever down, Angus. You need to keep it on." He didn't even stir as she placed the cloth over his body.

Knowing there was little more she could do just then for her brother, Emmalyne drew back and took a deep breath to steady her nerves. Tavin stood not four feet away, but it seemed only inches. "You rest, Angus. I'm going to go make you some tea." He didn't even acknowledge her, and Emmalyne couldn't help but frown. He was very sick. Worries crowded into her already churning thoughts about Tavin MacLachlan.

Tavin left the room, and Emmalyne followed him out toward the front door. She paused at the end of the hall, watched him for a moment, and tried to think of what to say. He was as handsome as he'd always been, but now he was a man full grown and hardened by life.

Tavin seemed to sense her gaze. His eyes met hers, and he scowled. Hand on the doorknob, he appeared in no mood for conversation.

"Wait, Tavin."

For a moment she wasn't sure he had heard her, but then he turned and looked at her, saying nothing.

"Thank you for bringing Angus home. He's very sick." Her voice sounded shaky in her ears.

"I guessed that much," he replied evenly.

Nervous, Emmalyne licked her lips. "I think it's the measles."

"Most likely. Lots of that going around."

For a moment neither one said anything, and Emmalyne couldn't help the warm rush of joy she felt just seeing him.

She smiled. "I didn't know you'd come back. I'm . . . I'm so glad to see you again."

His eyes narrowed. Emmalyne thought he looked displeased, but there was no point in retracting her statement. "Would you like some shortbread and tea? I was going to make Angus some tea, and I'd be happy to make you some, as well."

He shook his head. "I don't want anything . . . from you." He turned again for the door and yanked it open.

Emmalyne was shocked by his rudeness. "Wait just a minute," she demanded and followed him onto the porch. "What in the world is wrong with you?"

He turned to her with a look of such anger and bitterness that Emmalyne stopped short, as if struck. She trembled. "Why are you . . . why are you being so hateful?"

For a moment she didn't think he'd answer, but then he drew a deep breath. "Because hating you is the only way I've been able to live without you, Emmalyne Knox."

Chapter 12

Emmalyne followed Tavin outside, hoping she could stop him. "Tavin, please don't go. Not like this."

He didn't even acknowledge her, but stepped into the wagon and released the brake before even sitting down. Taking up the reins, he bellowed an order for the horses to move out. Emmalyne watched in disbelief. He said he hated her. Said that hating her was the only way he'd lived without her. Her eyes welled with tears.

"But I love you," she whispered to his retreating form. She watched and waited until the wagon turned at the bend in the road and was out of sight before going back inside. She dabbed her apron hem to her eyes. She might still love him, but it was obvious that he wanted nothing to do with her.

She headed back into the house, defeated. "He hates me."

"Emmalyne! Where are you?" came faintly from the back bedroom.

She drew a heavy breath. "I'm here, Mother." Emmalyne went to her mother's bedroom door and opened it.

"What's going on? I heard voices."

"Angus is sick. I've been tending him."

Her mother sat up in bed. "What's wrong with him?"

"I think it's the measles. Dr. Williams says there are many families in the area who are sick with it. Angus is running a high fever and has red spots on his chest. I couldn't recall if he'd ever had measles."

Mother surprised her by pushing up off the bed. "No. He hasn't. I must go to him." She pulled on her dressing gown and sat down at her vanity. "Is your father here, too?"

"No. Tavin brought him."

Mother looked up, shock filling her face. "Tavin is here? I thought he was far away. Your father assured me he was gone."

"I thought so, too. Apparently he's come home." Emmalyne wondered what else she should tell her mother.

Her mother didn't give her time to ponder for long. "Help me with my hair and tell me what you've done for Angus."

Emmalyne did as her mother instructed and ran a comb through her mother's graying brown hair. "I covered him in a wet sheet, and I'm planning to make him some willow tea." She quickly braided the bulky mane and reached for hairpins.

"Don't bother. Just tie off the braid." Emmalyne nodded and did just that. Mother quickly got to her feet and hurried to Angus's room. Emmalyne followed and waited in silence while Mother assessed Angus's condition. "We should send for the doctor."

"Yes, I was planning on that." Emmalyne watched her mother take up the cloth in the basin of water. "Mother, I can go to town for Dr. Williams if you can watch over Angus and make the tea."

"Of course I can. Go." Her mother frowned and shook her head. "I wish we had an extra horse. You'll be hard-pressed to walk all the way."

"Don't be worried about that, Mother. I can go quite fast."

Emmalyne began to doubt her mother's ability to tend the situation. "Are you certain you want me to go? You've not been well yourself."

"I'm fine. Your brother needs me." She wiped the cloth over Angus's face. "Just hurry."

With little thought to her appearance, Emmalyne threw off her apron on the way out the front door and hiked up her skirts to run. She made it to the first turn before having to slow to a walk. Breathless, she couldn't help but wonder how long it would take her to make the journey to town.

She prayed that she would remember the way, then added another request, as well. "Lord, I could sure use a little help here. A ride would be wonderful, or maybe you could just have Dr. Williams come along about now." She looked down the long road, but saw no one. A light breeze touched her damp skin but did little to cool her. The sun overhead heated the humid air, making it heavy and difficult to breathe.

Her hair loosened from the run, Emmalyne wished she'd thought to don a bonnet. She tended to the mass falling around her shoulders as she walked, her fingers working with quick, nimble grace to secure the pins. "Lord, you could at least put the sun behind a cloud," she suggested, looking skyward.

With her hair in better order, Emmalyne put her mind back on the reason for her trip. She knew measles could be deadly, particularly for an adult, and the thought of losing her brother was unbearable. "Lord, I was kind of selfish in my earlier prayers. Please heal my brother. Lord, the measles are a terrible thing, as you well know. Please help him—don't let him die."

She was murmuring the latter part of her prayer over

and over when a distant sound caused her to look over her shoulder. An older man sat atop a buckboard with milk cans lined up behind him. Emmalyne waved him down, and he drew the single roan to a stop.

"Could you please give me a ride into town?" she asked.

"Oh sure," he said with a smile. "You betcha."

Emmalyne climbed up quickly lest the man change his mind. "I need to find Dr. Williams's office. Do you know him?"

"Ja," the man said, nodding. "He's that young fella what works with old Dr. Schultz. He saw my wife a few weeks back. He's a good man."

Emmalyne breathed a sigh of relief. "My brother is sick, and I need to get the doctor as quickly as possible."

"Ja, I know just the place." The man flicked the reins. "Old Nellie will getcha there in a quick minute. My Nellie is old but sturdy. She's been pulling the milk to town for nigh twenty-two years." The man rattled on about his horse, but Emmalyne couldn't focus on the words.

Nearly twenty "quick" but awfully long minutes later, Emmalyne found herself ushered into the doctor's waiting room by a stern-looking older woman dressed head to toe in black. "The doctors are with a patient, but should be out soon."

"But I can't wait. Please, my brother is very ill, and I need Dr. Williams to come back to the house with me . . . immediately. Please."

The woman frowned. "And what is your name?"

"Emmalyne Knox. Please tell him that Angus Knox has collapsed, and I think he has the measles."

The woman continued to look at her for a moment, then nodded and disappeared into another room. Emmalyne paced the small entry and wondered how her mother was faring. Had it been foolish to leave her with such a grave task?

"Miss Knox, how nice to see you again," Dr. Williams said as he entered the room several minutes later. He wore no coat and was rolling his shirt sleeves back down. "I apologize for my attire. We were doing a bit of surgery."

"I'm sorry to bother you, but my brother is quite ill. Mother is with him, but if you could come to the house as soon as possible . . ."

"Of course. Let me get my bag."

Emmalyne waited while he gathered his things. He motioned her to a door at the end of a narrow hallway. "The buggy is waiting out back. I was just getting ready to make my rounds when our young patient arrived." He sent her a smile. "Five years old and five stitches to the head after falling out of a tree."

"Oh dear. I hope he will be all right," Emmalyne answered, following him to the door.

"He'll be fine. Not to worry."

"I'm so glad. I feared you'd be too busy to come. I know you said there were many cases of measles. I think Angus has joined their ranks. He came back to the house and collapsed. He's running a high fever—his skin is very hot to the touch."

Dr. Williams helped her into the buggy, then pressed in beside her. His nearness was rather unnerving, but not for the reasons she just recently might have thought. With him so near, all she could think about was that she had once sat like this with Tavin. The doctor's shaving cologne reminded her that Tavin had once worn a similar scent when courting her. She tried to keep her focus on the matter at hand, but it was no use. Her thoughts kept going back to Tavin. She finally pressed her hands to her head.

"Are you all right?" the doctor asked. He had already set the horse into motion and turned the buggy abruptly at the end of the alleyway.

She let go of her head to take hold of the side of the buggy, but the sharp turn sent her leaning into Dr. Williams all the same. "I'm worried about Angus," she finally answered.

"Is that the whole of it?"

"Yes," she said. Then, "No."

He chuckled. "Why don't you tell me what's got you so flustered?"

"Flustered? I didn't think of myself as being flustered." Emmalyne shook her head and gazed out on the passing buildings. "I suppose I'm also worried about Mother. She took it upon herself to tend to Angus since I needed to find you."

"That's very good. She needs to have something to occupy her other than her own misery."

Emmalyne nodded and fell silent. She hoped that Dr. Williams would let matters drop, but of course he didn't.

"And what else is on your mind?"

"Nothing that talking about will help."

"It might." He turned to smile at her. "I can be a very good listener, and sometimes I even offer sound advice."

She thought of the past, of all she'd endured for the sake of her family. "I . . . well . . . I wouldn't know where to begin."

"Why not at the beginning?" he offered casually, his gaze fixed on the road.

"I just saw someone . . . a man. He was . . . I was . . . we were supposed to marry a long time ago." She bit her lower lip and tried to think of what else to say. "It wasn't a pleasant meeting."

"Did he hurt you?" Jason asked, looking her over from head to toe.

"No . . . well . . . just my feelings." She was surprised at her candor. "He brought Angus home from the quarry. His father owns the quarry."

"So he's a MacLachlan. I'm guessing he must be the son who has just returned. His mother was quite happy about it. She told me he'd been gone for years."

"Yes," she said, feeling somewhat relieved to have it out in the open. "Tavin is his name. We were engaged eleven years ago. Then . . . well . . . it's a long story, but our engagement ended abruptly."

"But not your love for him?" Dr. Williams's voice was barely audible.

"No," Emmalyne whispered back.

Jason tried not to let his dismay show at Emmalyne Knox's reply. He hadn't expected her to be in love with someone else, particularly a man who'd left her life eleven years ago.

"Were you engaged for a long time?" He needed to know more about this rival, unknown until now.

"We were. We'd known each other for a good many years. We grew up together. His sister, Fenella, and I were best friends. I think I told you that."

"Yes, I seem to remember something along those lines."

"She and I were as close as sisters. It seemed only natural that I should fall for her brother. She and I used to laugh and say that one day we would truly be sisters." She frowned.

"So what happened?" He held his breath, hoping she would continue.

Emmalyne said nothing for several minutes. Jason could see that she was deep in thought; perhaps the question was too painful to answer. "I'm sorry," he offered. "That was rude of me. The matter is certainly none of my business."

Emmalyne looked at him for a moment. "It's difficult to explain. There isn't an easy way to tell the story without speaking ill of one person or another."

He said nothing further, hoping that she would eventually feel at ease enough to offer a brief explanation. They were over half the distance to the Knox house, however, and still she hadn't continued. Jason had all but given up when Emmalyne finally began to speak.

"Neither one of us wanted to end the engagement. It wasn't planned. We were just a few short weeks from our wedding, in fact. Then the tornado came, and my sisters were killed. It was a horrible time for all of us, but especially for Mother and Father. They lost everything—the house, the girls. Their grief was more than they could bear."

"And you canceled the wedding so they wouldn't lose yet another daughter?"

She looked at him oddly and shook her head. "Not exactly. Like I said, it's difficult to explain."

He made the final turn and headed toward the small house. "I'd very much like to understand."

She laughed rather bitterly. "So would I."

Her comment only served to confuse him more. "Is there anything I can do to help?"

Emmalyne shook her head. "Some things can't be helped, Dr. Williams."

"Jason. Call me Jason, please. I'd like very much for us to be friends."

She put her hand up to cover her eyes. She rubbed her temples for a moment before answering. "I don't have any friends—my responsibilities have been too great for such a luxury."

"Everyone needs a friend," he countered. "Responsibilities or no. You shouldn't consider friendship a luxury, but rather a necessity."

Emmalyne stopped rubbing her head and rested her hands once again in her lap with a sigh. "There already have been a great many necessities denied me, Dr. Williams."

"Jason," he insisted. The buggy came up even with the porch, and he reined the horse to a stop.

Emmalyne jumped down almost before the buggy completely halted. She looked up with an apologetic expression that vexed him. "I'm sorry, but I can't."

She hurried into the house, leaving Jason to stare after her. Whatever it was that was troubling her went even deeper than a broken engagement. He took up his bag and followed after Emmalyne, his mind whirling with questions and suspicions on what was truly at the root of her despair. Hopefully they would have a little time alone after he saw to her brother. Maybe then he could get some answers.

Chapter 13

For days after his unexpected encounter with Emmalyne, Tavin wrestled with his conscience. He should never have treated Emmalyne so poorly. He honestly hadn't meant to, but seeing her again sent all of his thoughts reeling back to the days when they had been so deeply in love . . . and all that had been lost by her decision to follow the tradition. Her scent, the way the sun glinted on her hair, the blue of her eyes—they all haunted him like nothing he'd never known.

Even now, as his father and Luthias Knox tried to figure out the production numbers, Tavin could think only of Emmalyne and the dreams they once had.

"I think if we can get another couple of men," his father was saying as he looked over the paper work, "we'll be just fine. Losin' Angus's help will definitely cause some problems, but not as much as if we'd lost an experienced cutter. I'll find some lads to hire who can work as common laborers. Mebbe there'll be a man or two down on their luck and just out of the state reformatory. They have 'em quarryin' over there to build the prison walls. Could be we might find men already well trained."

"Aye," Luthias said, nodding his agreement. "The deadline cannae be ignored. Angus's sickness need nae set us back."

"Father, can I have a word?" Gillam asked from the office door.

"I'll only be a minute," Robert told Tavin. "Wait here."

The last place Tavin wanted to be was alone with Luthias Knox. The older man hated him, and Tavin was only too glad to return the sentiment.

Tavin tried not to think about his terrible rage toward the older man. For many years he'd worked hard to forget that Luthias Knox even existed. For a time, he thought drink would help him drown his memories, his anger. But it wasn't long before Tavin realized that alcohol wasn't his friend. The memories and all the emotions surrounding them were always there, waiting for him after the booze had lost its power to make him forget. So then Tavin tried to throw himself into work. He would work such long, hard hours that he'd fall into bed exhausted at the close of each day. Even deep sleep couldn't keep the dreams away, however.

"I donnae like yer bein' here," Luthias said, pulling Tavin from his contemplation when Robert MacLachlan stepped out the door.

He threw the man a hard look. "I don't care for you being here, either."

Luthias flicked away a fly. "Ye stay away from ma Emmalyne. It can bode nothin' guid."

"Believe me, I have no intention of being near your daughter. You made your feelings quite clear eleven years ago, when you ruined my life and hers. I doubt you care what you did, since you were thinking only of yourself, but what's done is done. I won't be seeking to repeat it."

For a moment Luthias looked surprised. But just as quickly he gave a growl and hurled a string of curses at Tavin. "Yer a thorn in ma side. Yer the one that thinks only of hisself. I wiltnae have ye stirrin' up Emmalyne's feelin's. She's done jest fine these years without ye. Leave her be. Leave us be." The last words cut at Tavin like shards of glass.

Tavin could see the older man was livid with anger. Luthias maintained his distance behind the desk, but his hands were balled into fists that Tavin had no doubt would slam into him if the man dared.

Shaking his head, Tavin crossed his arms. "Ever the tyrant."

The old man's eyes narrowed. "What say ye?"

Louder. "I said you're a tyrant, and so you are."

"Ye should learn to respect yer elders."

"When my elders are due respect," Tavin spat out, "I show them a great deal of it. And to be truthful, I have shown you a lot of respect these last eleven years. I didn't come and set matters straight when I should have."

"I give ye my word, ye'll regret crossin' me," the older man hissed, his face growing more red by the moment.

"Your word means very little to me." Tavin shook his head again. "You broke your word, and as my father would say, 'Ye must drink the breest ye've brewed.'"

"Then yer faither would be wrong. There be no consequences for me to bear." The man's face and voice held a sneer.

"Donnae be so sure," Tavin replied in as strong a brogue as Luthias's. He paused, then said, his voice straight as an arrow, "You gave me your blessing to marry Emmalyne, then took it back. You are not a man of honor, Luthias Knox. If you were, you would have honored our agreement."

The older man looked thunderstruck. Tavin knew this had hit a nerve, since the man had always prided himself on maintaining his honor.

Deciding he'd said enough, Tavin moved toward the door just as his father returned. He could see from the look on his father's face that something was wrong.

"Is there a problem?"

"Aye." His father looked at Luthias and then back to Tavin. "There've been some shenanigans goin' on around the quarry. Gillam and others believe it to be the union men tryin' to get our attention."

"What kind of shenanigans?" Tavin asked.

"Some thefts. Some damage to two of the ladders. One man nearly broke his leg when one of the ladders' rungs gave way. 'Twas clearly because of tampering."

"What can we do?" Luthias put in.

"Bide the stour," Robert replied, shaking his head.

"But in order to bear the struggle," Tavin interjected, "we need to know what the struggle is. If our problem is with the unions, then we should figure out our next step."

"Do we give in to 'em?" Tavin's father crossed the room and hit the wall with his fist. "It's nae that I cannae see the good in unions, but I resent bein' forced. If they cannae treat us as equals, why should I be givin' 'em the time of day?"

"Perhaps you could go and speak to the union leaders. Let them know that you won't be bullied."

"Aye, mebbe I will, and take a rifle with me." His father's words grew more menacing. "Mebbe they should know a taste of their own medicine. See how they are likin' it. We'll send an even stronger message than they have."

Tavin knew from the past that when his father was in this

frame of mind, there would be no reasoning with him. It was best to let him pour out his anger, then later, after the worst of it had passed, they could talk rationally about what should be done.

"I need to get back to work," Tavin told his father. "We're setting off powder charges, and I want to make sure the young lads do it right."

"Be sure no one has tampered with the powder," he answered gruffly. "Ye sure donnae want to end up like poor Sten. Yer sister is a ghost of a woman for the loss, and I'll nae have ye mither goin' the same road."

His mother's letter about the tragedy had hinted that his father considered Tavin's brother-in-law's death to be more than just an accident. The entire matter smacked of an underhanded threat gone awry. Sten had been an expert in the use of explosives. He'd learned to handle powder and dynamite from his own father and wouldn't have made such deadly mistakes. Of course, no one could prove anything—at least that was his mother's summation. No one could even say for certain what had happened to cause the explosion to go off sooner than it should have.

"I'll be careful, Father. Maybe it's time to post some of the men as guards, or hire some new men to watch over the quarry."

His father's face grew as red as Luthias's had. "Mebbe it's time to teach those troublemakers a lesson."

Tavin could see that Luthias was unaffected by the discussion. He was sitting at his desk, rummaging through a stack of papers.

Tavin looked back to his father and chose his words carefully. "Maybe so, but you'd not want Mother to bear the possible consequences of that tactic either. No matter if you set the men straight at the end of a gun or they reinforce their beliefs on you . . . Mother will be the one who suffers."

His father obviously calmed himself a bit at this. "Aye." He released a heavy breath. "It's prayin' that we should be doin', not threatenin'."

"Well, I'm not convinced that will help, either," Tavin said, "but at least it won't break the law or leave anyone worse for the wear. So I'll leave you to your praying and get back to my drilling." Tavin gave his father a nod and exited the building in search of his tools. There were still a good number of hours left in the day and rock to be blasted. With any luck at all, he could use the work to help him forget about Knox and his lovely daughter.

Tavin gave a harsh laugh. "But then, if I were the lucky sort, I wouldn't even be here now."

"You look madder 'n a wet hen," Gillam said, stepping up to walk in perfect stride with his brother.

"Leave me be, Gillam."

He only laughed. "You're in a fine mood. Old Mr. Knox get under your skin?"

Tavin said nothing and continued walking. Gillam couldn't seem to take the hint and said, "I suppose he found out that you'd seen Emmalyne. I don't know how the man could expect it not to happen. They live less than three miles down the road."

"Gillam, shut up."

Still the younger man refused to stop. "You haven't said much about your encounter, even if it was over an attack of the measles. Is she still as beautiful as you remember, or has she grown into an old hag?"

Tavin stopped and looked straight into Gillam's face. "You would do well to let the subject go. I find my patience has run out."

Gillam gave a nonchalant chuckle and pushed his hat back. "My, aren't we testy today. A body would think you were still in love with her."

Tavin put his fist into Gillam's face without so much as a word. Blood spurted from his brother's nose, but the younger man remained standing. He looked utterly shocked by Tavin's actions, and in truth, they had surprised Tavin himself. Even so, he wasn't going to admit to it.

"I said . . . let it go."

"Reverend Campbell, it was so good of you to come by and visit," Emmalyne said, offering the man another piece of shortbread. "Your sermons were always some of my favorite."

The man smiled, shook his head, and waved off the plate. "Thanks, but I'd best not have a second delicious piece of that shortbread," he said with a chuckle. "You are kind, Miss Knox, to remember my sermons from that long ago. And I remember your family well. You're quite welcome to join us on Sundays. We'd be glad to have you and your family back with us."

"I would be glad for that, too," Emmalyne said softly, putting the plate aside. "However, it would be difficult to get to town. We have but one wagon, and my father is generally using it."

"Would he not take time out on the Lord's Day to accompany you and your mother?"

"No, I'm afraid he wouldn't." Emmalyne offered no explanation, and the kindly reverend did not ask for one.

"Perhaps there are others in the area who might offer you and your mother a ride. The MacLachlans, for example. They live just to the west of you, and I'm sure they'd be willing once they are out of quarantine and can resume their usual attendance."

The last thing Emmalyne wanted was to ride to church on Sunday with the MacLachlans and Tavin. They used to attend church together . . . back in the good days. They both felt church not only their duty, but their privilege. They had enjoyed the fellowship of other believers and had experienced great comfort in attending. They had praised the Reverend Campbell's sermons, discussed them on occasion, and thought him a wonderful pastor.

"I can't say at this point," Emmalyne finally replied. She sipped her tea and shrugged. "With our own quarantine, it's hard to say when we might be able to come to town. I know Mother will be grateful that you visited, however. I'll let her know of your invitation when she wakes up. She'll be sorry to have missed you."

"I'm sorry, too. Sorry to hear there has been so much trouble for your family." He looked at her in his gentle way and smiled. "You know, Emmalyne, God may seem far away in times of trouble, but He isn't."

"Yes . . . at times it certainly feels like it." She didn't want to pour out the details of her life to the pastor, but at the same time Emmalyne sensed Reverend Campbell would truly understand.

"It can feel quite difficult," he commented quietly.

She tried to smile. "Life used to be so much better than

this, Reverend. I thought it would always be so, because I belonged to God. I believed all the things the Bible said, and I tried hard to live by the Word of God. I really didn't think He would allow bad things to come my way."

"You certainly never heard me say that it would be so," the elderly man replied, slowly raising his eyebrows.

She shook her head. "No, I suppose I didn't. Call it girlish whimsy if you would." Emmalyne smoothed her skirt and lifted her face to the ceiling. "I just somehow had it in my mind that Christians were protected from such things. And I suppose that was how my life had been up until . . ." She didn't finish the sentence.

"I think God's care for His children is often misunderstood. But we must remember that God 'spared not his own Son, but delivered him up for us all.'"

Emmalyne nodded. "That's from Romans eight, verse thirty-two. I know it well. Even so, the rest of the verse says, '. . . how shall he not with him also freely give us all things?'"

"But has He refused you all things?" the pastor asked. "Is God keeping good things from you?" His expression betrayed just a hint of amusement.

"Well, He's certainly refused me a good number of them," Emmalyne replied, feeling slightly irritated.

The old man nodded knowingly. "Still, my dear, the entire eighth chapter of Romans offers great insight. Think on this. 'For I reckon that the sufferings of this present time are not worthy to be compared with the glory which shall be revealed in us.' That's verse eighteen."

Emmalyne nodded and admitted a bit sheepishly, "'Likewise the Spirit also helpeth our infirmities: for we know not what we should pray for as we ought: but the Spirit itself maketh

intercession for us with groanings which cannot be uttered.'"
She and Tavin had once memorized the entire chapter of Romans eight. They had declared it would be their life chapter.

"Ah, verse twenty-six." The reverend leaned forward as if in a debate. "And twenty-seven tells us, 'And he that searcheth the hearts knoweth what is the mind of the Spirit, because he maketh intercession for the saints according to the will of God.'"

Emmalyne sighed and eased back in her chair. "'According to the will of God,'" she repeated. "But I'm not always sure what His will for me might be. Just when I think I understand it, something comes to vex me and steal away my peace."

"Such is the way of the world," Reverend Campbell replied. "You must go back up to verses five and six. 'For they that are after the flesh do mind the things of the flesh; but they that are after the Spirit the things of the Spirit. For to be carnally minded is death; but to be spiritually minded is life and peace.'"

She drank in the words as if water for her parched soul. The reverend's gentle instruction finally broke through the brittle façade she'd tried to keep around her wounded soul. "Yes. I must set my mind on spiritual matters. That is where I have strayed." She looked at him and felt the burdens of her life ease a bit. "I'm so glad you came here today. I have been putting my mind on the wrong things, and with this visit, you have helped to set my mind right again."

He got to his feet and handed her his teacup and saucer. "I am glad we could speak of such things together. Putting one's mind right is the larger part of such battles."

Emmalyne nodded. Now if she could just get her heart to follow suit.

Chapter 14

Angus's condition went from bad to worse. Despite all their efforts, he continued to weaken. And then pneumonia set in.

"You will want to keep moving him," Dr. Williams instructed them. "Elevate him so the fluid in his lungs can drain. Don't leave him in one position for more than an hour or two. If you keep turning him and encouraging him to cough, he will be able to rid himself of the mucus."

Mother's eyes welled with tears. "I cannot lose him." She wept softly, and Emmalyne wrapped her arm around her mother's shoulders. "God is dealing most severely with us, Emmy," she said, shaking her head. Emmalyne wished Pastor Campbell were there to comfort them and provide the wise instruction he'd recently given her.

She watched as Jason Williams finished examining her brother. Angus was barely conscious, almost oblivious to what was happening around him.

"Angus, you must take in more fluids, and you must do your best to practice taking in deep breaths. I know you have pain when you breathe, but it is imperative that you do as I instruct. Do you understand?"

Angus said nothing but gave the doctor the slightest nod. Dr. Williams looked to Emmalyne. "You must work with him to get him to breathe deeply. I would also recommend you pound on his back for a good ten or fifteen minutes at least four times a day—more if you have the time. This will help to loosen the mucus and make it easier for him to cough." He rolled Angus onto his side and showed Emmalyne how to use the flats of her hands to perform the task.

"I will do it," Mother said, stepping forward, her voice firm. "I will see to it that he recovers." She brushed aside her tears and fixed the doctor with a most determined gaze. "I am his mother, and he needs me."

Emmalyne was delighted to see her mother take initiative. It apparently pleased Dr. Williams, as well, for he flashed a small smile before continuing to demonstrate.

"The rash is clearing up, but he's weak. With the added complication of pneumonia, he is far sicker than I would have liked to see," the doctor explained. "However, he's a strong young man, and he should be able to overcome this with the proper care."

The doctor finished his demonstration, looking pleased to hear Angus cough, and eased him back onto the pillows. But Angus hardly acknowledged the action, and Emmalyne worried that he was far more ill than Dr. Williams was letting on. She intended to question the doctor about it once they were away from Angus and her mother.

"It's good to see you looking better, Mrs. Knox," Jason said, gathering his equipment. "Your color is much improved. Sometimes just having a sense of purpose gives us a healing all its own."

She nodded but kept her gaze on Angus. "I will nae leave

him until he's recovered. 'Tis the only purpose I have." Emotion made her Scottish accent thicker.

"I have some refreshments in the kitchen if you'd like," Emmalyne offered Dr. Williams. "I'm sure you'll have a great many more patients to see before you can get to your supper."

He smiled and tucked the medical bag under his arm. "I do have patients, but I'd like very much to enjoy some more of your shortbread—if you have it."

Emmalyne nodded. "Mother, we'll be just down the hall if you need us."

"I will be fine," Mother replied, turning back to Angus.

Emmalyne led the doctor to the kitchen. She arranged a cup and saucer on the table, then brought a small plate to add to the arrangement. Next came the teapot.

"I have some shortbread," she told him, "but perhaps you'd favor a piece of pie instead."

"I am quite fond of pie," he said, rubbing his hands together.

His enthusiasm pleased Emmalyne. "I hope you like gooseberries. I picked them myself." She went to a kitchen drawer to retrieve a knife and fork. "I found a great many bushes down by the water. They were so heavily loaded I couldn't help but put them to good use. I've made jam and jelly and now this pie."

"I do like gooseberries, especially in pie. My grandmother and mother both made it for me as a child. We often collected the berries as a family when I was very young."

"It's tedious and painful work," Emmalyne admitted, "but I find the tart flavor so refreshing." She handed him the plate and turned her attention to the tea. "Would you like cream or sugar for your tea?"

"No, this is quite all right." He picked up the fork. "Won't you join me?"

"Not for the pie, but perhaps a cup of tea," she said and hurried to take down another cup and saucer. "I want you to be honest with me," she began carefully as she took a seat at the table and poured herself some tea.

"I'll do my best. What's on your mind?"

Emmalyne met his curious expression and took a deep breath. "Will my brother recover?" She hated to even voice the question, but she had to know the truth.

"He's quite sick, as you no doubt can tell. And his recovery will depend largely on his care and God's will. I would like to see him moved to the hospital, but your mother has made it clear that this is not acceptable to her. I don't suppose you can change her mind on that, can you?"

"No, it's not so much her mind that must be changed. My father won't hear of money being spent for something he believes can be attended to at home. And not only that, but both Mother and Father see hospitals as a place one goes to die. It would be akin to giving up, in their eyes."

"I understand. However, your brother is very weak, and because of that he will have a harder time clearing his lungs. It's one of the main difficulties with measles. Often the disease itself doesn't kill, but the complications do. Pneumonia is particularly serious."

She considered his words. "Would poultices help?"

"I doubt it. I know there is some speculation that vaporized herbs can help, but I can't actually recommend them. Pounding on his back as I showed you will do him the most benefit. That and keeping him from lying in one position too long." He picked up the fork and sampled the pie. "Ummm, this is delicious. My compliments."

Emmalyne gave a distracted smile. "I'm glad you like it."

She sipped her tea and thought about Tavin and his family. How were they doing? Had they fared just as poorly with the measles as Angus?

"Can you . . . would you be able to tell me how Fenella and her sons are doing?"

"Better, actually," he replied. "The boys are very nearly over their outbreak, and Fenella is improving. At least where the measles are concerned."

Emmalyne frowned and shook her head. "I don't understand. Does she have some other ailment, as well? Did she contract pneumonia also?"

"No. It's just that her mental lapses have continued in the same manner."

"What does that exactly mean?"

"She's . . . well . . . emotionally unbalanced, I'm afraid." He took a long drink of tea and studied the pattern on his cup. "She's taken leave of her senses since her husband's death. I thought you might have heard by now."

"No," Emmalyne said, shaking her head in disbelief. "No one has said a word. Oh, this is terrible. Poor Fenella. Will she . . . I mean . . . can she recover?"

He shrugged. "There's no way of determining when or whether that will happen. When her husband's death was reported to her, Dr. Schultz told me she screamed for hours on end. They medicated her to calm her down. Keeping her in a state of near unconsciousness was the only way to control her behavior. Dr. Schultz was afraid she might hurt herself or others. I've spoken to Mrs. MacLachlan about the matter on several occasions, and I tend to believe Fenella should go to a hospital or institution, where she can receive the latest care for such trauma."

"I've heard awful stories about those places," Emmalyne said with a shudder. "I read an article in the Minneapolis newspaper that spoke of all sorts of experiments being practiced on the mentally ill."

"It's true . . . such things do take place. Doctors cannot always know what might help a patient without first trying it. Often that has negative results."

"I would hate for someone to experiment on Fenella." Emmalyne pictured the cheerful, attractive friend she had known so well. Her heart ached, imagining the poor woman unable to handle her misery. "Is she able to speak?"

"Not really. She rambles from time to time, but it's usually nonsensical. She can be quite violent at times, and that is the most important reason I believe the MacLachlans should send her away. She's hurt her boys on several occasions and now cannot be allowed to go near them. She's even a danger to herself, the result being she's kept locked in her room with nothing in it with which she could do harm to herself."

Emmalyne's hand went to her mouth. "Oh, please, say it isn't so."

"I'm afraid it is most grave," Dr. Williams replied. "She is seriously ill."

"Do you think I could visit her? Might that help?"

"It's possible that seeing someone from her past could help her." He paused and shrugged. "It's also possible it could cause further trouble. The mind is so complicated, and we know very little about it. I wish I could be more encouraging to you on this matter."

"She was always so happy," Emmalyne said, shaking her head. "We both dreamed of marriage and having children. I remember our plans to live close enough to raise our families together. We talked of how much fun it would be to have babies close in age." Emmalyne felt the heaviness of her sorrow and fell silent. She had never expected to hear such horrible news, and the very thought of Fenella's situation on top of everything else left her feeling truly overwhelmed.

"I'm sorry," Dr. Williams said, true sympathy in his expression. "I can see this has been most upsetting. I really thought by now that someone would have told you."

"It wouldn't have mattered when the telling came or who did it." She met his gaze and forced a smile. "You did me a favor in sharing this. I thank you for your honesty."

He reached out and placed his hand over hers. Emmalyne quickly pulled her hand back as if he'd burned her. She very nearly knocked over the teapot in doing so. "I'm . . . oh dear . . . I'm so sorry."

Dr. Williams shook his head. "Don't be. I apologize for being . . . less than a gentleman. I should not have been so forward." He got to his feet and looked down at Emmalyne. "You should visit Fenella, if you think you can bear it. I'd give it another week or so, and by then she should be feeling better—at least physically. I'll come by to check on Angus tomorrow."

"Thank you," Emmalyne said, wishing she could offer something more tangible than mere words. She didn't want to encourage the good doctor, however. The sooner he accepted limitations where she was concerned, the better they both would be. Emmalyne knew that nothing could ever come of his obvious interest in her, and he needed to be clear on that. As did she.

Feeling all the worse after Dr. Williams departed, Emmalyne went to check on the patient and his nurse. To her surprise she found her mother kneeling beside the sickbed.

"Mother?"

The woman lifted her head and looked at Emmalyne. "Come pray with me, daughter. We need to ask God to lift this wretched curse. We won't be free of these sorrows until He does."

Emmalyne wasn't sure whether they were truly under a curse or not, but she did believe it was time for them to refocus their hearts on God. She wished her father could see the truth in this. She went to her mother and knelt beside her. The hard wooden floor was most uncomfortable, but Emmalyne didn't mind. Maybe such an act of sacrifice would show God just how sincere she was with her requests.

She lost track of the time as they prayed in silence. From time to time her mother would pray aloud and plead with God to deliver them. The entire matter reminded Emmalyne of Jacob wrestling with God. Jacob had declared that he would not let go until God blessed him, and Emmalyne could imagine her mother saying the same thing.

"He's my only son, Lord," she heard her mother whisper. "You must allow him to come back to us."

Emmalyne wasn't sure God was obligated to do anything of the sort, but she knew it was her deepest desire. She glanced to where her brother lay. He looked so still—almost lifeless. The rash had faded somewhat from his face, but in its place Angus's skin was a pasty yellow-gray color, suggesting death.

Please don't take him from us, Father, Emmalyne prayed in silence. *He's so precious to me—to all of us. Lord, let us know what to do. Let us know how to help Angus recover from this terrible sickness.*

"O God," her mother sobbed beside her, "hear our cries. Hear us and answer, O Lord our God. You are all we have now. So much has been lost to us. So much has been taken from us. Forgive us our sins . . . forgive me, Faither." Her mother's voice rose in earnest petition. "Please, Faither, I know I've been a selfish woman. I know I've not lived life in the fullness of your will. I've oft taken my own way, and now I am paying the price. I beg you, Lord, to take this misery from my family. If need be, take me as payment."

Emmalyne heard something behind them and turned to see her father standing in the doorway. Their gazes met only for a moment, and then he was gone. It was probably just her imagination, Emmalyne told herself, but she thought she saw something akin to regret in his expression.

Tavin stood on the front lawn and stared up into the night sky. The stars looked like tiny candle flames set against a coal-black curtain. He had long ago learned to navigate by the constellations. His father had told him that man needed to know where he was, even if he didn't know where he was going.

"But where am I?" he asked no one in particular.

He thought of Emmalyne Knox, less than three miles away. She was no doubt sleeping safe and sound in her own bed, dreaming whatever dreams might come. Did she ever think of him? Did she ever regret the decision she'd made? He certainly did.

Tavin slammed his fists against his hips, wishing he could

forget it all. Yet at the same time he knew he didn't ever want to lose those good memories of Emmalyne. It was the dichotomy of his life. He constantly found himself torn between the ideals of love and hate. His misery was acute.

The sound of frogs croaking nearby mixed with the wind rustling overhead in the trees gave Tavin a strange sense of unease, like a chill down to his bones. He was thirty-one years old, and what had he done with his life except attempt to run away from it all? He had no wife, no children, not even a home of his own.

Gazing back at his father's house, Tavin stifled the urge to release a scream from somewhere deep within his soul. A tightness in his chest gripped him hard, and for a moment he found it difficult to breathe. What kind of new anguish was this? Was God so displeased that He found it necessary to punish Tavin even before Judgment Day?

"If you hate me, God, why don't you just kill me now and get it over with," he said, his teeth gritted in frustration as he looked heavenward once again. "I have nothing. You've taken it all. You might as well take my life, as well."

For a moment, just a very short moment, Tavin wondered if perhaps God would indeed strike him down. His mother had raised him to respect the Almighty and never to speak in such a manner lest God's ire be raised. However, instead of facing the wrath of God, Tavin felt a strange sense of His presence nearby. It was the last thing he'd expected, and certainly the last thing he thought he wanted. And yet . . . he found himself longing for such a union with his Creator.

"Perhaps I'm just as mad as Fenella," he whispered, gripping his head between his hands.

Chapter 15

When Angus showed remarkable improvement the next day, Mother declared that God had heard their prayers and lifted His curse on the Knox family. Emmalyne was glad Angus was better, but she was less than convinced that a curse had been lifted. When Reverend Campbell came by once again, Emmalyne couldn't help but question him as she walked with him back to his carriage.

"Does God put curses on His children?"

The pastor looked at her for a long moment. "Why do you ask such a thing?"

"My mother believes our family was cursed because of things she did wrong in the past. I thought, however, that God was forgiving and that if we asked Him, He would forgive our sins and cast them as far as the east is from the west."

"That is true."

"But God also punishes," Emmalyne continued. "The Bible shows examples of God's punishment. When the Israelites sinned and built idols, for example."

"Yes, those events did happen," the reverend replied. "But you forget another very important event." The man smiled at Emmalyne. "Calvary. Jesus took on the curses and sins and wrath of God against all evil at Calvary. As God's children we might endure discipline, but surely not God's wrath. Jesus paid the price for that already."

"So my mother's belief that her sins—and I would question that they are truly sins—have brought curses upon our family would be false."

"In my understanding of God's Word, yes." The man grew thoughtful. "There are, of course, *consequences* for sin, and often people equate this with God's punishment. Or curse, if you will."

"And how does that differ?" Emmalyne asked. "Suffering is suffering. If the innocent suffer for the sins of others, how is that something the Lord allows?"

"Ah, the theological dichotomy of why bad things are permitted to happen to good people."

They were stopped alongside the buggy by now. Emmalyne folded her arms. "Why *does* God allow it?" She thought of Fenella and the loss of her husband and the subsequent loss of her mind. "If God loves His children as the Bible says, then why would He allow them to suffer?"

"Emmalyne, this world is far from perfect, and suffering is all around us. God in His infinite wisdom holds the world in His hands. His power over all is unequaled and without question. However, He has also allowed Satan—for a time—a certain amount of power and say-so. Would you not agree that we are challenged by Satan's ploys on this earth?"

"I would, but I don't understand why it must be so. I gave my heart to Jesus as a little girl. I heard the gospel message of God's love for us, how He sent Jesus to take our place on the cross. I've studied the Scriptures, and I've done my best to live by them, even losing the love of my heart in seeking to honor my father and mother." She paused and lowered her head in a moment of embarrassment. She wished she could take that last statement back.

"Please don't think that I'm saying I believe myself to be perfect," she finally continued. "I'm not." She raised her face to meet the older man's gaze. "I just don't understand why my family continues to endure so many awful things. My father blames my mother for every problem—every turn of despair. Why does God allow him to do that?"

"Why does God allow it?" He smiled. "Tell me, Emmalyne, why do *you* allow it?"

Her brows knit together as she frowned. "How can I not? How can I honor my father and mother and not? I am not my father's master to make demands of him."

"That is true. But you have an intercessor, Jesus, who is your father's master. Have you pled your case to Him? God does not call us to tolerate or accept sin. He would have us overcome sin with His love."

Emmalyne considered the man's words for a moment. In truth, while she had prayed that things would change, she'd never specifically prayed for God to change her father's heart. Nor had she prayed for insight to change her own where he was concerned. "I suppose I have been remiss in my prayers. I have ranted at God to tell Him of my misery and ask that He take it away, but I suppose I've not truly looked to Him for answers beyond my own ease. And I've certainly not worried overmuch about love."

Reverend Campbell nodded. "I would encourage you to spend time in prayer and to seek God's heart. He will reveal to you what is to be done. He is a God of reconciliation. We need look no further than the cross to prove this."

"Reconciliation." Emmalyne murmured the word. "Perhaps my pain has blinded me to God's true purpose for my life. Maybe I am to help facilitate reconciliation in my family."

The pastor smiled and reached out to pat her hand. "Perhaps you are."

Emmalyne thought for a long while on Reverend Campbell's words. That afternoon she decided to approach her mother on the matter. With Angus sleeping peacefully, Emmalyne drew her mother out to the dining table and surprised her with fresh-brewed tea.

"Mother," she began, sitting down across from her with her own cup, "I know you feel God cursed this family because you encouraged Father to run away and marry you." Her mother started to say something, but Emmalyne held up her hand. "Please, just hear me out." Mother nodded and took a sip of tea.

Emmalyne thought for a moment. "I don't think it has been God's punishment, so much as the consequences that naturally befall us when we make any number of choices." She fiddled with her teacup.

"I was speaking with Reverend Campbell, and he said that God's wrath toward us was paid out at the cross. He said that when we are reconciled with God through Jesus, His wrath against our sins is no longer on us. Jesus took on our sins, and we are made clean by His sacrifice."

"But even so, we are not without sin. We are not perfect," Mother interjected.

"No, we aren't. But we are forgiven, and if we are forgiven, how can we say that we are under God's curse?"

Emmalyne's mother must not have been able to answer that, because she took a new tack. "Suffering is a way of life," she said. "Jesus himself said we would have suffering—trials and troubles."

"True," Emmalyne replied, "but He also said that we could take heart because He had overcome this world. Mother, I think we do God a disservice to believe we are cursed by Him when we have sought to be reconciled to Him through Jesus. I do not believe this family has been cursed because you and Father fell in love and eloped. Granted, there were consequences for your actions, but the death of Father's family wasn't God exacting payment. There is nothing in the Bible that I can see that would support that belief."

Mother sipped her tea quietly as Emmalyne continued to lay out her thoughts. "I am determined to see this family come together in love. I know Father is a bitter and hate-filled man, but I also know that God's love can change that." She looked at her mother with a feeling of growing hope. "We can pray for Father and for ourselves. We can ask God to change our hearts and Father's, as well. Let's watch for ways to show him that we care about him." Mother and daughter stared at each other for a moment at this new, somewhat daunting, thought.

"I want you to be happy, Mother," Emmalyne went on. "I want you to know peace of mind. You have not brought a curse upon this family. You are a loving woman who seeks to do God's will. Satan is the only one who benefits by your believing otherwise."

Her mother looked rather stunned. She said nothing for several minutes, and Emmalyne used the silent moments to pray.

God, this isn't easy for her to hear, much less accept. Please open her heart and mind to the truth. Help us, Lord. Please help us to love one another. Help us to love Father.

The next morning Angus was sitting up on his own, and though extremely weak, he was able to feed himself. Emmalyne stood at the end of his bed and proclaimed his progress a miracle.

"We had feared losing you, but now you are restored to us . . . at least in part. I know you'll continue to grow strong. I have prayed for it to be so."

Angus's pale complexion and weary expression did not deter her positive proclamations. "Before you know it, Angus, you'll be fully recovered. God is to be praised for this."

"I agree," he replied, then gave way to a bout of coughing. When he finally regained control, he looked up at Emmalyne with watery eyes. "I remember you and Mother praying for me. I don't think I've ever heard anything like it before."

"Hopefully you'll hear a lot more of it in the days and months to come." Emmalyne squared her shoulders. "I have resolved to see this family mended from the rips and tears Satan has delivered us."

"And that we've delivered to each other," Angus added.

"Aye. We are responsible for allowing Satan's ill will and bad feelings. We must turn our hearts ever toward the light—toward God's mercy. We need to pray for Father to find peace and to know God's love again. He has been angry so long that he won't even try. But if we show him love, perhaps Father will be drawn back to his heavenly Father."

Angus shrugged. "I'm not sure any of us are very knowledgeable about loving."

Emmalyne smiled. "Then it's high time we learned."

Mother entered the room with a stack of freshly washed bedding. "Emmalyne, help me get Angus from the bed to the chair so I can make his bed with fresh linens."

"I'll help you make the bed, as well," Emmalyne said, coming around to the side. She pulled back the covers and reached out to take hold of her brother. "Come then, little brother." She threw him a grin and pulled him toward her. Angus was stronger than she'd expected and, grinning back, gave her arm a yank. Emmalyne very nearly lost her balance. "Mother, I believe he might well be able to get himself to the chair."

Angus chuckled and eased to the edge of the bed. "I wouldn't go that far. My legs feel as though they're no better than a rag doll's."

Emmalyne helped him put his arm around her neck, then eased him into a standing position. "Just take your time," she told him. "Get your bearings, and then we can move to the chair." She helped Angus to the rocker and gently lowered him to sit. Weeks in a sickbed had taken their toll, and she could feel his bones where before were muscles.

"Mother," she said, "I think it might be a good idea to have some beef for supper. Angus is skin and bones, and a good hearty stew would do him well."

"Have we the needed ingredients?" Mother asked.

"We will." Emmalyne went to the bed and helped her mother secure the clean sheet. "There's a beef roast in the icebox that Father procured yesterday. We can cut that up for stew. Also, Morna MacLachlan sent a note offering us some fresh produce from her garden. I thought you and I might walk over there and pay a visit. After all, we've been here over two months and have yet to see them."

"I cannae leave your brother," Mother said quickly. "But you go. I can start stewing the meat and care for Angus."

Emmalyne considered arguing, but then changed her mind. She hadn't wanted to go alone to the MacLachlans'; she worried that she would find herself in another difficult encounter with Tavin. But it was early in the day, so he would be working. There was no reason to think she would have to face him.

"Very well. I'll go and bring back vegetables. I'll take Morna some gooseberry jam and fresh rolls."

"Aye, that would be good. Give her my best," Mother said, shaking out Angus's quilt. "I believe I will let this air on the line while you sit in the chair awhile."

Angus nodded. "It feels good to be upright. I can manage this for a time. Maybe you could bring me a book to read."

"Nae, you mustn't yet strain your eyes. I'll get the meat to stewing and bring a Bible to read to you," Mother declared. "It will do us both good."

Emmalyne couldn't help but smile at the words. She was feeling more hopeful that the mother of her childhood would return yet again.

On her walk to the MacLachlans', Emmalyne pondered how she might help to change her father. She knew that she couldn't change him herself, but she prayed that God might. Father had been very quiet of late. She knew he'd been fraught with worry over Angus's sickness, yet even this hadn't brought him to words of kindness or love.

He's not just angry and bitter; he's like a crippled man. He can only limp from task to task, reeling from the pain. Yet he has no choice but to keep moving. Emmalyne looked up at the bright sky. *Haven't I felt that way myself?*

She thought on this for a while. The day was hot and humid, and sweat trickled down the middle of Emmalyne's back, but still her mind stayed fixed on her father and what she could do. When she looked into her own heart, she found little love for the man. It troubled her to face that truth.

"O Father God," she said, looking to the canopy of trees over the narrow lane, "teach me to love him."

You can begin by doing and saying loving things. The words were so clear, Emmalyne stopped dead in her tracks and looked around her. Soon another powerful statement filled her mind: *Love is not an emotion but an act.*

She moved slowly to the side of the road and sat down on a stone. "Thank you, Father, for loving me," she whispered through the tears brimming in her eyes. "Thank you for showing me how to love Father—even when he doesn't deserve it. None of us deserved your love, yet you have still given it freely." She wiped her eyes. It seemed so simple, yet Emmalyne knew it to be quite difficult to show love to those who were less than loving in return. "I will endeavor to do so, however," she promised.

After she resumed her journey, it wasn't much longer before she reached the end of the road and spied the MacLachlans' two-story house. It looked to be in much better repair than the Knox place, but that didn't surprise her. Robert MacLachlan was not nearly so tight-handed with money as her father. *But I'm going to start thinking kind, good thoughts about him rather than dwelling on the difficulties.*

Emmalyne shifted the basket she'd brought and knocked on the screen door.

A young boy came running full speed, halting just short of the screen. "Hello! Who are you?"

"I'm Emmalyne," she replied, beaming a smile at him. "Who are you?"

"I'm Gunnar, an' I'm four," he told her, his little blond head bobbing from side to side.

"Gunnar, who are you talking to?" Morna came to the door with another blond-haired boy on her hip. "Emmalyne! Oh, bless my soul." She opened the door and extended her free arm to hug Emmalyne close. "I can scarce believe you're here."

"I'm sorry it's taken so long." Emmalyne relished the embrace. This woman had been like a second mother to her, and they had shared a great many things in the past. Even now, it felt as if those eleven years of separation had simply vanished.

"Come in, child. Come in and tell me about your family." She released her hold as the baby began to protest. Morna laughed. "This is Lethan, and he doesn't hesitate to let his will be known."

Emmalyne laughed. "I am pleased to meet you handsome boys."

"Where do you come from?" Gunnar asked.

Morna led the way into the sitting room. "She comes from just down the road, Gunnar. Now, why don't you play with your brother while Emmalyne and I have a wee visit."

"I wanna visit, too," Gunnar said, coming to Emmalyne's side. "What's in the basket?"

"I brought you some jam and fresh rolls. Maybe your grandmother will let you have some."

Gunnar looked to Morna in expectation. "Can I?"

"Certainly." She turned to Emmalyne. "Will you stay for lunch?"

"I really shouldn't today. I came with more than just the visit in mind." She chuckled. "I had hoped to take you up on the offer of garden vegetables. I'm happy to pick my own if you—"

"Oh, goodness no," Morna answered quickly. "I have the entire back porch full of produce. We've been picking and eating and canning as fast as we can. I'm weary to the bone trying to keep up. 'Tis why I hinnae been to visit. Oh, and you must think me such a bad friend."

"Not at all. I know you have more than enough to tend to with the measles and all. Dr. Williams told me about Fenella." Emmalyne bit her lower lip, hoping she'd not said too much.

"Aye. She's not the lass you remember." Morna looked at the boys and smiled. "These are her sons, but they scarce know her."

Gunnar lost interest in the new visitor and went to the corner of the room, where he began to play. Seeing this, Lethan wanted down to join his brother. Morna placed the boy on his feet and chuckled as he ran across the floor. "They are growing up so fast," she said with a shake of her head.

"They are handsome lads. Gunnar looks quite like his mother."

"Aye." Morna motioned to the settee. "Please, sit." She pulled up a small chair for herself.

"Mother sends her love. She's got her hands full with Angus's recovery."

"Tavin told me he was ill." She pressed her lips together, looking stricken.

Emmalyne tried to ease her discomfort. "Yes, thank the good Lord Tavin was able to bring Angus home. He was very sick. Measles and then pneumonia. He's doing much better now."

"I'm so glad," Morna said, seeming to relax. "We prayed for him at church. Reverend Campbell said he's been to see you a couple of times." '

"Aye," Emmalyne replied. "It was so nice to see him again."

"Lethan, no!" Gunnar shouted, but too late. Lethan knocked over the towering block structure.

"Grandma, Lethan's being bad." Gunnar stood with arms crossed, his lower lip quivering as if he might break into tears.

Morna quickly interceded. "Gunnar, he's just trying to play with you. Show him how to stack the blocks again. In time, he'll learn."

From the expression on his face, Gunnar wasn't really satisfied with this explanation. "It's gonna take a long time to build it," he muttered and began to pick through the blocks again. Emmalyne heard him admonish the younger boy to be good and couldn't help but smile.

"With Fenella unable to care for them and needin' so much attention herself," Morna said, her voice low, "it's a wonder I get anything done."

"I'm sure they keep you very busy, Morna. May I see Fenella?" Emmalyne asked. "I know her condition is not good, but . . . well . . . she was such a dear friend."

"Of course you may see her." Morna shook her head. "But donnae expect much. She probably wiltnae ken who you are."

Emmalyne nodded. "I understand."

"Boys, you play here for a minute while I take Emmalyne to say hello to your mither."

Gunnar looked up. "My mama is sick."

"Aye, but you be a big boy and watch Lethan here while I go check on her."

The boy nodded in a most sober fashion, his expression quite unusual for a child. But Emmalyne supposed he'd had to endure a great deal.

She followed Morna upstairs and down the hall. At the end, Morna took out a key and unlocked the bedroom door. "She can be harmful to herself and to the boys, so we have to keep the door locked."

The room was quite warm. Emmalyne couldn't understand why the windows weren't open. Morna seemed to read her mind.

"I usually try to move Fenella elsewhere during the heat of the day. We had to nail the windows closed lest she climb out and harm herself."

Thinking on this, Emmalyne stepped into the room and immediately saw the wild-haired, glassy-eyed woman who only vaguely resembled her old friend. Fenella looked up from where she sat on the floor pulling threads from her skirt. She looked at Emmalyne for several seconds, then let out a shriek. Emmalyne jumped at the shocking noise.

"She does that whenever we come into the room," Morna explained. "I told the boys it was her way of saying hello." The older woman looked so sad. "She's so lost within herself."

Emmalyne stepped closer, then crouched down. "Fenella? It's me, Emmy. Remember?"

Fenella looked at her but said nothing. She stared blankly for several silent moments, then turned her attention back to the threads. Emmalyne longed to reach out to her friend, but she didn't know how to start. Standing, she looked back to Morna.

"Is there no hope she'll come back to us?"

Morna shook her head. "Very little. We've taken her to a great many doctors, and they all say the same thing: Losing her husband caused her mind to . . . well, to break. And they know of no way to repair the damage."

"I'm so sorry." Emmalyne looked back at Fenella. "She seems at peace."

"For the moment. She's had her morning medicine," Morna replied. "In time she'll be ranting and screaming. Sometimes it goes on for hours. Usually I take the boys out to the garden or to care for the animals when she has one of her fits. It's quite hard on them."

"I can imagine."

"We'd best leave before she gets agitated. I can't always manage her very well when she's excited."

Emmalyne looked one last time at Fenella. Her skin was pale, and Emmalyne saw scratches and scars where she'd obviously done harm to herself. "I will come to see you again, Fenella," she said with a smile. Fenella never looked up or even acknowledged her best friend from the past.

Once the door was locked and the two women were walking back downstairs, Emmalyne couldn't help but remember Dr. Williams's comments about sending Fenella to an institution. "What will become of her?" she asked softly.

Morna paused at the bottom of the steps. "I donnae ken. She's in the good Lord's hands is all we know."

Emmalyne reached out and embraced the older woman. "I'm so sorry. So very sorry. I will pray for her . . . and for you."

Chapter 16

"You must be the doctor," Tavin said as Jason Williams descended the stairs.

"I am." The man smiled and extended his hand.

Tavin shook it and introduced himself. "Tavin MacLachlan."

The smile faded a bit, and the doctor studied Tavin for a moment. "You're the newly returned son."

Feeling slightly uncomfortable, Tavin nodded. "The prodigal son and all that goes with it." Williams continued sizing him up for a moment, making Tavin feel even more out of place. "How's my sister doing?"

"The same, I'm afraid. I've encouraged your mother to let me find a place for her. Perhaps you can help to convince her."

"A place? You mean an institution? Lock Fenella up somewhere? She's a human being, you know." Tavin couldn't contain his fury at the idea.

"Yes, but she's a danger to herself and to those around her. Did you see the bruising on your mother's arms? You may not know this yet, but there have also been incidents in the past when she's hurt the children."

Tavin shook his head slowly. "I had heard about the children, but didn't realize Fenella had hurt my mother."

171

"Unfortunately, she did." The doctor and Tavin faced each other at the bottom of the stairs. "Fenella hit your mother multiple times when she was trying to clean her up. Your mother is worn out, Mr. MacLachlan. Besides the physical and emotional burden of your sister's care, she is raising those two young boys at the time in her life when she should simply be enjoying her role as a grandmother. I fear before much longer I'll be making visits out here to see to your mother, too."

Tavin regretted his earlier outburst. "Maybe Mother needs to have my father or me take part in helping her."

"That is a gracious offer but would probably be most difficult and at times inappropriate, Tavin. When your sister has physical needs or has torn off her clothing, it wouldn't do to have her brother or father caring for her. In fact, the job is quickly becoming one for properly trained attendants. Your sister often needs to be sedated, and although your mother tries to get her to take her medicine, it isn't always easy."

"But we get by" came his mother's voice from the top of the stairs. The men turned to face her as she made her way down. "I know that the guid doctor is tryin' to convince you that we should send Fenella away."

"He is," Tavin admitted. "But why didn't you tell me she's hurt you?"

His mother shrugged. "If I mentioned it every time, we widnae speak of much else."

"It's that bad?" Tavin asked, shocked anew. For some reason he had presumed that Fenella's spells were few and far between. He'd heard her screaming and throwing herself around the room, but he'd not once considered that she might be causing harm to their mother.

"As I was saying," Dr. Williams continued, "there are some good places—some alternatives to large institutions. Some private hospitals have sprung up in various areas for the purpose of treating the mentally ill. I could check into one of those locations and see what they might have to offer."

"You can check into it if you wish, Doctor," she told the man. "But I cannae make a decision about it today. Nor on my own. I will speak to my husband and sons on the matter."

Dr. Williams nodded. "Very well. I'll be back to check on her again next week. In the meanwhile, it might serve you well to at least have one of the men present when you deal with her episodes. You can always send them into the hall to wait until you're finished, but I fear for your safety as she becomes more violent."

"Donnae worry, Doctor. I'll see to it." She pulled some coins from her apron pocket. "Will this cover today?"

"It's exactly right," the doctor said, taking the money. "You're spoiling me. Your family is one of the few that pays their expenses upon service . . . and in cash." At the door, Dr. Williams reached for his hat on a nearby table.

Just then, Lethan woke up from his nap and began to call for his grandmother. Tavin knew it would only be a matter of minutes before Gunnar did likewise.

"I'll walk the doctor out, Mother," Tavin said. "You go ahead and see to the boys."

"Thank you, Tavin." She stretched up to offer him a kiss on the cheek. "You're a good lad."

Tavin followed Dr. Williams outside and down the walkway to the buggy. He was surprised, however, when the doctor paused and looked him in the eye. "You are the one who used to be engaged to Miss Knox, are you not?"

He had never imagined that such a question would be posed by anyone who hadn't been around back then, and for a moment Tavin was without the words to reply. He looked at the doctor for a moment, then gave a curt nod.

"Well, just so you know, I happen to care about what happens to that young woman. She has become a friend, and I wouldn't want to see her hurt by you—again."

Tavin sized the man up. They weren't so different in height or weight, but he figured he probably had more muscle than a man who treated the sick for a living. The doctor's statement riled him, but Tavin wasn't about to admit it to the man.

"I hope you understand," the doctor added firmly.

"I think you'd do better to keep your thoughts to yourself," Tavin said through gritted teeth, attempting to hold back his desire to plant a fist in the man's face.

He thought back to how he'd treated Emmalyne on that recent unfortunate encounter. Had she told the doctor—was that the reason he brought it up now? Guilt mingled with irritation as he sarcastically spat out, "As a physician I'm sure you have everyone's welfare in mind, but you'd do well to remember your place."

Dr. Williams held his gaze a moment longer as he climbed into the small buggy. "I do know my place, Mr. MacLachlan. I only hope you will remember yours. Otherwise, it may get a little crowded." He flicked the reins and was gone before Tavin could think of a reply.

Watching the doctor drive away, Tavin had the strangest mix of emotions. There was a part of him that wanted to pummel the man, while another felt a jealous possessiveness that he'd not known since Emmalyne had been his betrothed. But even as those feelings were awakened, Tavin remembered only too well that Luthias Knox would allow *no* man a place in his daughter's life. The good doctor would be hard-pressed to get past that obstacle, no matter how much he cared for Emmalyne. And, for the moment, that provided Tavin great comfort.

With her evening work done, Emmalyne decided to risk her father's ire and seek him out for a conversation. She sensed less anger in him since Angus had begun to recover, but nevertheless he remained aloof. Tonight he was in the barn sharpening tools.

Emmalyne hung her apron in the kitchen and poured a cup of coffee for her father—a good excuse to interrupt his work. She made her way out back without the benefit of a lamp thanks to the warm glow of the evening light. The late-summer days were such a blessing. She paused just inside the barn door and watched her father at work. He seemed quite intent, gripping the back of the axe head so he could place the blade against the grinding stone. His foot easily mastered the pedal while his hands expertly guided the edge of the axe over the stone.

Emmalyne waited until he lifted the axe away from the stone to call out. "Father, I've brought you some coffee."

He looked up and narrowed his eyes. "I dinnae ask for coffee."

"I know. I just thought you might appreciate some. You've been hard at work for some time now. Angus and Mother have already retired for the night. I know tomorrow is Sunday and you aren't overly concerned with getting to bed early tonight, so I thought we might talk a bit."

He growled, "Talk? What about?"

Emmalyne stepped forward and handed him the mug. Despite his less than gracious response, her father took a good long drink before setting the cup aside.

"Do you love me, Father?"

Her question took him by surprise, and for just a moment she saw his blue eyes widen. Then the careful mask was back in place. He turned back to the grindstone. "Git on with ye. Such nonsense."

Emmalyne moved to stand beside him. "I don't think it's nonsense, Father. I need to know. Do you love me?"

He muttered an oath and put the grindstone back in motion. "I hinnae the time for this."

Dropping to her knees on the dirt floor of the barn, Emmalyne waited a moment to speak. Her action startled her father, and he stopped pumping the grindstone. He scowled at her. "I'm busy, girl. Git on with ye."

"Please, Father, give me just a moment." Emmalyne looked up at him, and she felt herself tremble. She had known him to slap her hard when he didn't like her attitude. He had even raised welts on her back after taking a thick switch to her, although the last time that had happened had been a decade or more ago.

When he said nothing more, Emmalyne took a breath to calm herself and continued. "I know you've had a lot of bad things happen to you in life. As a family, we have known a great deal of sorrow. But I can't help but ask if you have any love for me. You see, Father, I find myself asking the same question about my feelings toward you."

Now he looked puzzled, and Emmalyne hurried to explain, lest he lose interest. "Father, I realize that mostly I fear you.

I respect you, and I know that it is my place to honor you. But—" she paused for another breath—"I cannot say for sure . . . that I love you." She frowned. "It pains me to admit this, because I had always thought I held love for you. After all, you are my father. But to say differently would be a lie."

It might have been her imagination, but Emmalyne was almost sure her father's expression softened just a bit. She wondered if she had reached him, at least in part.

"I owe you an apology, Father. I'm sorry I've not shown you the love you deserve."

To her surprise he countered with, "I donnae deserve love. Especially from ye." His eyes seemed to fill with regret, and for a moment Emmalyne thought he might say more. But just as quickly, the façade of harsh indifference went back in place. He turned back to the grindstone and studied the axe across his hands in silence.

"Father, I want very much to learn to love you," Emmalyne said, bravely soldiering on. "I hate that there is so much anger and bitterness in our family. God does not intend for it to be that way. I know you are angry at God for taking Doreen and Lorna. Mother told me as much."

Her father looked at her with a dark scowl. "We wiltnae speak their names."

"But *why*, Father? They brought us great joy, and their loss hurt all of us deeply. We can't change that fact just by not speaking their names." She knew she was risking much with her forthrightness, but Emmalyne couldn't stop now. "Wouldn't it be more to our benefit to remember them and the love we shared?"

"'Tis wimen's feelin's ye speak of. I have nocht to say." He began forcefully grinding the head of the axe once again.

Emmalyne got to her feet but stayed at her father's side in silence. She prayed for the strength to continue. She wanted to feel a measure of love for this man—this unlovable, angry man. She wanted to forgive him for what he'd stolen from her, even though he didn't believe himself in need of forgiveness.

"Father, forgive me for not loving you."

He growled in frustration. "I've got ma work to do. There is nocht to forgive—now be gone."

Emmalyne put her hand on his well-muscled arm. For a man who spent most of his days working in an office, he had maintained a sturdy, firm body that could meet most any task.

"Please, Father. I won't be able to rest if you don't at least try to forgive me."

Finally he looked her in the eye. She could see his irritation, but also something else. She couldn't really tell what it was, but it seemed to make him less imposing.

"There's nocht to forgive. I ne're gave ye reason to love me. I dinnae ask for love, and dinnae deserve such."

Emmalyne felt her chest tighten at this declaration. It was clear her father not only felt undeserving of love, but wanted nothing of it when offered. In fact, if she didn't know better, she'd think he was afraid.

"I'm praying that you will change your mind. Our heavenly Father is offering love, and I believe He wants very much for us to love one another. I think He has called me to repent of not loving you as I should, and I will endeavor to show you that love." She paused and wondered for a moment if her next words would undo any progress she might have made with the man.

"I have but one more thing to ask of you, Father."

"And what is that?"

"Forgive Mother. She needs your love. She's very nearly died from the lack of it. Angus's sickness caused her to feel needed again, but I know her greatest desire is to know she is loved by you."

Her father was clearly disturbed by this comment, and Emmalyne realized the time had come to leave him with his thoughts. She turned and walked from the barn without another word.

She wasn't at all surprised by her father's return to silence. "Lord," she whispered in the damp night air, "please let him see the truth of it and be willing to do something about it."

Tavin finished his coffee and watched as his mother straightened her hat. She had a quickness in her step that he'd not seen in some time—all because he'd offered to stay home and care for Fenella while the rest of the family attended church.

"I've not been in a month of Sundays," his mother had admitted. She clearly had missed it most dearly.

Tavin knew that prior to the boys' bout with measles, his mother and father had taken turns taking the boys to church. Fenella was usually medicated and quiet during this time, but they still didn't dare leave her alone.

"Are you sure you donnae mind staying?" his mother asked.

"I wouldn't have offered if I did. I can see how difficult this situation has become."

"Aye. We may well have no other choice but to do as the doctor suggests," Mother said quietly, resignation in her tone.

"We can't just throw people away like so much garbage," Tavin muttered, not yet convinced. "They have feelings and needs, even if they are sick or injured."

His mother paused and gave him a sad smile. "I seem to remember you cast Emmalyne away in that manner."

Tavin sat back in the chair, astonished at such a comparison. "No, *she* cast *me* away. She's the one who refused to marry me. She's the one who decided her mother and father's needs were more important."

"You must admit, the situation was exceedingly difficult for her. I believe she still cares for you, Tavin."

He got to his feet so quickly he knocked over the remainder of his coffee. The dark liquid soaked into his mother's linen tablecloth. "Now see what you've made me do," he grumbled, though he knew it wasn't his mother's fault. He went to retrieve a dish towel and tried to sop up the spreading stain.

"'Tis no matter, Tavin. It doesn't change the truth." She touched his shoulder. "I will be praying for you today. I ken there's a great bit of pain inside of you. I ken, too, that it's the kind of pain that only God can take away."

Tavin looked up and met her gaze. He didn't want to hear her words. Why couldn't she understand that even God couldn't take away this much hurt?

Chapter 17

"Remind yer mither that I'll be helpin' Gillam tonight," Robert MacLachlan told his oldest son as they stood in the office of the quarry.

Tavin nodded. "I'll remind her."

"And ye'll be goin' right home?"

"Aye. The men invited me to come share in libations and games, but I'm not in the mood for such things. I'll just head home and see what I can do to help Mother."

His father's expression changed to one of concern. "Yer sister isnae gettin' any better."

"I know."

"Do ye ken the doctors want to put her away?"

"I do," Tavin admitted.

"What think ye?" his father asked.

The frank question surprised Tavin. "I've been thinking on that very thing. Mother is so tired, and she's often injured while caring for Fenella. She said that twice recently Fenella has escaped her and harmed the boys, as well."

"Aye. I fear our lass is no more the Fenella we once knew." The anguish in his father's voice was so clear that Tavin had to turn his head away for a moment.

"Maybe the doctor is right," Tavin finally said. "Perhaps they could even help her. Maybe she needs to be in a hospital or someplace where doctors can work with her all the time. Maybe something can be done that we're unable to do here at home."

"Aye. Mebbe." Father gave Tavin's shoulder a sorrowful pat. "It's guid to have ye back, son."

Tavin waited until his brother and father were on their way. He wanted to make certain the other men had secured the equipment and were off the premises before leaving the quarry. Despite an undercurrent of grumbling and rumors, there hadn't been any additional vandalism or conflicts with the union—and Tavin wanted to be sure that it stayed that way.

Seeing nothing out of place, Tavin headed home. It wasn't a long walk, but tonight it felt like it took forever. He couldn't help but feel weighed down by the problems of his sister's condition, as well as by memories of Emmalyne Knox. He thought of his mother's comments last Sunday. She believed Emmalyne still cared for him, and if he was honest with himself, he thought as much, too. She had looked at him with the same expression that he'd once known so many years ago. The love and joy in her eyes might have been more subtle and guarded, but it was there nonetheless.

He was nearly to the back porch door when he heard a terrible scream. Running for the house, Tavin was through the porch and kitchen and up the stairs before the second ear-piercing sound. At the end of the hall, Tavin spied Gunnar squatting in the corner with his hands over his ears. He was crying and didn't seem to notice his uncle.

Tavin had no idea of where Lethan might be, but he could

see from the open doorway to his sister's room that their mother was in the midst of an awful battle with Fenella.

"You need to take your medicine, Fenella," his mother was saying in a calm tone, even as she wrestled with her daughter. "It will make you feel better."

Tavin stepped into the room and called out, "Mother, let me help you."

The sound of his voice caught Fenella's attention, and she stopped struggling. She looked up at Tavin, appearing much like a little child caught doing wrong. "What seems to be the problem?" he asked, lowering his tone.

Mother relaxed her hold and straightened. "She needs her medicine and doesn't want to take it."

Tavin stepped nearer to his sister. "Maybe now she'll be willing."

Their mother nodded and retrieved a small tin cup. "I have it in here with a little cocoa. She seems to like it best that way. At least sometimes."

Taking the cup in hand, Tavin lifted it to his sister's lips. "Now, drink this like a good lass," he instructed.

Fenella didn't offer a single protest, quietly accepting the medicine. When she'd finished, Tavin smoothed back the hair from her face and kissed her cheek. "There, now that wasn't so bad, was it?"

She didn't say a word, but something in her expression seemed to suggest understanding. Mother gently but firmly took Fenella's hand and led her to a small table and chair. "If you would see to the boys, Tavin, I'll finish feeding your sister."

He nodded and stepped back into the hall, where Gunnar was still crying. Lifting the boy into his arms, Tavin carried him downstairs, talking the entire time, assuring Gunnar that he was safe.

"My mama hurts me," Gunnar told him, his lip trembling. "She twisted my arm and hit me."

"Your mama is very sick. She doesn't even know what she's doing when she hurts you."

The boy nodded. "She is sick. Grandma said she's bad sick."

Tavin wiped tears from the child's eyes. "I'm sorry to say you are right, Gunnar." He looked around the foyer, then into the front room. "Where's your brother?"

"Sleepin'. In his bed upstairs."

"Good. Then we can have some fun."

Gunnar perked up at this. "What kind of fun?"

"You'll see." Tavin put the boy down and went in search of the newspaper he'd seen. His father often brought a paper home to read, and Tavin didn't figure he'd mind if Gunnar made use of it just this once.

Once he found it, he motioned Gunnar to sit down at the table. "When I was away, I spent my days working hard at a great many jobs. One of my jobs was on a freighter that sailed the Great Lakes."

"What's a freighter?" the boy asked.

"It's a big ship that carries supplies." Tavin unfolded the newspaper.

"What kind of supplies?"

"Just about anything—food, lumber, coal, and lots of other things," Tavin explained. "There were a lot of men who worked on the ship, and I was one of them. Sometimes storms would come up, and we had to keep the freight from getting damaged or falling into the water."

Gunnar seemed to have completely forgotten the earlier

scene with his overwrought mother. "Did *you* ever go in the water?" he asked, his eyes wide.

"No, but I saw other men who did. Some we never could get back, and others we were able to rescue." Tavin began folding the paper first one way and then another. "The water is a dangerous place to work. Many a man has lost his life to the sea."

"My papa died, but not in the sea," Gunnar declared.

Tavin was sorry the conversation had gone in such a direction. He didn't want to pretend the death hadn't occurred, but neither did he want the boy to dwell on sad things just now.

"I know he did. There are a lot of dangerous jobs that need to be done," Tavin admitted. He hurried on with his story. "I liked being on the big ship even though it was dangerous. Our captain was a big man, and he always wore a very big hat." Tavin finished his folds and held it up. "It wasn't *exactly* like this hat, but I thought you might like to pretend you're a sea captain."

He opened the bottom of the triangular hat and placed it on the boy's head. Gunnar reached up and carefully touched the paper, his face full of delight. "I never saw a big ship, Uncle Tavin. How do they go in the water?"

"Steam powers the engine, like it does for the trains. Maybe one day I'll take you to see the steamboats on the river."

"Maybe I can go on one?" the boy asked hopefully. "And wear my hat?"

"Maybe," Tavin said with a smile and a pat on Gunnar's head. "It's hard to say. Maybe one day *you* will be the captain of a ship."

"I want to blow up rocks like my papa did," Gunnar countered. "But I can still wear this hat, can't I?"

Tavin laughed. "Of course."

Later, when Tavin's mother appeared with Lethan, Gunnar was full of stories that Tavin had told him. He danced around the room in an animated fashion while Tavin's mother put supper on the table.

"And then Uncle Tavin had to hang on to the rope, or he was gonna fall into the water," Gunnar exclaimed, eyes wide as he finished his version of one tale.

"Goodness, that sounds a wee bit frightenin'." Morna had already placed Lethan in the high chair and turned to Gunnar for inspection. "Are your hands clean, lad?"

Gunnar nodded and held them up. Unfortunately he'd handled his newsprint hat so much there was ink on his fingers. Tavin rubbed his head. "Come on, we'll both wash up."

They quickly tended to the task, Gunnar mirroring Tavin's every move as he washed and dried his hands. "I like you, Uncle Tavin."

Tavin smiled. "I like you, too, Gunnar."

They joined Mother and Lethan at the supper table. "Father told me to remind you he'd be helpin' Gillam tonight," Tavin said to his mother. "I all but forgot to mention it."

"I remembered," his mother replied. "Let us offer thanks for the food. Tavin, would you care to say grace?"

He looked down at his hands, then up at her. "Ah, well, I can't say that God and I have exactly been speaking much." He looked away again, feeling rather embarrassed. He hadn't really meant to say that aloud.

His mother offered the prayer herself without further comment, then saw to the boys' plates before taking a portion of the potatoes and cabbage dish for herself.

Tavin felt uncomfortable in the silence and tried to think

of something to say. Apparently Gunnar did, as well. He touched Tavin's hand. "I know how to pray," the little boy said. "If you want, I can show you."

Tavin felt like his heart was being squeezed with the emotion of the moment. He met his mother's gaze. She was smiling. "'From the mouths of babes,'" she said. "Sometimes I think the wee ones have more sense than we have ourselves."

"No doubt." Tavin looked at the boy and tousled his hair. "And Gunnar is extra smart."

The boy beamed proudly. "Did you know that Uncle Tavin worked on a big ship, Grandma?"

"I believe you did mention something about that," she said as she buttered a piece of bread and looked at her son. "Still, I have a feeling there's a great bit I don't know about him. But I'd like to hear it all."

"I wanna hear it all, too. He tells good stories" was Gunnar's enthusiastic comment.

Tavin laughed in spite of himself. "There's a good bit of it I'd just as soon forget."

"You seem to work very hard to do that with a great many things," his mother noted with a knowing glance.

"Sometimes," he countered, "it's the only way to get by."

"And sometimes it's good to face what has been and look forward to what can be."

"Some things were never meant to be," Tavin shot back, hoping his mother would just let the subject drop. But of course she didn't.

"Like your love for Emmalyne Knox?"

Tavin swallowed hard. "I'd really rather not discuss it."

"I ken that." She had the audacity to smile at him. "But that doesnae mean you shouldnae. Tavin, you've battled this beastly anger of yours for over ten years. Donnae you think it's time to let it go—give everything over to God?"

"As I said, God and I aren't exactly on good terms."

"So you think that means He's ignorin' you? Forgotten about you?"

Tavin clamped his mouth shut. He pretended to focus his attention on cutting Gunnar's pork into pieces.

"Do you remember when you brought home a stray dog," his mother said, obviously not daunted by his irritation, "and I widnae let you keep him? You widnae speak to me for days. You thought by ignorin' me, I would just go away and leave you alone. But, if anything, your actions only made me think on you all the more. I figure if humans are that way, God must be even more so. You may think you've been hidin' from Him by ignorin' Him, but I'm bettin' you're all the more on His heart because of it."

Gunnar looked up at Tavin. "Are you 'norin' God, Uncle Tavin?"

Tavin looked at the boy for a moment, then lifted his gaze toward the ceiling. "It doesn't appear I can ignore anyone. Mother, I think we'd better get to eating this very good meal. I'm hungry, even if the rest of you are set on keeping me uncomfortable."

To his surprise, Mother laughed. When she did so, little Lethan thought it something he should do, too, and joined in, clapping his hands. Gunnar looked around at the other three and grinned. It only served to make Tavin feel all the more foolish.

"Son, I think maybe your discomfort is God's way of tryin' to get your attention. Mebbe it's time to have a wee talk with Him and see what it is He wants to say."

Tavin blew out a breath and lifted a bite to his mouth. He knew she was right. The only conversation he'd had with God in the last months was to accuse Him of not caring or to beg to be taken from this world.

"You ne'er ken, my son. He might've brought you and Mr. Knox here near the same time to mend the past and set a new path for the future."

This shook Tavin out of his morbid thoughts. "That's the last thing that God could ever bring about," he muttered.

His mother raised her eyebrows and smiled in a most indulgent manner. "Aye. I suppose you would ken best what God wants. What with you spendin' so much time with Him and all."

"Sarcasm from my own mother? I really hadn't expected that of you," Tavin said, trying his best to sound nonchalant.

Morna met his look with one of her own. "There's often a great deal we dinnae expect in life, son, but sometimes the unexpected is exactly what we need. I just dinnae want you to close your heart to the possibilities. God has a way of comin' to us in most unusual ways, and I think you may be in for a surprise."

"I've had enough surprises to last a lifetime," Tavin said, his frustration growing once more. "I would think you have, too."

"Aye," his mother replied. This time all hint of amusement was gone from her face. "But God has sent blessin's in those surprises, too. After all, you're here sharin' our table. That's somethin' I've prayed a guid many years to see come true." She looked at the boys and smiled. "And my grandsons are one of the best blessin's to be set at my door."

She turned back to Tavin and gave him a sympathetic nod. "I think if you open your heart to what God wants to show you, you'll find a blessin' or two, as well."

Chapter 18

The steel cables of the derrick moaned against the pulley as the horse teams strained, lugging the seventy-ton slab of granite into place. Tavin signaled a go-ahead to the man handling the teams, and the horses moved forward. The tension was palpable as the granite block rose in the air, for if the horses spooked or got disturbed in any way, there could be all manner of trouble. It took a strong, steady handler and driver to keep the beasts under control, the slab from toppling over, and the crew and horses safe.

The goal of the crew—bosses and laborers—was to make sure the stone excavation was properly and safely executed. But even the granite itself was unpredictable. If the cables weren't properly affixed, a shifting of the load could mean seventy tons of rock moving in the wrong direction—a death sentence for anyone in its way. Tavin had seen men killed by similar events and never wanted to witness it again.

Laborers were paid the lowly sum of seventeen cents an hour and often toiled for ten or twelve hours a day. They counted themselves lucky, however. Many were unskilled at any other type of job and were grateful for the pittance they earned. Some wanted the freedom to do nothing more than this kind of physical labor, and they moved around from quarry to quarry, city to city whenever they needed more cash. The stonecutters themselves earned more. Tavin knew a skilled stonecutter could command as much as five dollars a day, but that was only for the very best ones. Being able to eye the rock and see the fault lines and natural cuts wasn't that difficult, but assessing the stone for precise extraction was a valuable talent.

The quarry master was Tavin's brother, Gillam, and he stood not far from the derrick, making sure that everything proceeded in perfect order. He had developed a true skill for reading the rock. He could tell from years of experience how the rock would break apart and where the best places were to cut. Tavin, too, had developed an eye for the same, though he'd not really brought it to anyone's attention. He had little desire to continue quarry work once he helped his father meet his current demands. Tavin found his ability to read the stone was useful in artistically styling the piece. He loved running his hands over granite, feeling the patterns inherent in the rock.

Tavin looked back at the large slab. It was to become paving stones—nothing artistic or lovely, but definitely beneficial. He reminded himself that both aspects were needed in life.

The granite rose ever higher and strained every line on the derrick. The thick wooden beams of the derrick held fast, however, and the cumbersome monster was very nearly in position to be lowered into place for further cutting. It seemed as if the world held its breath.

Just as Tavin started to signal the horse handler, he heard

a strange whining noise. "Hold up," he hollered, waving his arms, and the handler and driver quickly complied. He went into the pulley shed and quickly checked the equipment to see if something had happened to clog the lines. Nothing seemed amiss.

Tavin walked back outside. His brother called down from his perch, "What's the problem?"

"I heard a strange sound. I thought maybe the pulley had frozen or that something had gotten into the lines. It looks to be all right. Let's finish with this."

The words were no sooner out of his mouth, however, than Tavin heard the unmistakable snap of cable. "Loose line!" he yelled.

The cable whipped away from the derrick in a frenzied fashion. En masse, the men hit the dirt, knowing they could easily be cut in half or decapitated by a wild line. Tavin feared the granite slab would create even more danger, but he didn't have time to worry over it. Back in the pulley shed, he crouched in the doorway, hoping no one would be hurt.

It was over in a matter of seconds, although it felt like an eternity. Tavin rose to see if anyone was injured and found the laborers collecting themselves off the ground. Gillam was nowhere to be found, and Tavin could only assume he'd gone to fetch their father.

"Anyone hurt?" he called. "Are the horses all right?"

Mumbled comments and curses filled the air, but no one reported any injury. Tavin quickly went to work assessing the situation.

The granite slab hung precariously at an angle. Tavin called one of the derrick operators to his side. "Will the rig function well enough to get that rock lowered?"

"We'll do what we can," the man replied. "We can't reset that cable without easin' the tension."

"Coordinate with the handler and driver—they should be able to control the teams and help you," Tavin instructed. "Just put that slab anywhere, and we'll get it in a proper place later. Right now, safety is more important."

Tavin motioned the man back to his business. Next he went to the horses and spoke to the handler. "You're going to have to work with the operator to get that slab down on the ground before another cable breaks." He glanced to where another of the handlers was talking in a soothing tone to one of the large teams of Belgians. It was truly a miracle no one had been hurt.

"Do what you can to get the slab down safely. Don't worry right now about where it ends up; just get it down."

He glanced up to find his father making his way toward him. Tavin met him halfway. "I figured Gillam would get you right away."

"I've sent him for the sheriff," his father replied.

"The sheriff? What's he got to do with this?"

His father ignored the question and kept searching the area with great intensity. "Is anyone hurt?"

"Miraculously, no."

His father breathed easier. "Praise God. What happened?"

"Cable broke. Haven't been able to inspect the line yet, so sending for the sheriff may be premature."

"Nay. I checked all those lines myself jest yesterday. They were perfect." His father's eyes narrowed. "I cannae believe they failed overnight. Someone did this."

"Maybe, but shouldn't we figure that out before getting the law involved?" Tavin felt sweat trickle into his eyes and brushed at his face with the back of hand. He could see his father's jaw clench.

"The line's been cut," one of the men called from across the way.

"See, I knew 'twas no accident," Robert MacLachlan said, slamming his fist into his hand as he moved out to inspect the line for himself. Tavin followed.

"Somebody cut in different splices," the muscular man said, holding up the cable. "You can see the marks here and here." He turned the piece in his hand. "And here and here. Weakened the line, but didn't let it break first thing."

Tavin's father looked to the derrick's other lines. "Inspect every inch of every cable. I don't want anything overlooked. If they did this to one line, they very well may have done it to others."

"Who?" the man asked, looking first to Tavin and then to Robert, who was already walking away.

"That's the question," Tavin muttered.

"I can ask around," the sheriff told Robert MacLachlan. "There are plenty of men who'll do such deeds for a few bucks. After all, we have an entire prison full of crafty fellows not all that far from here. Could be you have an enemy, Mr. MacLachlan."

"I'm tellin' ye, 'tis the stonecutters' union. They're behind this." Tavin's father pounded his fist on the desk. "I wiltnae believe otherwise. They've kilt my son-in-law, and now they're after more blood."

"Now, Mr. MacLachlan, your son-in-law's death was an accident. As I recall, the explosion proved to be worse than expected or went off quicker than the young man figured. That hardly constitutes murder."

MacLachan's face reddened. "Sten Edlund was an experienced man—expert in usin' explosives. I donnae ken how anybody can possibly think it wasnae murder."

The sheriff lowered his head and picked at a thread on his coat. "Seems like all men are capable of making mistakes, Mr. MacLachlan. There's no way to prove that anyone did anything to hasten your son-in-law's death. Certainly no one is going to come forward after all this time."

"But the troubles continue. Men might've died today."

"And the line was clearly tampered with," Tavin threw in. "That much we know for a fact."

"Can you give me an idea of any enemies you might have, Mr. MacLachlan? Someone who would want to see harm come to you?"

"The stonecutters' union officials," the man repeated firmly.

"You truly believe that union men are responsible for this?"

"Aye." Robert MacLachlan leaned forward. "They've been after me since I bought the place. Said we needed to 'stand together' to better life for all."

"But you were against this?"

Tavin's father sputtered wordlessly for a moment. "I'm nae against it! I believe a man has a right to decide for himself. Personally, I donnae need the union tellin' me what to do to treat a worker fairly. I'm an honorable man, and I ken what is expected."

"But you believe your refusal to force your crew to join the union is behind all of these problems?"

"Aye. I'm thinkin' it may well be a matter for me to handle."
He locked gazes with the sheriff.

"I can't have you doing that, Mr. MacLachlan," the sheriff
said. "I'll check into your allegations and do what I can to
get to the bottom of this, but you need to refrain from interfering." The sheriff looked to Tavin for support. "Someone
will get hurt or killed if your father goes around taking the
law into his own hands."

"Someone may well get killed if he doesn't," Tavin shot
back. "Have you ever seen what happens when a derrick cable
snaps? As the tension is released, it whips through the air like
a knife. It can cut a man's head from his shoulders. I've seen
a man lose a leg to such an . . . an accident."

"It was only by the Almighty's grace that it dinnae happen
this time," Robert MacLachlan added, shaking his head.

The sheriff nodded and got to his feet. "If you'll accompany
me, I'd like to see the site and question the workers. Once
I have a better understanding of the situation, I'll have an
easier time of figuring out what to do next."

"I ken what to do," Tavin's father growled.

"I'll take the sheriff around to meet the workers," Tavin
said quickly. He knew it would be best to get the man out of
the office before his father truly lost his temper.

By the time the workday concluded, Tavin had made the
rounds with the sheriff to interview each of the workers.
Satisfied that he had all the relevant information, the sheriff headed back to town without another word to Tavin's
father. Tavin was just as glad for this. He knew his father's
nerves were stretched taut. He was worried about his men,

worried that someone would destroy his livelihood. It had taken every cent his father could scrape together to buy the quarry in the first place. All he had to do to make back his investment was to meet this large contract. Tavin supposed it might be public knowledge that this was the case. Perhaps someone out there wanted his father to fail and lose it all. Maybe the sheriff was right. Maybe Father had an enemy other than one related to the union. To fail now would rob Robert MacLachlan of everything he'd worked a lifetime to gain. Surely the union officials would see that as more harmful than helpful. How could his father's business failure benefit them?

Tavin knew there was little he could say to assuage his father's fears, but he hoped to try. Heading back to the office, Tavin considered the events of the day and how he might approach his father. He finally decided it was best they just sit down and talk man to man with the union officials. If they were truly behind this, Tavin seriously doubted they'd shy away from the fact. Oh, they wouldn't admit to criminal activity, but Tavin felt positive he'd be able to read the truth in their actions and statements.

"Father?" Tavin called as he entered the office. His father's desk was empty, and the lamp had been extinguished. At the far end of the building a light still glowed. Perhaps his father was speaking with Luthias Knox. Tavin waited a moment, listening for the sound of voices, but he heard nothing.

The last thing he wanted was yet another encounter with Emmalyne's father. It was bad enough that Tavin had been tortured by dreams of the young woman every day for the last eleven years; seeing her father and brother at the quarry caused him to daily reconsider his agreement to stay. His father knew how difficult the situation was, yet he did nothing to help avoid the unwelcome meetings. In fact, he had on two different occasions instructed Tavin to go and speak to Mr. Knox on one matter or another. Tavin mustered his courage. It was foolish to be afraid of one old man. "But I don't fear him as much as I fear myself around him," Tavin said, moving toward Knox's office.

Looking into the room, Tavin could see that Knox was alone. With his head bent over the ledgers and pencil in hand, Luthias seemed not to hear his approach. It was just as well. Tavin had no desire to speak to the man. He started to back away when Knox spoke.

"Are ye jest gonna stand there a-hoverin'?"

"I was looking for my father," Tavin replied and turned to go.

Knox halted him with one simple yet astounding statement. "I would have a word with ye."

Tavin's jaw tightened and his breath seemed to catch in the back of his throat. He squared his shoulders and faced his enemy. The older man's icy blue eyes narrowed, and his thick reddish-brown brows pulled together as he frowned.

Waiting in the uncomfortable silence, Tavin thought perhaps to just leave without hearing the old man out. After all, why should he show this man any respect? Luthias Knox had done nothing but treat him with contempt since his arrival.

Knox continued to size Tavin up a moment longer, then slowly stood. Finally he spoke. "I have jes one question for ye."

"Very well," Tavin said evenly. "And what would that be?"

"Do ye still love ma daughter?"

Of everything Tavin could have imagined, he had never expected such a question. He looked at the man and tried to push aside the bitterness and hate that had been his companions since losing Emmalyne. He had no desire to give Knox an answer to this question fraught with such anguish, and so he posed one of his own.

"Why would you care?"

Knox seemed surprised but stood his ground. "I asked ye a question. Ye can have the decency to answer me."

Tavin shook his head, backing away. "I owe you no answer."

He was halfway out the door by the time Knox caught up with him. "I ken yer anger and hatred of me, but what I donnae ken is yer intentions toward her."

Tavin doubled his fists and whirled around so quickly it actually produced a look of fear on Knox's usually dour expression. "You made sure my intentions toward her were put aside years ago," he spat out like sharp daggers at the old man. "Now you toy with me—ask if I still love her. I think you know the answer to that, Mr. Knox. But if you don't, I see no reason to enlighten you." He reeled away as quickly as he had confronted his archenemy, not waiting for a response.

Marching across the grounds, Tavin shook in anger. It was as if a storm had risen up and been unleashed inside him, certain to destroy everything in its path.

"It was a mistake to come back," he spat out once more. "I would have done better to fall off the face of the earth. Better that I should drown in Lake Superior than face these demons." He glanced around him at the thicket of aspen and oak, grateful that no one was around to hear his tirade.

Promise or no promise, Tavin knew now it would be impossible to stay. How could he? Emmalyne was just down the road—a few short miles away. She was as lovely and appealing—inside and out—as ever, and it was killing Tavin to know that she could never be his.

"Do ye still love me daughter?" The words came back to haunt him.

Of course he still loved her. He'd always loved her.

I will always love her.

Chapter 19

Even with the arrival of September, the temperatures held fast in the nineties. Angus was well again and back to work, and Emmalyne worried that Mother would slip away again into her sorrows. However, to her surprise, that didn't happen. She wasn't sure why. A part of her liked to think that perhaps her talk with Father weeks earlier had something to do with it. Father had been less demanding of late, and in truth, Emmalyne thought he seemed even a wee bit happier.

Of course, it could just be wishful thinking. I want so much for things to change, and it would be like me to see improvement where none truly exists.

"You look so deep in thought, I'm hesitant to ask what you're pondering," her mother said from across the kitchen table.

Emmalyne looked up from the creel basket she was weaving. "Oh, you know me. I'm thinking of all the work that needs to be done before the cold sets in." Then she shook her head. "No, that's not the truth, Mother." Her mother looked surprised and opened her mouth to speak, but Emmalyne quickly continued. "I was thinking about Father. He seems . . . well, he doesn't appear to be as unhappy as he's been in the past."

"I think seeing Angus's health return has helped him appreciate life more," Mother replied. "He's been much more patient with me, as well."

"I'm so glad. I worried that it was just my imagination. I want to believe that a change is truly happening—that my prayers are being answered."

Mother paused in her own basket work. "And exactly what did you pray for?"

"That Father would learn to love again. That he would find peace with God. That he would treat you better—give you the love you deserve."

"And what of prayers for yourself?"

Emmalyne shrugged. "Those prayers were as much for me as for you and him. If you are happy and at peace with Father, that will make me happy, too."

Mother frowned and put aside her handiwork. Leaning forward, she reached out to still Emmalyne's fingers on the basket. "I would have thought you might have prayed for your father to change his mind about your marrying Tavin MacLachlan."

She hadn't expected this comment from her mother. In eleven years they had never talked in detail about what had happened between Emmalyne and Tavin. It seemed strange that Mother would bring this up now.

"What's done is done." Emmalyne pulled her hand away and continued her work. "Besides, Tavin hates me."

"Bah! He doesn't hate you. He couldn't. I remember the way he used to look at you—care for you. I was happy for the both of you. I knew it was a true love match."

Emmalyne sighed and pushed wispy strands of hair away from her face. This was not a conversation she wanted to have, and she wondered if the pain would ever leave her. *Will I ever be able to talk about Tavin and not feel as if my life is ending all over again?*

"I never felt right in putting an end to your engagement, Emmalyne. I argued with your father about his decision. But he wouldn't be moved. His heart was so broken over the loss of the girls." Her mother's lower lip quivered, and her eyes shone with tears. "The loss cut him deep."

"It affected all of us. But instead of taking it out on each other, we should have come together." Emmalyne lifted her gaze to meet her mother's regretful nod.

"Aye, we should have. It is funny how death brings some close and tears others apart."

Emmalyne figured her mother was referencing the death of Father's family as much as the girls. She couldn't help but wonder how her mother had ever managed to continue keeping house and raising children for a man filled with such bitterness, such cold indifference.

"I think your father was afraid more than anything," Mother said, her voice low. She glanced around the room, as if fearful that someone might overhear. "I think death frightens him terribly, because he feels at odds with God."

"I'm praying that this will change," Emmalyne said, her voice also hushed. "God alone is the one who can reach through to Father's hard heart. God is the only one who can change any of us."

"'Tis true. I only hope Luthias won't wait until it's too late. He's not a young man anymore." Rowena paused a moment, considering her next words.

"Emmalyne," she finally said, "we did you wrong in keeping you from Tavin. I've told your father that on many occasions. I know he will never admit it, but I believe he regrets his actions. I wanted you to know that, because I believe in his own way he . . . well, he cares about having made the wrong decision."

The tightening in her throat left Emmalyne unable to speak. She wanted to rage at her mother. *How can you say Father regrets his actions? He shows no signs of remorse. He's controlled his family like a tyrant.* Her father had made a decision and inflicted his judgment on all of them, no matter the cost, the pain. Everything had to be his way. *He is cruel . . . how can Mother expect me to believe otherwise?*

Yet how could she ever grow to love her father if she refused to forgive him? Emmalyne gave her head a brief shake at how easily bitterness could grow from a single thought.

"Emmy . . ." Her mother's voice interrupted her inner dialogue. "I'm so sorry for what we took away from you. If I could go back and see things done differently . . . I would."

Emmalyne looked up and saw her mother's sincerity, her genuine love. "I know you would have, Mother. Sometimes . . . just once in a while . . . I like to think Father would, as well." At least she hoped that might be true. "I'd like to believe he's sorry for what he did."

A knock at the front door startled both women. Emmalyne stood, abandoning the basket and her discomfort.

"Dr. Williams, what a pleasant surprise," she said at the front door, ushering the tall man into the house. "Come see what Mother and I have been up to." Emmalyne brought him into the kitchen. "Look, Mother, Dr. Williams has come to pay us a call."

"I'm happy to see both of you looking so well," Jason said, his smile widening. "Ah, those must be the baskets you told me about, Miss Knox. May I?" he asked Emmalyne's mother. She nodded and Jason picked up the partially woven container. "This is quite grand." He handed back the piece and turned to Emmalyne. "I know you must be wondering why I'm here today."

"Yes. It is a surprise to both of us," she admitted.

He sobered considerably. "I hope you will forgive me, but I've actually come to ask a favor."

"And what would that be?"

The doctor looked to Mrs. Knox first, and Emmalyne couldn't help but wonder if what he had to say would upset her.

"I'm on my way to the MacLachlans'. I have some information regarding a . . . a place where Mrs. Edlund might be able to receive help. However, I need to convince Mrs. Mac-Lachlan that it's a good establishment, one where Fenella isn't simply locked away but where she could be treated." He returned his piercing gaze to Emmalyne. "I hoped you might come with me."

"And how is it you know that it is a good place?" Emmalyne wondered. "I feel just as concerned as Mrs. MacLachlan when it comes to the matter of Fenella's care."

Jason nodded. "I completely understand. That's why I went to visit this particular establishment myself. It's in St. Paul."

"A mental institution?" Emmalyne asked.

"No. Actually it's more along the lines of a convalescent home, much like those set up in the mountains for patients with tuberculosis. It has a home-like setting. A doctor of psychiatric studies, along with another physician, has arranged this in the belief that it will bode better for the mentally ill patient. It provides a much calmer environment with more personalized care. The entire place has room for just twenty patients. It's costly, but I think it might be the kind of home Mrs. MacLachlan would approve of."

Emmalyne nodded. "It sounds like a possibility. However, do they lock the patients in their rooms?" The fact that Fenella could never sit outdoors bothered Emmalyne a lot. She couldn't help but think that fresh air would do her good, but she also understood that Fenella's violent acts forced Morna to keep her under lock and key. To be honest, that hardly seemed better than an institution to Emmalyne.

"They do lock them in at night. That's for their own safety as much as for the others. During the day they try to engage the patients in various activities."

Emmalyne tried to imagine Fenella actually participating. "And what of the hideous tortures I've heard some institutes use?"

"They use a variety of methods to help them handle their patients, but this doctor uses humane treatments and believes in therapies that will help the patient recover their sense of well-being."

"Such as what, Dr. Williams?" Emmalyne's mother asked.

"Well, walking outdoors, planting in the garden, water therapy. They read to the patients and have art classes for them to participate in. And music—they had the most amazing pianist there playing for the residents when I visited. Not only this, but the doctors are both good, godly men. They arrange for a minister to come on Sunday afternoons to share Scripture and pray with the patients."

"I think Morna would like the sound of all that very much," Mother replied. "How might we help?"

Emmalyne was surprised that her mother was including

herself in the matter, but said nothing. Instead, she looked back to the doctor. "Yes, tell us." Emmalyne suddenly realized she had left him standing and hadn't even offered refreshments. "In fact, why don't you sit here with us and have some shortbread and tea while you explain."

After Jason enjoyed three helpings of shortbread and gave the details of how they might assist him, the trio headed over to the MacLachlans'. The buggy was too small for more than the doctor and her mother, so Emmalyne walked briskly alongside the entire way despite the doctor's protests. The day was warm but the air was cooler under the canopy of shade. The trees were just starting to change color, and in another few weeks, the entire land would be a riot of beautiful oranges, yellows, reds, and browns.

"This is such a pleasant time of year," she commented. "Even though it's warm, the humidity seems far less. I suppose it will return soon enough, however, in the form of icy rain and snow."

Dr. Williams smiled down at her as he kept the horse moving forward. "I have to admit I am rather worried about the winters. We didn't get much snow in Kansas City."

"The winters can be dreadful," Mother interjected. "You'll need a sleigh."

Emmalyne nodded. "She's right, you know. I hope Dr. Schultz has already thought of that for you."

Jason chuckled. "He has. He told me he has a sleigh and snowshoes and a variety of other equipment that he assures me are necessary for living through a Minnesota winter."

They weren't far from the MacLachlan house when they heard screaming. Emmalyne looked at the doctor for a moment, then hiked her skirt and began to run. Something was terribly wrong. Another scream tore through the air.

Dr. Williams urged the horse to pick up speed and easily bypassed Emmalyne on the road. He'd just brought the buggy to a stop in front of the house when Emmalyne rounded the corner and saw the problem. Fenella was on the roof.

Morna MacLachlan stood on the ground, pleading with her daughter to go back inside. "You cannae stay out here, Fenella. You'll get hurt. Please haste ye back inside," she begged.

Fenella gave another scream and swayed back and forth on the lower roof. Emmalyne clutched her throat in fear. Dr. Williams was already heading to where Morna stood, so Emmalyne helped her mother from the buggy before joining them.

The doctor and Morna were attempting to reason with the crazed woman. Emmalyne looked up at Fenella and wondered if there was anything left inside her mind that could recall their days together.

Dr. Williams leaned toward Emmalyne. "Talk to her. I'm going to climb up the trellis and see if I can get ahold of her. It's not such a long fall should she lose her balance, but I fear she could get hurt nonetheless."

"Of course." Emmalyne looked to Morna, who had collapsed into Mother's arms. "I'll do what I can."

She walked to a position where Fenella could see her better. "Fenella, it's me, Emmy!" she called.

Fenella stopped swaying and cocked her head to the right. She appeared to understand Emmalyne's words. Encouraged by this, Emmalyne continued. "Fenella, do you remember when we were in eighth grade, and we had a harvest party at school? Remember? You and I were in charge of baking one of the cakes for the cake walk. We worked so hard on that cake." Fenella said nothing, but neither did she seem to notice Dr. Williams stealthily approaching from the other side.

"Then we put the cake on a chair while we helped Mrs. Morton hang the banner, and Horus Kaberline sat on it." Emmalyne chuckled at the memory. "Do you remember, Fenella? You told him it was a cake walk, not a 'cake sit,' and he'd have to pay a dollar for ruining a perfectly good prize."

Just then Dr. Williams reached Fenella and grabbed her from behind. She cried out and fought him like a wild animal, but Jason easily overpowered her and dragged her to the window of her room. Emmalyne grabbed his doctor's bag from the buggy and rushed past Morna and her mother.

She dashed up the stairs and burst into Fenella's room. "Is she all right?"

By this time, Dr. Williams had wrestled the woman through the window. He had Fenella pinned on the floor of her room while she kicked and screamed in a most hideous fashion.

Emmalyne approached and knelt beside them. She grasped Fenella's hand and smoothed back the girl's wild hair. "Fenella, you're safe now. Be calm, dear one."

Her voice seemed to immediately quiet the young woman. Emmalyne continued to stroke her hair. "You gave us a fright. We thought you might get hurt. I'm so glad that you didn't."

Morna stepped into the room, panic clearly written in her expression. "Oh, thank you, Dr. Williams. Thank you. She'd been up there for over an hour. Somehow she got the window open, and afore I knew it, she was out there on the roof. I tried to go out there after her, but it only served to agitate her more."

"Well, I'm thankful she didn't get hurt," he said, getting up from the floor.

Fenella scooted away to the corner, and Emmalyne stood up. "It would seem our coming here today was rather timely,

Morna. Dr. Williams wanted to discuss something with you. I think you will be happy to hear what he has to say."

Morna MacLachlan looked at Emmalyne, then gave a heavy sigh. "Is this about sending her away?"

Emmalyne went to the woman and squeezed her hand. "Yes, but not to an institution or hospital. Listen to what Dr. Williams has found, and I think you'll be pleased."

The older woman brushed a hand across her eyes. "I suppose there's little choice. Would you go be with the boys, please, Emmalyne? I left them in the front room with their toys. Your mother is there right now, but maybe you can . . . They have so much energy," she finished, her voice drifting off.

"Of course. I'd be happy to help." Emmalyne gave the older woman a quick hug, then paused at the doorway and glanced to Fenella with a smile. "I hope to see you later, Fenella dear." The young woman's expression showed no sign of having heard Emmalyne's words. It was all Emmalyne could do to keep back her tears. There was very little left of her old friend, and she couldn't help but wonder if anyone would ever be able to help Fenella find her way back.

As if understanding, Morna nodded, then turned to the doctor. "Dr. Williams, I will hear you out, but perhaps we'd do well to board up the window first. I donnae want a repeat of what we just endured."

Downstairs, Emmalyne found her mother and the boys in the front room just as Morna had said. "You look to be having fun," Emmalyne said as she approached the boys.

"Is my mama gonna die today?" Gunnar asked, looking up at her with a sober expression.

"There's no way to know when any of us will die," Emmalyne told him. She knelt beside him and picked up one of his blocks. "But we don't have to be afraid of such things. If we love Jesus, then our life is just the beginning. One day we will get to go be with Him in heaven." She placed the block atop one of those already stacked.

Gunnar seemed to consider both her words and the block's placement. Finally he nodded. "My papa went to live with Jesus." He put another block on top.

"Yes, I'm sure he did," Emmalyne said. Lethan toddled over to her and reached out for the block she'd just picked up. She handed it to the boy without hesitation. Lethan let out a little chuckle and squatted to position his block atop the others. Emmalyne held her breath. The block stayed in place, much to her relief.

Gunnar looked back at Emmalyne's mother. "Is she your mama?"

"Yes. You may call her Mrs. Knox."

He nodded. "That's what she said." He frowned and looked past Emmalyne to the foyer. "My mama is hurt. Grandma says she got sick in her head."

"Your mother used to be my very best friend, did I tell you that?" She didn't wait for his answer, but continued, "We went to school together, and we loved to play together."

"Did you have a dog?" Gunnar asked.

"We did. There were several dogs, as I recall." She looked to her mother. "Weren't there?"

"Oh goodness, yes. It seemed there was a dog for each child," her mother said with a laugh.

"I wanna dog, and Grandma says we can get one soon. They used to have a dog, but my Uncle Gillam took him."

"I think getting a pet would be great fun."

Gunnar seemed to have recovered from his earlier trauma. He jumped to his feet and reached for Emmalyne's arm. "You wanna see where we're gonna put him?"

She smiled and looked to her mother. "Yes, I'd like to see that. Mother, would you excuse us for a moment?"

Emmalyne felt Fenella's younger boy take hold of her skirt. "Why don't we take Lethan with us, and you can show us both." She lifted the younger boy in her arms, hopeful that he wouldn't protest. He didn't, but instead reached for her nose. Emmalyne laughed and pretended to nibble his hand. Oh, how she wished she might have had children to love.

Chapter 20

Emmalyne and the boys returned to the house just as Jason and Morna descended the stairs from Fenella's room. She wondered if the doctor had been able to tell Mrs. MacLachlan about the place he'd found for Fenella, possibly even convince her of its potential. Lethan yawned and laid his head on Emmalyne's shoulder. She loved the way his head felt against her neck. She nuzzled him with her chin and gave a sigh.

"I thank you for everything," Morna said, looking first to Emmalyne and then to the doctor. "Both of you."

"Why don't we continue our discussion while you sit down for a rest," Dr. Williams suggested. "You must be quite exhausted, Mrs. MacLachlan."

Morna nodded and led the way into the front room. "Aye, that I am." She went to sit beside Emmalyne's mother and patted her on the arm. "It's such a treat to see you again. I'm sorry the situation couldn't be more inviting for a visit."

"You've nothing to apologize for, Morna. 'Tis I who owe you an apology. I should have come by sooner."

Morna clung to Mother's hand. "I cannae tell you how it comforts my heart to have you here."

Emmalyne took a seat, still cradling Lethan. Gunnar lost interest in the adults and went back to his toys. "Mrs. MacLachlan, Dr. Williams told me about the home he found. Didn't it sound lovely?"

"Aye, it did, Emmalyne. I cannae imagine sending her away, though. It seems cruel—like I'm abandoning her."

"I fear that with the threat her behavior is to the boys and to you," Dr. Williams began, "it would be even more cruel to keep her here. Besides, you have no one to help you. With two small children to look after as well as a sick woman—a most unpredictable sick woman—you really have no choice."

"How long would it take for arrangements to be made for Fenella to move there?" Emmalyne asked.

Dr. Williams shrugged. "Probably take a week or more to get everything in order."

Emmalyne was surprised when her mother spoke up. "I could lend you my Emmy in the meantime. I'm feeling much better these days, and she could come over here and help you with the chores and anything else that needs doing."

She had never expected her mother to suggest such a thing. Unable to fully hide her reaction, Emmalyne sputtered, "I . . . well . . . do you think that would . . . well . . ." She looked from Morna to her mother. Then, "What would Father say?"

"Bah! I care not." Her mother's candor was even more startling. "He'll be working and won't know the difference. You could come over here two or three times a week after he goes to work and be home before he returns. He needn't even know."

"I think this would be a good solution while I make arrangements for Fenella," Dr. Williams put in. "Emmalyne obviously has a way with children." He threw her a smile.

"I donnae ken," Mrs. MacLachlan said. "About Fenella. I mean, I have approached the idea with Rabbie, but we made no decision."

"I think today made the decision for you," the doctor said, eyebrows raised meaningfully. "You can't endure another event like that, Mrs. MacLachlan. You both could have been seriously injured, and then where would the boys be?"

Morna looked to where Gunnar was playing. "I suppose 'tis the right thing to do. The wee ones cannae defend themselves."

"Goodness, Morna, you can scarcely defend yourself," Emmalyne's mother said, giving the woman's hand a squeeze. "You've done all that a mother could. I think Dr. Williams is right. Now it's time to let someone else help."

"And, as I said," Dr. Williams interjected, "There is a chance that Fenella could recover with the proper help. Doctors are learning more and more about the mind every day. It's possible that your daughter would be one of those patients who benefits from new treatments."

"That would be wonderful," Emmalyne said, shifting the now-sleeping boy in her arms. "Imagine if you could have Fenella returned to you in her right mind. Think of what that would mean to the boys."

"'Twould be a miracle," the woman replied. She fell silent for a moment, then nodded. "Aye, go ahead and make the arrangements. I'll speak to her faither and brothers."

Dr. Williams gave Emmalyne a rather rueful smile. "And Miss Knox will come and help you as time permits."

"Oh, that isn't necessary," Mrs. MacLachlan replied. "Although 'twould be wonderful to have her company."

The doctor leaned forward. "Mrs. MacLachlan, I insist you allow for this help. I am prescribing you to take an afternoon nap each day. If you do not, I fear you will suffer a collapse. I will speak to your husband and sons if need be."

Emmalyne could see the surprise on the older women's faces. It was clear neither woman took seriously the threat to Morna's own well-being. Despite her concerns about assisting the MacLachlans, Emmalyne quickly interjected, "I'd be happy to come and help you with whatever you need." Even so, the idea terrified her. After all, what if she had to deal with Tavin? Or Father?

Tavin had spent days wrestling with his heart since he'd walked out on Luthias Knox. He knew he'd erred in how he'd handled the situation, but the old man had gotten the best of him. Not only that, but the entire matter served to prove how ridiculous it was to expect that things could change.

He walked the path between the quarry and the house as he did every day, but this time it was in hopes of clearing his mind and figuring out if he should talk to his father and mother, tell them he had to leave.

His parents would be hurt. Worse, his father would believe he'd gone back on his word and point to the promise he'd given. Tavin regretted that promise now, but the idea of having his own shop to work in had been so enticing. He'd turned his hand to dozens of jobs over the years, but carving stone was the one that gave him the most satisfaction. There was something about handling the hard stone that exhilarated him. It was as if with each careful stroke he was able to reveal the story that the rock had to tell. With all the betrayal he'd endured, how could he not do everything in his power to bring about this one dream?

"But how can I remain here with Emmalyne just down the road?" he wondered aloud. "How can I stay, knowing she's so near . . . and yet we can never be husband and wife?" How was he to endure such a thing?

Straying from the path, Tavin climbed up to an outcropping of rock. He sat for a time, wrestling with what he should do. His mother had urged him to have a talk with God—to set things right between them. Would it help? Sweat ran rivulets down the side of his face. After several cooler and drier days, the temperature had climbed once again, and the humidity made the air feel thick and heavy. But more than the heat was making him sweat.

Taking out his handkerchief, Tavin gazed up to the cloudless blue sky. "Is that what it will take?" He wiped his forehead and neck. "Will prayer really help?"

An aura of silence wrapped around him. The quarry work had stopped for the evening, and the heaviness of the air muffled sounds that might otherwise have filled the day. Even the birds seemed to have turned in for the night. Tavin ran his hand along the granite. This rock had been a part of his life for as long as he had memory.

There was another Rock that had accompanied him through life, as well. The Rock of Ages—Jesus. Tavin couldn't remember a time in his life when God hadn't been a part of conversations and his training. He could recall how his mother would sit him on her knee and tell him Bible stories about men who'd made hard choices to serve God.

He'd been taught to serve God—to look to God for help. So why should it be so hard now? But Tavin needn't seek the answer; he already knew fear was why he hesitated. Fear that

God wouldn't listen. Fear that God would abandon him just as Tavin had abandoned God.

"I don't know what to say," he murmured, still running his hand over the rock. "I know I've done wrong. I suppose I should start there. But, Lord, I don't know how to make my way back through the mess of my life. You'll need to show me."

He stood and looked again to the sky. "Forgive me." The words seemed too few, too simple—yet Tavin knew it was exactly the right place to start. He thought of his promise to his father and wondered if he could ever find the strength to endure. If Luthias Knox cornered him again, Tavin wasn't sure what he might do.

"I'm so angry at what he's done to me . . . to Em and me," he said aloud, as if God didn't already know. "I have spent most of the last few years wanting to cause him as much pain as he caused me. And now . . ." And now what? What did he want?

Tavin pushed his hands deep into his pockets and turned back to the path that would take him home. *I want Emmalyne.*

But wanting something—or someone—didn't mean getting it. Tavin knew that better than most. Now he was facing his future once again, and once again it would continue to be without the woman he loved. Could he do that? Could he see her from time to time and not yearn to find a way to have her for his own?

Approaching the house, Tavin saw the doctor's buggy and wondered if something was wrong. His mother had said nothing about the doctor coming today. He picked up his pace and bound into the house without warning. And there she was. The one woman he'd hoped to avoid.

Emmalyne.

She was sitting there so sweetly, holding a sleeping Lethan against her breast as she might have done their own children. The boy had entwined his fingers in Emmalyne's hair, and Tavin could remember the silky touch of that mane. He'd always loved her hair. He wondered if it still smelled of rose water. Was her skin still like satin, smooth and unblemished? Tavin clenched his jaw tight to keep from saying something he'd regret.

"Tavin, Dr. Williams has come to tell me about a home for Fenella," his mother said, rising from her chair. "It's located in St. Paul, and it's a private facility run by two men of God. They are both doctors, and they are working to find ways for patients to be restored to their right minds." She sat back down.

He had a hard time focusing on her words as he tore his gaze from Emmalyne to the doctor and finally to where his mother and Mrs. Knox sat together. "I thought—" he paused and drew a deep breath to steady himself—"you were against such an idea."

"I was," his mother admitted, "but that was with the idea of sending our poor girl to an institution, where they would do all manner of things to her. This, the good doctor assures me, is an entirely different place."

"Your mother is pushing herself to exhaustion and risking not only her life, but Mrs. Edlund's and her children," Dr. Williams said.

Gunnar tugged on Tavin's shirt. "My mama was on the roof," he said, eyes wide.

Tavin picked the boy up and could see the fear in his eyes. "The roof?" he asked.

Gunnar nodded in a most solemn manner. "She climbed

out the window. I think she was tryin' to fly to heaven to be with my papa. Grandma made me stay here with Lethan. I was scared."

Tavin felt his heart clench. "I'm sure you were." He looked to his mother. "Is Fenella all right?"

"Thanks to the doctor. He was just arriving with Emmalyne and her mother to talk to me about the new home. Fenella had been out on the roof for so long, I was beginning to despair. It was an answer to prayer that they came when they did."

Tavin put Gunnar back down and turned to the doctor. "I'm grateful for what you did." Dr. Williams stood, and Tavin wearily extended his hand in thanks.

"I'm glad I could be here. However, next time the scenario could unfold in an entirely different manner."

Tavin nodded in agreement. "I suppose we've run out of possibilities." Without meaning to, he cast his gaze at Emmalyne.

"Uncle Tavin, Emmy is gonna come and play with me. Lethan too," Gunnar announced.

Hearing her called Emmy very nearly choked off Tavin's breath. He tried to appear untouched by the boy's words, but he feared he wasn't doing a very good job. "I'm sure Miss Knox is much too busy."

"No she's not," Gunnar insisted. "She's gonna help Grandma."

Tavin looked to his mother, but didn't bother to voice the question. She nodded. "The doctor said I needed the help. Just for a time."

"I did, indeed. Have you noticed your mother's weight loss and pale complexion? I've only been in St. Cloud a short time, and I can see it."

Tavin's mind had been so fixed on himself that he hadn't

noticed much of anything. He looked at his mother now as if seeing her for the first time. She had more gray in her hair, and her eyes betrayed a weariness that he couldn't deny. She was thinner—much more so than he'd ever known her to be. How could they have all just ignored this?

"It is essential that your mother rest each and every day."

"We could hire someone, Mother," Tavin said. He squatted down beside her. "Surely there are women in town who could come here to keep house for you."

"That isn't necessary," Mrs. Knox declared. "I have already told your mother that I can spare Emmalyne while Dr. Williams makes arrangements for your sister."

Tavin frowned. Before he could speak, however, Gunnar was at his side. The boy put his hand on Tavin's shoulder. "I like Emmy. She's real nice, Uncle Tavin. I think you would like her, too."

Seeing the innocence in the boy's expression, Tavin tried to soften his words. "I think it would be better to have someone . . . else. Someone . . . older."

Gunnar shook his head. "Emmy's more fun, and Grandma said she loves Emmy just like she loves Mama."

Tavin knew he'd been defeated. He supposed the only thing he could do was to push for the immediate removal of his sister so his mother's workload would lessen. "Why don't we take Fenella to this facility tomorrow?" He stood and looked to the doctor. "After all, I could escort her there by train. It wouldn't take that long. I'm sure Father could spare me, and that way Mother's workload will be lessened immediately and there would be no need for . . . for Miss Knox to be here." *No need for me to worry about seeing her. No need to risk saying the wrong thing.*

"The fact is," Dr. Williams replied, "it will take some time to make arrangements for Fenella. At least a week, maybe more. Your mother needs the help now, and Miss Knox is available. I think it's the best solution, and obviously your nephews are comfortable with her." He waved his hand toward Emmalyne and the sleeping baby. "Quite comfortable."

Tavin felt his hands balling into fists, and his anger rose from a deep sense of frustration. He knew he needed to leave or he would say something he'd regret. "Well, since you seem to have this all figured out, I hope you'll excuse me."

He left as quickly as possible, wanting nothing more than to let loose a guttural cry. He denied the urge, and instead turned to God. "Is this how you answer my prayers, Lord? Is this how you ease my pain?" Now not only did he have to deal with her father and brother, but given this new development, Tavin would have to see Emmalyne herself. Possibly every day.

"I don't think Tavin was very happy about my offer to assist his mother," Emmalyne said as Dr. Williams helped her mother from the buggy. The trio had said little on the way home, but Emmalyne couldn't help but express her thoughts now. Perhaps it was because she felt safer now that they were back on Knox property. Perhaps it was just that she needed the time and distance from Tavin.

"He'll come to see the sense of it," Mother replied matter-of-factly. "He's probably pretty worried about his mother's failing health but doesn't want to acknowledge how serious it is. Now, if you'll both excuse me, I'll get supper started." She strode toward the house, Emmalyne and the doctor staring after her. A small smile graced Emmalyne's face. It was awfully good to see Mother back among the living, finding purpose in life and doing what came naturally to her.

I want to focus on the good, Emmalyne thought. *I want to keep my eyes on God and all that He has made right, rather than what man has made wrong.* She stared at the front door for several moments, struggling to eliminate thoughts of Tavin from her mind. This wasn't how she had pictured things. She wasn't against the idea of helping Morna, but being so near Tavin, hearing his mother speak about him . . . well, it made her most anxious.

"If you keep worrying your lip like that, you're bound to bite clear through," Dr. Williams said.

Emmalyne looked at him in surprise. She couldn't quite read his expression. "What?"

He shrugged. "Just a doctor's observation, but the way you're chewing on your lip can't bode well. . . ." He shook his head and gave her a sad little smile. "I really had plans for you, Miss Knox."

She was even more surprised. "Plans?"

"Yes, I had hoped to court you, Emmalyne. Ever since you dropped into my arms, I'd entertained pursuing your hand in marriage. I can see now, however, that you are in love with Tavin MacLachlan. I don't know what all happened between the two of you, but I can tell he still has feelings for you, as well. So my question is this: Why are you two fighting the inevitable?"

Chapter 21

Emmalyne thought about Jason's comments all that evening and into the next morning. She hadn't explained the situation—there had been no time, for he'd no sooner asked that last question than she heard her father and brother approaching. She had given him a hasty promise to speak more about the matter at a later date before hurrying inside to help her mother.

Now, she was still contemplating Jason and his observations—about both Tavin and herself. Emmalyne was attracted to the doctor's kindness and good character, and she found him very handsome. She would have enjoyed a courtship, had it not been for her feelings for Tavin and her parents' tradition. Dr. Williams was the kind of man a woman would feel fortunate to have in her life. Emmalyne was grateful for their friendship.

But it was Tavin who held her heart. The comments Dr. Williams had made were most intriguing to her. He wasn't the first to suggest that Tavin still had feelings for her, and if the doctor could recognize it, then there was little doubt others could. Especially her father. The thought of what he might say or do made her stomach lurch. It was best to put such thoughts out of her mind. She turned her attention to the dishes that needed washing.

"Emmalyne, I'm going to the hen house to collect the eggs," her mother announced. "I'll see the chickens fed and watered."

"Thank you, Mother. I was just about to wash up the morning dishes." Emmalyne tested the hot soapy water to make sure it wouldn't scald her, amazed at her mother's return to health . . . body, soul, and spirit.

"Maybe we can finish up those baskets today," her mother suggested. She paused at the back door. "Who knows, perhaps we can get into town and see about selling them. That would give us a little extra spending money. You could use some new clothes, daughter."

"My clothes are fine, Mother."

The older woman smiled in a knowing way. "You wouldn't want to shame your family when you go helping out at the MacLachlan house." She left the kitchen before Emmalyne could reply.

Emmalyne added dishes to the water and let them soak while she wiped down the dining room table. Mother's comment was so out of character. Why did she care what Emmalyne looked like? Her mother knew full well that Morna wouldn't care, and if she had in mind to fancy Emmalyne up for Tavin . . . well, Mother knew as well as Emmalyne that nothing could come of it.

Once the table was clean and shining, Emmalyne spread out a freshly pressed linen tablecloth. It was one of her mother's favorites and had been in the family for generations. Emmalyne ran her hand over the smooth cloth and its lovely embroidery. When she'd been a girl she'd dreamed of inheriting such things for her own family. Emmalyne lifted her shoulders, took a deep breath, and fought back the urge to cry. There was no need for tears. They wouldn't change anything.

Emmalyne was up to her elbows in soapy water and dishes when she heard the approach of horses. She hurried to wipe her arms dry before going to the front door. They were so isolated out here that they could hear the approach of visitors well before their arrival. She waited and watched the road, knowing it was possible whoever it was might pass by and head on to the MacLachlans'.

She was rather surprised to find Dr. Williams riding up on horseback, leading a fully saddled bay gelding. She stepped out onto the porch and tipped her head to one side as Jason halted the horses at the end of the walkway.

"Are you afraid the first horse will tire out?" she quipped with a smile.

"Good morning to you, Miss Knox." He tied off the mounts and made his way to the porch. "I come bearing a gift."

"A gift?" She looked at the horses and shook her head. "What gift?"

"The extra horse. I have purchased it, and I thought to bring it to you for your use. I know you will be traveling back and forth to the MacLachlan place, and I figured you might need it." He held up his hand as she started to protest. "I know you are quite healthy and capable of the walk, but this will add precious hours to your day. You can cut your travel time considerably, and that in turn will give you more time at home as well as at the MacLachlans'."

"But—"

He put a finger to her lips. "Furthermore, you won't have to hitch rides into town. Should Fenella get ill or have another situation occur like the other day, it won't be so difficult to get into town. You can simply ride old Buster here." He waved to the bay, then turned to her in a somewhat abrupt manner. "You do ride, don't you?"

"I do. That, however, is not at issue here," Emmalyne said, feeling self-conscious with her sleeves rolled up and apron still on. She smoothed the material of her sleeves down and tried to pretend it wasn't bothering her.

"Then what is the issue, may I ask?"

She met his warm gaze and continued to button her sleeves. "I appreciate your consideration, but I cannot accept such a gift from you. My father would never understand, even with your kind explanation. He would never spare the money for feed, either. No, I'm sorry, but you must take the horse back."

Dr. Williams shook his head. "I realized something yesterday."

Emmalyne felt her frustration mounting. "And what would that be?"

"I realized that I care more about your happiness than my own. Call me a glutton for punishment, but I intend to see you and the rather inhospitable Mr. MacLachlan back together." He gave her an impish grin. "I'm a hopeless romantic."

"That can't happen," Emmalyne said flatly, refusing to fall in with his lighthearted demeanor. "I'm sorry you made a trip here for nothing." She turned to step back into the house, but Jason's words stopped her.

"Look, I don't know what the problem is, but I truly believe you and Tavin were meant for each other. Now, you must realize that this epiphany hasn't been easy for me. I am dealing with a very disappointed heart at the moment. However, I am no fool. You two belong together."

"I don't deny that," she said sadly. "I do deny the possibility of it happening."

"But why on earth not?"

She looked at the horse and drew a deep breath. Letting it out slowly, she made up her mind to tell Dr. Williams about the tradition. "Maybe you should step inside. There are some things I need to tell you. It will help you to understand the impossibility of my situation."

That evening Emmalyne sat silently while her mother chatted with Angus about his day. Father, though, dug at his shepherd's pie as though the thing might well rise up and attack him at any moment. He was clearly unhappy about something, but there was nothing new about that. Unfortunately, it made what she had to say all the harder. She tried to think how she might explain Jason Williams's gift. The beast was tied up to graze behind the barn down by the stream. He would have enough food and water for the present, or so Dr. Williams figured. He had assured Emmalyne that he would return with feed to see the animal through the next two weeks. After that they could revisit her need for the horse.

She knew her mother had no plans to tell Father about Emmalyne's new duties, but the discovery of the horse would make it difficult to keep the secret. Father often took a stroll down by the "burn," as he called it, to clear his head. If he did that this evening, he would see the horse and know that something was afoot. Be that as it may, Emmalyne still hoped she could find a way to lessen the severity of her father's displeasure, maybe even convince him of the merit of this loan from the good doctor.

"The horses respond well to me now," Angus was explaining to their mother. "I thought since I was away so long they would be difficult, but they are handling it quite well. I seem to have a way with them."

"I'm so glad to hear it. And you like what you're doing?" Mother asked.

"Very much so. I hadn't thought to work with a team before, but now I'm considering how it might be a good investment to purchase my own. If I save my money, I could buy a strong draft team and hire out to transport freight. There's good money to be made."

Father gave a disgruntled snort. "Always lookin' to greener grasses. Ye'd do well to stop yer dreamin' and focus on the job at hand." He drank down the rest of his coffee and held the cup out to Mother for refilling.

Emmalyne thought now might be the time for her to interject her news. "Speaking of horses, I was surprised today with a horse." She met her father's shocked stare and hurried on. "Dr. Williams thought it would be good for us to have a mount here at the house. You know, in case something happened to Mother . . . and to be able to get back and forth to town." She thought her words sounded rather lame by the end of her announcement.

"We've no money for a horse, and ye cannae be takin' such a gift from a man." Her father snatched the refilled cup and slammed it down. Coffee sloshed onto Mother's beautiful linen tablecloth. "I grow awful weary of folks interferin' with ma family." His Scottish brogue thickened and his r's rolled heavily. "Reasonable folk would understand." He blew out a breath and turned his attention back to the meal as if the matter were completely settled.

To Emmalyne's surprise, her mother firmly put down her fork and looked directly at her husband. "I believe the good doctor was kind in the offering," she said. "I think it wise that we have a mount. When you are gone and the wagon and horse are with you, there is no hope for us should there be an emergency."

"Wheesht, woman! Yer nae the man of this hoose. It costs a guid amount of coin for the feed and care of such a beast. We donnae need another horse."

"Dr. Williams has provided for the feed, as well," Emmalyne said in as nonchalant a manner as she could muster. "Would you like another bannock, Father?" She held out the plate of biscuits, hoping it would distract him.

"I'll nae allow it!" Father slammed his fist on the table, causing all the china to clatter.

"You will allow it," Mother stated, standing to her feet. "Emmalyne needs the beast to make her way back and forth to the MacLachlan place. I've agreed to let her help Morna for a spell. Morna is near to exhaustion with . . ."

Emmalyne lost the thread of the conversation as she nearly choked on her bite of buttered bannock. The last thing she had expected was for her mother to let the cat out of the bag with such a declaration. What was she thinking? Emmalyne fixed her gaze on her mother, unwilling to face the wrath that was sure to be upon her father's face.

But Mother was acting as though nothing were amiss. ". . . and you know their poor daughter Fenella hasn't been well since she lost her husband. The lass has suffered a complete nervous disruption. She's all but worn out Morna, what with the care she needs and that of Fenella's two wee lads." Mother sat down again. Emmalyne dared a side glance at her father. She could see that his face had reddened, but he seemed to have lost the ability to speak. Angus took that opportunity to add his thoughts on the matter.

"I think it's great that Emmy can go and help them. I'm sure it will ease Mr. MacLachlan's mind, and the horse will make it a whole lot easier for Emmy to get there and home." He took another portion of the shepherd's pie and lifted a forkful to his mouth.

Mother nodded and smiled at Emmalyne. "Morna was so good to us all those years ago. I doubt I could have gotten through losing . . . Well, she was a great comfort. I know Emmalyne will be a great help to Morna because she's been so useful to me."

Father finally found his voice. "And that is what she's expected to be," he roared. "She's here for our care, nae our neighbors."

To Emmalyne's surprise, Mother was undaunted. "They won't need her for long. Fenella is to go to a special home where the doctors can help her regain her mind. It's the Christian thing for us to help as we can until that occurs."

"Christian? Ye wimen are always bletherin' about religion to excuse yer actions."

Mother folded her hands and raised her chin. "The Bible makes it clear."

"Ye forget yerself, woman!" This time it was Father who rose from the table to stand at his place. "Who are ye to tell me what's in the Guid Beuk? Emmalyne's duty is to us. 'Tis the tradition that we agreed upon long ago."

"Well, I don't agree with it any longer," Mother said. She sat calmly, looking at Luthias without even a hint of nervousness or fear in her expression.

Emmalyne thought she might be dreaming. She'd never

seen her mother stand up to Father in this way. What was Mother thinking? She had to know this would only serve to make Father angrier. Emmalyne looked to Angus, searching his face for an explanation of this extraordinary turn of events. He only shrugged.

"I do believe, Luthias, that we made a mistake in denying Emmalyne her marriage to Tavin. 'Twas selfish of us, and I believe God would have us make matters right."

Emmalyne's heart nearly stopped, and this time she couldn't help but look to her father for his reaction. To her amazement he simply stood stock-still, staring into the distance, his icy blue eyes narrow slits, his jaw clenched tight.

"I don't want the tradition to continue at the price of Emmalyne's happiness," Mother said quietly. "She's been a good and honorable daughter to us, but I can see her heart is still with Tavin MacLachlan and his is with her. I would see them together."

"I would, too," Angus declared, seeming to have taken new courage from his mother.

"So ye've conspired against me. The devil has played his hand in ma hoose and won!" Father knocked the chair backward with a growl and stormed from the room.

Emmalyne shook her head and looked at her mother. "Mother, dear Mother . . . but why did you say those things to him?"

"Because they are true," she replied, hands folded on the table. "I've had plenty of time to think on this. A good deal of my heartbreak has been because of the problems we caused for you and Tavin. Seeing the two of you together again made me realize what a mistake it has been to keep you apart. You two should never have been separated."

"But, Mother, I won't have this come between you and Father." Emmalyne felt heartsick. She had wanted to see her family knit back together. She'd hoped her father would learn to love and to seek God. Now she feared this would drive him even further away.

"It came between us a long time ago," Mother said, looking more determined than Emmalyne had ever seen her. "I should have stood my ground when your father blamed me for what happened to his family. Don't fret over this, Emmalyne. Nor you, Angus. 'Tis time for your father and I to deal with the ghosts of the past."

"I'll go speak to him," Emmalyne offered. She got to her feet. "He needs to know that no matter what, I will always be here for you both."

"Speak to him if you must," her mother replied. "He'll not be in much of a mood to hear it, however."

"I'll take that chance. I am trying so hard to show him gentleness and respect. Love. I'm sure he thinks we're all against him—even hate him. But that isn't true."

"No, it's not true," Mother agreed, "but he does need to face what he's done and be responsible for it." Nodding, Emmalyne took her leave.

Her mother's words echoed through her head as she slowly walked to the barn. She felt certain this was the only place her father would go, and she was right. The dim light from a single lantern showed him sitting at the grinding stone, completely still. His hands were empty, and he was obviously deep in thought.

"Father." She whispered the word and drew near him. Kneeling beside him, Emmalyne touched his arm. "Father, please hear me."

She expected his wrath, perhaps even the back of his hand, but instead he looked defeated. When he said nothing, Emmalyne took this as his agreement to hear her.

"Father, I will never allow you or Mother to be left alone. I will always take care of you. No matter what. I love you. I love you both. Do you understand that?"

Still he said nothing. He just faced the grinding stone with the same vacant stare. Emmalyne stroked his forearm, feeling the strength and warmth of it. Her father had always been a good provider, and now that he was moving up in years, she knew he wanted only to know that he could continue to care for them.

"I've long thought about our earlier talk here in the barn. I've prayed about my heart and my words. I want to please you and to be useful to you. But that doesn't mean I can't be useful to others, as well. Fenella was my dearest friend at one time. Now she only has a vague memory of those years. She doesn't know me when she sees me, and she very nearly brought an end to her life yesterday. Mrs. MacLachlan's strength is giving out. She can't keep up with Fenella's needs and those of her grandsons, too. Not to mention the duties of the house. She's near to collapse, the doctor says. I know you wouldn't want ill to befall her. You know how hard it would be on Mr. MacLachlan and . . . the others."

"Ye mean yer Tavin." Still he didn't look at her.

She shrugged. "Tavin and anyone else who relies on Mrs. MacLachlan. Gillam and his wife are expecting a baby. They will need her to help, because Irene's mother has passed on.

"Father, I don't pretend to know what the future holds or how God intends to see it managed, but I do know that He is faithful, and we can believe His Word. Father, I know

237

your heart is heavy, but please . . . for the sake of the love you once held for us . . . please make peace with God. He loves you dearly."

The older man kept his gaze fixed on the grinder. "And ye love Tavin MacLachlan."

Emmalyne leaned back against her heels as she thought on that statement. She finally allowed her heart to declare the truth. "I do, Father. I love him more today than I did eleven years ago. I will go on loving him . . . for as long as I have breath." She paused and reached up to gently touch his cheek with the back of her fingers. "But so, too, will I love you and Mother . . . and Angus. I will never allow you to go in want if I have anything to offer. I will always care for you and Mother, not just because it's my right and duty, but because I want to."

Wordless, he turned to look at her. Emmalyne thought it might just be a trick of the lantern light, but she thought she saw moisture in his eyes. He did nothing but gaze at her for several minutes. Emmalyne had never known a moment quite like this with him. The silence offered her a glimmer of hope—hope that things could change. Hope that her father might yet learn to love again. Love his God and his family.

Chapter 22

"Mr. MacLachlan, I don't believe I understand the purpose of your visit today," the union official said. "If you aren't here to join, then what can I possibly do for you?"

"You can get your men to stop causing problems at my father's quarry. Someone's going to get hurt or killed. In fact, someone already has."

"What you talking about?" The man stood to his feet, a scowl on his face.

Tavin tossed his hat to a chair. "I'm talking about the vandalism and tampering going on at the MacLachlan Quarry."

The older man stared down his nose at Tavin. "This has nothing to do with me or the union. We do not approve bully-ragging of any kind."

"Well, somebody apparently does, and it would seem my father's quarry has been targeted. Who but union supporters would be out to cause problems for us?"

"That, sir, is a question you should ask yourself." The man sat down again and leaned forward in his chair. "I have encouraged your father to join the union for the sake of protection, as well as coming under its hospices of scheduling and rates. We are honorable men. I respect that your father wishes to give his men the right to choose. I can't say that I agree with it, but I do respect it."

Tavin got the distinct impression that the man was telling the truth. "But what of some of the union members?"

"My men are used to following orders. I have made it clear that we are not in the business of causing problems for our fellow stonecutters. However, I have clearly stated the advantages of joining our union to any man who would listen. Your father might even be persuaded to change his mind."

"And force his quarrymen to join your union?" Tavin raised a brow. "I thought the attraction of America was freedom to choose whatever is right for each individual. In the old country, a man was under the limits set by the queen or king. Even owning land was impossible without the approval of someone else. Here in America, if a man has the will to work the land, he can own property. If he has enough money, he can own most anything. Why should he be put back in the chains of having to bow and scrape to somebody else's decision?"

The man sputtered and coughed. "Mr. MacLachlan, no one is bowing to anybody else around here. The union is here to provide help. Protection and provision are our main focus. You would do well to better understand our organization before condemning it."

Tavin shook his head. "I do not condemn it. I have, in fact, at times paid my dues to belong."

The man calmed down and seemed to reconsider Tavin. "Then you are not opposed to your father unionizing his quarry."

"Not at all. I'm opposed to being forced to do so or having men threatened until they comply. We've had a variety of so-called 'accidents' at the quarry. The last one could have killed several men. A derrick cable was cut just enough so that when strain was put upon it, it snapped. It was just the . . . well, the grace of God that kept death at bay. I intend to see that these events end . . . here and now." He paused, hoping his declaration would be understood and heeded. "Even if you aren't the one behind it," he said, looking directly at the union boss, "I would appreciate it if you would put the word out that whoever is responsible should cease. My brother-in-law died in one of those accidents a year ago, and I want to prevent another loss of life."

"I am sorry for your loss. Sorry, too, for the accidents. Tell your father I had nothing to do with those events. If he decides to join the union, I will see to it nothing like that happens again. We take the protection of our members very seriously."

Tavin retrieved his hat and headed for the office door. Before stepping outside he looked back at the union leader. "I'll tell him. I hope, however, that should you get wind of something planned against us, whether union members or not, you would do the right thing in seeing us forewarned."

"We do not support violations of the law, Mr. MacLachlan. You have my word."

Back out on the street, the last person Tavin wanted to encounter was Dr. Jason Williams. But that was exactly who now stood before him, looking equally surprised.

"Dr. Williams," Tavin said, inclining his head.

"Mr. MacLachlan. I had no idea you were in town today, but I'm glad you are. I wonder if you might join me at the café for the noonday meal. I have some things I'd like to discuss about your sister's transfer to St. Paul."

Tavin had no desire to share a meal and conversation with Williams, but he nodded and followed the man to the nearby restaurant. They were seated immediately, and both men ordered the special of the day, German sausages and sauerkraut. As they waited for the food, Dr. Williams began to speak.

"The doctors in St. Paul are quite encouraging about your sister's condition. They believe the shock of her husband's death can be overcome in time. They feel she will need some very special care, however."

"She's already been receiving special care," Tavin muttered.

"Yes, but I'm referring to professional care that will differ from the care your mother has been giving. With a focus on the proper balance of medication, therapies, and encouragement, the consensus is that Fenella might well recover."

"But she also might not," Tavin replied. "Isn't that just as true?"

"Yes," the doctor said, nodding. "Only God knows for sure. But I like to keep a positive outlook. Life without hope is no life at all. We must have faith that God can help your sister recover."

"I believe God can do anything He chooses," Tavin spat out. "I just don't pretend to know what that might be."

Dr. Williams leaned forward. "You seem quite angry. I suppose I offended you at our previous meeting when I mentioned Miss Knox. I want to apologize for that. I was wrong to speak in such a manner."

Tavin was surprised at this confession. He didn't know what to say in return and remained silent. When the food arrived, he pretended great interest in salting and peppering the dish.

Dr. Williams began to speak again. "The fact of the matter is that I've come to care a great deal about Miss Knox. I believe that she deserves to be happy, and I know she is not. I can clearly see that you are just as miserable. What I cannot come to terms with is how you could just walk away from such a woman."

Tavin's head snapped up, and he fixed Williams with a glare. "I didn't just walk away. Her parents drove me away."

"Ah, yes. So I've heard. But even so, a man who really loved her would have fought for her, no?"

Tavin wasn't about to just sit and take such talk from a man who knew nothing about him. "You'd do well to drop the subject, Doc. You can discuss my sister's move to St. Paul all you like, but leave Emmalyne out of this."

"Emmalyne. Such a beautiful name," Williams murmured, cutting into his sausage. "I've always thought so." He took several bites before continuing. "Mr. MacLachlan, I realize your anger is borne from the fact that you still love her. I believe this anger will ultimately destroy your health and well-being, and because of that I feel it only right that I speak to you . . . as a concerned physician and, I hope, a friend."

"Well, I don't." Tavin had lost all interest in the food and pushed the plate back. "It's none of your affair who I love or don't love."

"But because you love Emmalyne, and I have made Emmalyne my business, I feel it is somewhat my affair." He smiled. "Her happiness is most important to me. And to you also, I believe."

"Well, you can forget about courting her," Tavin said,

certain that was where the conversation was headed. "Her parents won't hear of it. They have a tradition that forbids it."

"Ah yes, the tradition. Well, can't new traditions be made?"

Tavin got to his feet and looked down at the doctor. He wanted to rage at the man and tell him he didn't know what he was talking about. But he held his temper in check. "Good luck with that. The day you can get Luthias Knox to do anything other than exactly what he wants will be the day St. Cloud is made the capital." With that, he threw down the coins for his lunch and went to retrieve his horse. Why couldn't folks just leave well enough alone?

"Do it again! Do it again, Auntie Em," Gunnar called to Emmalyne.

They were enjoying an unusually warm fall day at the pond, and Emmalyne had just showed Gunnar how to skip a stone on the water's surface. Lethan clapped and squealed as his brother jumped up and down enthusiastically. Emmalyne picked through several rocks and found one that was just right.

"It's all about finding the perfect rock, and then holding it just so." She demonstrated. "Your hands are small now, but when they grow you will be able to master this without any trouble." She positioned herself and drew back her arm. "Now watch how I hold my hand and how my wrist moves." She let go, and again the stone danced across the water.

"Let me try!" Gunnar picked up a random rock and heaved it toward the pond. It sank immediately, and he frowned. "I did it just like you."

Emmalyne rubbed his head. "You'll get it in time. Just keep practicing. For now, however, what do you say we take off our shoes and socks and wade in the water for a little while. The sun is high and hot. I don't think there's anything quite so pleasurable on a warm day."

Gunnar didn't have to be told twice. He dropped to the ground and began pulling his shoes off in wild abandonment. Lethan, seeing this display, was not to be outdone. He plopped down and started pulling at his own shoes. Emmalyne sat down and helped him before removing her own shoes and stockings. She held on to Lethan's hand as they waded into the water. Gunnar, however, was already splashing around.

"Uncle Tavin sailed on a big ship," he told her. "He went out on the big lakes."

"I'm not surprised," Emmalyne said, laughing as Lethan bent to slap his hand on the water's surface. He giggled with delight and did it again and again.

"Sing that song again, Auntie Em," Gunnar called as he waded a little deeper into the pond.

"Don't be going out too far. We don't want your clothes to get too wet." Of course, Emmalyne could see that it was a bit late for that concern. Gunnar and Lethan were doing a fairly good job of drenching themselves.

"I'm not too far. Sing that song about Jenny in the rye," Gunnar demanded.

Emmalyne laughed and began to sing.

"O Jenny's a' weet, poor body, Jenny's seldom dry:
She draigl't a' her petticoatie, Comin thro' the rye!
Comin thro' the rye, poor body, Comin thro' the rye,
She draigl't a' her petticoatie, Comin thro' the rye!
Gin a body meet a body Comin thro' the rye,
Gin a body kiss a body, Need a body cry?"

She leaned down and kissed Lethan on the top of his head and tickled him under his chin. The boy gave a shriek of pure joy and rewarded Emmalyne by throwing a handful of water at her.

"Oh, ho wee man," she said, feigning her best Scottish accent, "I cannae leave that go unpunished." She splashed him back, and soon all three were laughing and assaulting each other with handfuls of water.

"I'm gonna get you, Auntie," Gunnar declared. "You aren't hardly wet at all."

She chuckled and moved away easily. "I can outrun you, little man. Better still, I could catch you and cover your face in kisses."

Gunnar screwed up his face. "No! No kisses!"

"One day you'll cherish the kisses of a girl," stated a male voice.

Emmalyne stopped abruptly and whirled around. She caught only a glimpse of Tavin sitting on the grassy bank just before she lost her balance and fell backward into the water.

He was up on his feet and down to the pond's edge in a single motion . . . or so it seemed to Emmalyne. Gunnar was babbling on about something and running toward them. Emmalyne struggled to get to her feet and Tavin reached out to help her up, stretching as far as he could so as not to get his boots overly wet.

"Thank you," she said, grasping his fingers. But as soon as she was standing again, dripping like a wet hen, Gunnar came flying at her like a barn owl swooping down on prey. Once again she fell into the water, only this time Tavin was very nearly a dead weight atop her.

Tavin maneuvered quickly, however, and pulled Emmalyne up without delay. He drew her to her feet. "Are you all right?" He looked her over carefully. Emmalyne nodded, stunned by what had happened.

Letting go of Emmalyne, Tavin turned toward Gunnar. "Come here, you." Tavin raced after the giggling boy, caught him, and hoisted him high into the air. "It's the water for you."

"Don't throw me out there, Uncle Tavin! I can't swim," Gunnar shouted, his tone caught between gleeful and fearful.

"Well, don't you think it's time you learned?" Tavin asked. "Since there are lakes and ponds all around here, seems like a reasonable thing to learn. Let me get you started." He rocked the boy back and forth in his arms as if gaining momentum for the throw.

"No!" The boy laughed and squirmed against Tavin's hold.

Emmalyne noted that Lethan was taking it all in from where he sat in the water. Apparently he had given up on wading since everyone else was taking a swim. She moved over to where he was watching Tavin and Gunnar's clowning in silent awe.

What was Tavin doing here? Where had he come from? She'd planned to be long gone before the men returned from work. Feeling rather self-conscious, Emmalyne surveyed the damage to her clothes. She was drenched, and the bodice of her gown clung to her most conspicuously. She pulled at the material and pressed as much water from it as possible. Next she tried to do the same for her skirt. Goodness, but she was a mess!

She walked to the grassy bank and sat down to deal with her hair. Somewhere along the way she'd lost several hairpins, and now her braid dangled awkwardly to one side. Releasing the rest of the pins, she let the braid trail down her back. She didn't dare look to see what Tavin was doing. His unexpected presence had so confused Emmalyne that she wasn't sure whether to gather up Lethan and hurry back to the house or force herself to wait and see what Tavin might have to say. The choice was quickly made for her.

"Are you hurt?"

Tavin left Gunnar at the water's edge and made his way to where Emmalyne sat. He seemed so different than their earlier encounters. The bitter, hateful look was gone, and there was a mischievousness in his expression that reminded Emmalyne of the good old days. "No—no, I'm fine," she finally answered.

He extended his hand to her once again. "Well, we're far enough from the water that I don't think there's a chance of repeating that earlier mishap."

Emmalyne nodded without looking up. She allowed him to pull her to her feet, more than a little aware of the touch of his hand. When he said nothing but continued to hold her hand, she forced herself to look into his eyes. In that moment, the terrible years of loss and loneliness fell away, and she couldn't help but wish he would kiss her as he once had. Her wish was quickly granted.

Tavin pulled her into his arms and kissed her with the lost passion of eleven years. Emmalyne could scarcely breathe, but she didn't care. If she should die in that moment, she would go happy to her reward.

"See, Uncle Tavin, I told you Emmy was nice."

They looked down to find Gunnar and Lethan, hand in hand, watching them most intently. Emmalyne put her hand to her mouth and backed away as Tavin gathered up his nephews.

In his clear baritone, Tavin began to sing, "Gin a body meet a body, Comin thro' the rye, Gin a body kiss a body, Need a body cry?" He threw Emmalyne a wink and headed for the house.

Chapter 23

Tavin walked along briskly, each boy's hand tucked into his. He had not intended to kiss Emmalyne Knox—at least not then—but at that moment he'd found it impossible to restrain himself any longer. His actions confused and intrigued him, however. His last words to her were that he hated her, and now he was behaving as though they'd never been apart. What in the world had come over him?

After his noontime encounter with Dr. Williams, Tavin's long ride home had given him much to think about. He couldn't fault the man for his obvious attention and concern for Emmalyne's happiness. He couldn't even fault the good doctor for interfering as he did. The more Tavin had pondered the man's comments, the more he had come to realize that Dr. Williams was not a threat to him. It appeared that the man was actually attempting to encourage Tavin to reclaim his lady. This on its own was truly amazing, and he didn't know, had their roles been reversed, that he could offer the same gracious and unselfish attitude.

The longer Tavin thought about Emmalyne, the more determined he became to resolve the past. He wasn't sure how he would manage to go toe-to-toe with Luthias Knox, but Tavin realized it was now impossible to do otherwise. He loved Emmalyne. He'd loved her faithfully through all these years of separation. Why had he ever agreed to Knox's preposterous rule? Why hadn't he found a way to reason with the man—to assure him that he wasn't of a mind to take Emmalyne away from them, but rather would share her with them?

He threw a glance over his shoulder, seeing that Emmalyne was just a few steps behind him. The expression on her face revealed that she was just as perplexed about the kiss they'd shared as he was. She hadn't said a word since . . . but he figured she'd said more in her actions.

"You boys are going to fish in that pond someday soon," he said, trying to steer his mind away from what he would say to Emmalyne.

"Are you gonna fish with us, Uncle Tavin?" Gunnar asked.

"You bet I will, but it will have to wait for another day. You two need to get into some dry clothes. I won't have your grandma telling me that I caused you to catch your death of cold."

"But it's not cold," Gunnar argued.

"Good thing, too," Tavin replied.

Lethan babbled something incoherent and then started asking for cookies.

As they approached the house, Tavin's mother appeared at the door. "And what, may I ask, happened at the pond? I thought you were just goin' to wade."

"We decided to have a little swim," Tavin said with a grin. "Now we're done." He let go of the boys' hands and sent them running to their grandma.

"You two get inside this minute and get your clothes changed. Emmy, you can wear some of Fenella's things."

"Thank you," she said, her reply hardly more than a murmur.

"Somehow I can't help but think that you had more to do with this than anyone," his mother said, hands on her hips, eyeing Tavin in a most curious manner.

He put his hand to his chest. "Who, me? I was merely an innocent bystander trying to save everyone from further disaster."

Emmalyne thanked Mrs. MacLachlan again for the borrowed clothes. She marveled at the fit; it was almost as if they were made for her. The crisp white shirtwaist and full brown skirt were very much like something Emmalyne would have purchased or made for herself—though in truth she was a much better cook than seamstress.

She adjusted the pleating on the bodice and looked at herself in Morna MacLachlan's mirror. The glimmer in her eyes gave her away—Emmalyne could see the glint of hope and happiness in their depths. But she knew she could not allow herself to let it show. No matter why Tavin had chosen to kiss her . . . no matter how much she had appreciated that kiss—yes, wanted it—and had given it back . . . Emmalyne had to gain control of her feelings and whatever might be seen in her face.

She remembered her mother's declaration that she didn't want the tradition to continue. But Emmalyne also thought of her father's anger and the look he'd given the entire family. He clearly thought they were conspiring against him.

"But there was nothing planned, no secret plotting behind his back," she whispered to the face in the mirror. But she knew he'd never believe it. Especially after what had just happened with Tavin.

By the time she went downstairs carrying the bundle of wet clothes, Morna had already gotten her grandsons changed, and Emmalyne knew it was time to head for home. Mrs. MacLachlan secured Lethan in the high chair and turned to survey Emmalyne.

"I'm glad to see they fit so well," she said, approval in her voice. "You and Fenella were always close in size. But not anymore. Fenella has lost so much weight she's hardly more than skin stretched over bones," she finished sadly. Lethan fussed and slapped his hands against the wooden tray.

"Hopefully this new facility will help her to regain her health," Emmalyne offered as Mrs. MacLachlan retrieved a cookie for the little boy. "It would break her heart to know she's caused you and her boys harm. So we press forward in hope for healing."

"Aye, hope is all we have."

Emmalyne noted the clock on the mantel. "I need to get home. Mother will be expecting me, and if I arrive after Father and Angus get there . . . well, I'm sure to hear about it."

Mrs. MacLachlan seemed to understand. "You run along. I knew you'd need to go, so I told Tavin to go saddle your horse."

Emmalyne trembled. She both feared and longed for what she might say to him . . . what he might say to her. "Thank you. I'll bring the clothes back tomorrow."

"No hurry. Fenella will not be needin' them for a time. Come on, I'll walk you out. Lethan is content with his treat." Already the little boy was munching away on the cookie.

Emmalyne and Mrs. MacLachlan stepped outside to find Tavin and Gunnar bringing her bay around. Gunnar was quite excited and came running to Emmalyne.

"We saddled up your horse, and I got to help with the cinch."

"Thank you," Emmalyne said, hugging him close. "I'm sure Tav . . . uh, Mr. MacLachlan appreciated that very much."

"You can call him Tavin since he kissed you," Gunnar announced. "That means he likes you. I knew he would."

Emmalyne felt her face grow hot. She didn't dare look at Morna MacLachlan, but Emmalyne could sense the woman was looking at her, no doubt shocked. A quick glance at Tavin confirmed he wasn't going to say anything one way or the other. Emmalyne was mortified and knew she must be flushed from her head to her toes.

"I . . . I guess I'll see you tomorrow." Emmalyne hurried over to take up the horse's reins without even a glance at Tavin. "Thank you."

With the wet clothes in her arms, Emmalyne took the reins and pulled the horse forward, not even bothering to mount him. She needed to get away quickly, and she didn't want to take the time to tie the bundle onto the back of the horse first. Emmalyne never even looked to see if they were all still watching her. She led the horse at a quick pace down the road for home. She reached the road to the quarry just as her father and brother were approaching in the wagon. Her father reined back to slow his animals and looked at her with a frown.

"Why are ye nae ridin'?"

She straightened. "It seemed like a good day for a walk."

"What's that in yer arms?" Father asked.

"Clothes. They're wet. I went wading with the lads."

Angus chuckled. "Looks more like you went swimming."

"It was a hot day," Emmalyne offered with a little shrug.

"Aye, it was at that." Her brother seemed to understand that she didn't wish to continue the discussion. "I do wish the heat would break, although I suppose come December we'll all be longing for it."

"Ye ought to ride so that we can get to the hoose more quickly," her father said. "Angus, help yer sister mount."

Angus jumped down from the wagon and went to assist her. Emmalyne shifted the clothes in order to raise her skirt and fit her foot into the stirrup. She felt herself blush again, remembering how Tavin had kissed her. If Angus noticed her discomfort, he said nothing and lifted her to the sidesaddle.

Emmalyne arranged herself and settled the wet clothes in front of her. She noted their dampness but had no desire to delay them further by asking her brother to secure them behind her. Angus handed her the reins.

"Thank you," she whispered, hoping he'd realize it was as much for his understanding as for his help.

The three moved forward without comment, but as they drew closer to their property, Emmalyne couldn't help but notice the distinct smell of smoke. "What do you suppose is burning?" she asked, looking back at her father and brother. "Do you smell that?"

"I do." Angus lifted his chin and sniffed at the air. "Smells like wood rather than grass."

Emmalyne rounded a curve in the road and noted that the air seemed hazy. She felt a sudden fear. "I think it's coming from our place!" she exclaimed.

She kicked the horse into a gallop, very nearly losing her

seat as she fought to hold the clothes and keep her balance. She heard the wagon rattling behind her and knew her father had followed suit.

They came up the wooded lane and crossed into the yard to see thick smoke billowing up from behind the house. Emmalyne dropped to the ground and barely took time to tie up the horse before following her brother around back. Angus's long legs made him much faster, and when Emmalyne and her father arrived moments later, they found Mother weeping in Angus's arms. The barn was blazing out of control.

"What happened?" Father demanded.

"There were three men," Mother said, fighting to speak between her sobs. "They let me get the cow out. I tied her over there." Mother motioned to where the milk cow stood in nervous agitation.

"Who were they?" Father asked angrily. "Did they hurt ye?"

Mother shook her head. "They never touched me. They . . . they said next time it would be the house unless . . ." Another sob escaped her.

"Unless what?" Father strode over to where Rowena stood. Emmalyne watched as her mother pulled away from Angus and took hold of Father's arm.

"Unless you convince Rabbie to join the union. The men were quite clear. They said this was to be a warning."

A portion of the old barn caved in, drawing their attention. It hadn't been much of a structure, but at least it had offered the animals shelter from the weather. Emmalyne could see her father's jaw clench. She knew he would never stand for such intimidation.

"How long ago were they here?" he demanded. "What did they look like?"

"They left just a few minutes ago." Mother looked at Emmalyne and shook her head. "I couldn't see what they looked like. They had kerchiefs pulled up to hide their faces. Two of them were short with big chests and arms. They wore hats, so I couldn't see too much of their hair. But the one who seemed to be in charge, he was tall with blond hair—curls a girl would envy."

"We cannae save the bern. All we can do is let it burn out and keep it from settin' the hoose afire. Emmy, ye get some water. Wife, ye help her. Angus, fetch the ladder from the front porch, where ye were workin' last."

Emmalyne ran immediately to the pump while Angus raced to the front of the house and the ladder. Two buckets sat near the pump. They generally used these for watering the livestock, but now Emmalyne could only pray they would keep the house from burning down. She handed one bucket to her mother and took the other for herself.

Angus brought the ladder around and secured it against the back wall of the house. He climbed the rungs and reached down to take up the first bucket of water from Emmalyne. "Keep 'em coming."

Emmalyne hurried back to get the other bucket her mother was filling. Angus threw down the empty bucket just as she brought the second one. She hurried back to the pump, wishing they had more to work with.

By the time the house was doused to her father's approval the barn flames had lessened considerably. The old dry wood had been quickly consumed, and now the fire had much less to feed on as the charred black frame disintegrated before their eyes. Emmalyne stood back watching the fire, uncertain what else to do.

"Angus, come with me," her father commanded.

Mother looked up. "Where are you going?"

"After the men who did this," Father replied. "I wiltnae let any man threaten me this way."

Mother hurried across the yard to her husband and took hold of him. "Don't, Luthias. Don't do this. They are not good men. They might hurt you if you try to—"

"Donnae worry."

Emmalyne had fully expected her father to turn angry at her mother's entreaties, but he actually put his hand on her mother's arm.

"They'll nae get the best of Luthias Knox."

"But how will you find them?" Mother asked. "It's been at least half an hour."

Her father motioned to the dirt. "One of 'em is ridin' a horse with a bad shoe."

Emmalyne looked to the tracks and marveled at her father's ability to note such a thing. She'd always been amazed at his tracking skills, but this surprised her once more. There were a great many hoofprints in the dirt, yet her father had spied that particular set and knew it would help him to find the perpetrators of this crime.

"Oh, Luthias, please be careful." Her mother was almost in tears again.

Her father looked at his wife for a moment with a tenderness Emmalyne wasn't sure she'd ever seen in his face. Father nodded and patted her arm before calling to Angus, "Leave us go."

The angry expression returned, and Luthias Knox stalked away like a Scottish chieftain of old—proud and regal, ready to do battle on behalf of his clan. Emmalyne came to her mother's side. She knew she could say nothing to offer assurance or comfort. Her biggest worry was that this would cause her mother to slip back into her sorrowful state. But to her surprise, Mother took hold of Emmalyne's arm. "You must get help. Go to the MacLachlans'. Haste ye now!"

Emmalyne wasn't sure how she managed to mount the bay without help, but she was flying down the road toward the MacLachlan house before her mother said another word. The thought of turning to their neighbors for help had not entered her mind, but once her mother had made the suggestion, Emmalyne knew it was the right one. Robert MacLachlan would know what to do. He could talk sense into her father when no one else could. He'd surely be able to stop her father from doing something foolish.

She crossed the distance in what felt like record time. Throwing herself from the back of the horse, Emmalyne crumpled onto the ground. She wanted to cry out but forced her legs to cooperate and got back to her feet. Hurrying to the door of the house, Emmalyne began pounding and calling for help.

Tavin opened the door. "Em?" he said, his voice full of concern.

Emmalyne took hold of him. "We need help. Some men burned down our barn. They did it when Mother was alone. They told her next it would be the house if Father didn't convince your father to join the union."

"What?" Tavin shook his head in disbelief.

"It's true." Tears filled her eyes. "Oh, Tavin, my father and Angus have gone after the men. You must get your father and stop them. Those men . . . oh, there's no telling what will happen."

"We'll go." Robert MacLachlan stepped out from behind his son. "I'll get the horses."

Tavin looked at Emmalyne and reached up to wipe a tear trickling down her cheek. "Don't worry," he murmured. "Pray instead."

Emmalyne nodded. "Father was so angry, Tavin. I'm afraid of what he'll do if he finds those men."

"I know, but your mother will need you to be strong. Let me help you back on your horse. We'll ride back with you, then follow the tracks."

"I'm so sorry, Tavin. I'm so sorry."

She knew he'd understand that her apology was for everything that had happened in the past and the present. She knew the years meant nothing. They were still two parts of one heart, now joined once again as they always should have been.

He smiled and touched her cheek again. "I know, Emmy. I know. I'm sorry, too."

Chapter 24

Tavin and his father rode hard and fast to catch up with the Knox men. They figured the men responsible for the arson attack would have hightailed it back to St. Cloud, so they stuck with the main roads. They weren't far from the city when Tavin spied Luthias Knox's wagon stopped on the side of the road. Three saddled horses grazed nearby, suggesting a rather peaceful gathering. Tavin knew it most likely was anything but. As he and his father drew near, it was obvious tensions were high. Luthias Knox was waving his fist in the face of one of the men.

"Looks like Luthias found his attackers," Tavin's father said, slowing his mount. "This could get ugly."

"They started it," Tavin replied.

They came up behind the wagon and dismounted. Tavin and his father tied their horses onto the Knoxes' wagon and stepped forward to hear what was being said. Angus noticed them and gave a nod as Tavin approached. The other men had their eyes trained on Luthias Knox.

"It's a reckonin' I want." Luthias raised his voice and leaned closer to the blond man, who had a good five inches and thirty pounds on the older man. Tavin had to admire Emmalyne's father for his fearless nature. He didn't stop for a moment to consider that the younger man could most likely best him in a fight. He was ready to fight, and Tavin knew they would have to intervene lest the situation get out of hand.

"Ye'll pay to build me a new bern, or ye'll answer to the law."

The man just laughed. He exchanged a look with his friends, who immediately joined him in his amusement. "Ain't buildin' you nothin', old man."

"Ye destroyed me bern and threatened me guid wife. I'll nae be standin' for it." Luthias drew back his fist.

Tavin stepped forward and took hold of the older man's arm. All of the men now noticed the MacLachlans. Luthias looked at Tavin and narrowed his eyes. The scowl on his face left Tavin little doubt that Knox would just as soon hit him as strike the blond-haired man.

The tall man's companions stepped forward, and one of them spoke. "What do you want? This ain't none of your business."

Tavin dropped his hold on Knox. "I came to back up our friend here." Luthias's expression changed from anger to confusion. Just as quickly, however, he looked back to the trio and glared.

Tavin spoke, his voice even but clear. "Looks like you fellows have been causing trouble. A lot of trouble, the way I see it."

"Well, I don't reckon I much care how you see it, MacLachlan," the tall man sneered.

Tavin smiled. "Ah, so you know who I am."

"I know, all right." The man spit and cast another sneer at Tavin.

"And I suppose you are the ones responsible for the mishaps we've endured at the quarry?" Tavin asked.

The man shrugged. "Around here, ain't no way of knowin' who's responsible for what. Stuff happens sometimes. Bad things. Good things." He cocked his head to one side and grinned. "Just like life."

"Now, I'd never have expected someone like you to wax philosophical," Tavin said, eyes narrowed.

"I ain't waxin' nothin'." The man looked to his friends. "Sometimes a man needs to think about what's important. That's all I'm suggestin'."

Robert MacLachlan stepped forward. "Well, what I'm suggestin' is a wee bit different. I donnae ken who put you up to this, but I do ken who will end it."

"You, old man?" one of the trio asked, his sarcasm unmistakable. The man had dark brown hair and equally dark eyes. He looked as if his nose had been broken a time or two and his fists were the size of hams. "I'll fight you, and we'll see how well that goes." He raised his large hands in a menacing pose.

"It seems like you two could use some help," the blond man interjected, looking at Tavin. "But just two old men and their lads hardly make an army."

"You seem pretty familiar with who's who," Tavin responded. "But even so, you'd be surprised," Tavin said matter-of-factly.

The blonde smiled and crossed his arms. "Look here. It's a pity about the old man's barn, but he has no way of proving it was us. Same for you and your quarry . . . 'accidents.' If you were union members, part of the Granite Cutter's Brotherhood—why, we'd be more'n happy to help figure out who was to blame. Better still, folks would know not to mess around with you."

"That's right," one of his companions declared. "Union looks out for its own."

"I'm sure you do," Tavin replied. "However, as I heard directly from your union boss, he doesn't approve of these kinds of . . . incentives."

The blonde laughed. "Well, we figure what he don't know won't hurt him. The way I see it, getting folks to join is what matters. How we get them isn't really all that important. But, like I said, you can't prove that we're anything but honorable men."

Luthias Knox folded his arms against his chest. "Ye frighten wimen and destroy property and think it an honorable thing. I'd like to talk to that leader of yers and let him know jes what ye've been about."

"Our leader . . . as you call him . . . won't take your word over ours. He knows we're loyal." The blond-haired man gave a knowing smile. "Loyalty means a lot in these parts."

"So does honor," Tavin countered. "A man is nothing if he has no honor. The way I see it, you three lack much in that regard."

Again the tall man shrugged. "You can't prove a thing, MacLachlan. Go to the law if you want. There's nothing you can say to prove anything."

"My guid wife can identify ye," Luthias said, stepping forward, his hands again balled into fists. "And one of those beasties carries a bad shoe." He pointed to the horses. "Ye left tracks all around me hoose."

"Hardly proof, old man." The blonde elbowed his companions. "Let's get out of here. I'm bored with this conversation."

Tavin put himself between Luthias and the taller man, fearing Emmalyne's father might do something foolish. "You'd do well to listen. Whether or not the men of our quarry join the union will be left entirely up to them to decide. Be forewarned: We'll have armed guards posted, and if anyone so much as rustles the brush around the quarry, we'll shoot first and ask questions later."

The man frowned and narrowed his eyes as he stared hard at Tavin. "I don't take well to threats, mister."

Tavin nodded, his lips pulled down at the corners. "Neither do we."

The four returned to the Knox property and surveyed the damage. Daylight was nearly gone, and it was impossible to make much more than a cursory examination. Some of the boards were still smoldering.

"Good thing there wasn't a wind," Tavin said, shaking his head. "Even so, it burned faster'n dried kindling."

"'Twas an auld homestead," Robert explained, "and the hoose and bern werenae put together all that well." He looked to Luthias and slapped his back. "Me and my lads will come on the morrow and see what's to be done to rebuild."

Emmalyne was surprised when her father didn't refuse but politely thanked his friend. Her father's pride usually would not have allowed him to accept help of any kind. Perhaps the whole event of the fire, the loss of the barn, and neighborly help in accosting the union men had changed her father. She watched him embrace his friend and threw Angus a silent look of question. He shrugged while Mother dabbed tears from her eyes.

Is this an answer to my prayer, Lord? Has Father had a change of heart? Did it take this attack to make him see the truth? And then, most startling of all, she watched Father reach out and shake hands with Tavin.

"Thank ye for yer help."

Emmalyne couldn't suppress a gasp. She tried to quickly cover it with a cough, but she immediately felt Tavin's gaze upon her. The thought of his kiss caused her to move her hand to her lips. Worrying that Tavin would know what she was thinking, Emmalyne quickly pretended to push back a wisp of hair from her face. She looked away for fear of what his expression might hold. *Is he embarrassed about it, wishing it had never happened?* she wondered.

"Are you sure you won't stay for supper?" Mother asked Robert and Tavin.

"Nae. Morna had supper ready for us when Emmalyne showed up with the news. We'll go back to it now," Mr. MacLachlan replied. "She'll be worried sick until we return and tell her what has happened."

"She may be even more worried once she hears the truth," Mother noted, her gaze on the ground. "I worry they'll be back. . . ."

"They'll nae cause ye more harm," Father assured her.

Emmalyne heard the determination in his tone and knew her father wouldn't rest until the men paid for their deeds. She still didn't know the details of what had happened on the road, but she did know her father. He would press this matter with the law officials as soon as he could. And maybe even take things into his own hands . . .

The men walked to the front of the house, where the horses were waiting. Emmalyne and Mother stared at the mess that had once been the barn. The smoldering wood created a terrible stench. Mother drew her apron to her nose.

"Pray for rain, Emmy. There's no better way to clear the air and make certain that fire's no more of a threat to us."

"Father said he and Angus were going to tend to it after supper," Emmalyne said, putting her arm around her mother's shoulder. "I'm sure they're very hungry, so we'd best get the table set."

Mother looked to Emmalyne and shook her head. "What manner of man would do such a thing to honest, hardworking people?"

"I don't know, Mother. Hopefully Father and the MacLachlans were able to reason with them." But Emmalyne knew her father's wrath and feared his temper had probably trumped any hope of reason.

It was much later, when Emmalyne was preparing for bed, that she heard a noise outside. Had the arsonists returned? She went to the window to look at the yard below. In the moonlight she could see her father. He was striking a match to light his pipe.

Pulling her shawl around her, Emmalyne felt an urge to join him. She didn't know why or what she would say, but she was out the front door before she knew it.

"Father?" she said quietly into the darkness.

"Emmalyne, what're ye doin' out here?"

"I heard a noise and thought those men might have returned. When I looked out, I saw you here." She caught a whiff of his pipe tobacco—much different from the odor of the burned barn. The aromatic scent always reminded her of her father.

"Yer brother and I will keep watch, fear ye nae. Nocht will happen while we stand guard."

"I wasn't worried," she said. Emmalyne longed to acknowledge her father's kindness after the fire, but she didn't wish to offend him. For several minutes she stood in the darkness with him, listening to him draw on the pipe.

"Yer gonna catch yer death out here. Best ye haste to bed."

Emmalyne felt such an ache in her heart. She longed to know this man as a loving father. She had always yearned for him to be more like Robert MacLachlan was with Fenella, but he never had been so inclined.

"Father, may I ask you something?"

"Aye," he said in a barely audible voice.

Emmalyne swallowed her fear and pressed on. "Mother said that you blame her for forcing you to marry her. Is that true?"

He said nothing for a time, and Emmalyne thought perhaps he would refuse to answer her at all. Perhaps she had overstepped propriety, and his silence was her comeuppance.

Just when she figured she might as well head back into the house, he spoke. "Do ye think me a man to be forced into anythin'?"

She considered this a moment. "No, I suppose I don't. But Mother said—"

"Yer mother says a lot of things. It doesnae make them so." He paused again for a long moment, then finally added, "I married willingly."

"So then you loved her once?" Emmalyne asked, her heart beating hard at her boldness.

"Aye. I loved her then . . . and I love her now." He gave a heavy sigh. "Nae that ma ways would prove it. Tonight I saw her fear, and it shamed me. I hinnae been a guid man. I dinnae bide the stour well."

"Bearing struggles is always hard without turning to God," Emmalyne dared to say. She stepped closer to where her father stood. "But the Bible says we can always come back to Him."

"Aye."

Her father said nothing more, and Emmalyne knew what he'd already offered was more than she could have hoped for. Without asking, she leaned over and kissed his cheek.

"Good night, Father." She left him then, but paused on the porch steps. "I'll be praying for you—for all of us." For the first time in her life, Emmalyne felt hope for her father to finally find peace. She wanted to sing and shout in praise to God but knew it would only frighten her mother and brother, who were no doubt sleeping by this time.

She smiled to herself and all but danced up the stairs to her small room. God was at work, and it would be difficult to sleep just imagining all the possibilities that might await them all.

Tavin was surprised to find his father sitting at the kitchen table. It was late, nearly midnight. A single lamp and an open Bible were in front of him.

"Seeking answers?" Tavin asked.

"Aye, and seeking wisdom," his father replied.

Tavin nodded. "I've been remiss in that."

"There's no time like the present," his father said with a smile.

Sitting down across from him, Tavin met his father's weary gaze. "And where has God led you this night?"

"To the Psalms. Psalm one hundred nineteen. It's a long one, and my eyes are weary," he replied, rubbing them as if for emphasis. "But I am compelled by the words there."

"Yes," Tavin said. "Words of wisdom."

"And of grace," his father said, looking back at him. "Grace and mercy, truth and hope. 'Tis all there for man if we will but seek it."

Tavin looked away, then back at his father. "If we will but seek it," he repeated.

His father smiled and pushed the Bible toward his son. "I'll be headin' to bed now," he said as he rose. "Mayhap you'd like a moment to seek for yourself."

Tavin turned the Bible to view the Scripture his father had been reading. Because of the hour the sixty-second verse caught his attention. *At midnight I will rise to give thanks unto thee because of thy righteous judgments.*

He read on silently as the clock chimed the hour.

I am a companion of all them that fear thee, and of them that keep thy precepts. The earth, O Lord, is full of thy mercy: teach me thy statutes. Thou hast dealt well with thy servant, O Lord, according unto thy word. Teach me good judgment and knowledge: for I have believed thy commandments. Before I was afflicted I went astray: but now have I kept thy word. Thou art good, and doest good; teach me thy statutes.

He breathed deeply, feeling the Word of God in the very depths of his soul.

He continued through the verses like a starving man. How could he have neglected this for so many years when it had once been so important to him? How could he have set up a wall of anger between him and the only hope he'd ever known?

The last three verses of the chapter stirred Tavin, and he found himself murmuring them aloud as a prayer.

"'I have longed for thy salvation, O Lord; and thy law is my delight. Let my soul live, and it shall praise thee; and let thy judgments help me. I have gone astray like a lost sheep; seek thy servant; for I do not forget thy commandments.'"

He glanced into the flame of the lamp. "I have gone astray like a lost sheep, Lord," he said aloud. "But now I long to come home. Please, Lord . . . take me back."

Warmth spread throughout his body and comfort washed over him like a gentle summer rain. Tavin closed his eyes and rested in the peace of the moment. For the first time in a very long time he could feel God's pleasure.

He had come home.

Chapter 25

"Tavin will take the lead wagon," his father instructed. "The others will follow." There were eight wagons in all, and each was loaded to capacity with granite ready for shipping on the railroad. Despite the accident, they were meeting their contract deadline with time to spare.

In the days that had passed since the Knox barn burned down, Tavin and his father had gone with Luthias Knox and the local authorities to confront the union leader in St. Cloud. The man had been unhappy to hear what had happened, but both he and the sheriff were of the opinion there was no way to prove who the arsonists were.

Tavin disagreed, reminding them that Mrs. Knox had been present when the barn had been set afire. But the sheriff countered that it would be her word against theirs, and without further supporting evidence, he could do nothing. Mr. Knox promised that should the men step foot again on his property, there would be evidence enough because he would shoot all three without regard.

This announcement still brought a smile to Tavin's face. He didn't believe that Knox would really shoot them, but he

had no doubt that the older man would find some way to
restrain them long enough for the law to arrive. The union
man had been less amused. He declared he would speak to
his men to ensure such incidents didn't happen again. Tavin
looked at the sheriff to see if the man had also picked up on
this near admission of guilt by the union boss, but there was
no sign he'd noticed it.

"Might I ride with ye?"

Tavin looked down from the wagon seat to Luthias Knox.
He couldn't hide his surprise. "You can, but may I ask why
would you want to?"

"I have business in town and with ye. If ye donnae mind,
I thought we could talk on the way."

Nodding, Tavin offered the man his hand. "Come on up."

Mr. Knox quickly complied. He took his place beside
Tavin and said nothing more until the caravan of wagons
was headed to St. Cloud. Even then, they were a few miles
down the road before he spoke.

"Ye ne'r answered my question," Knox said without turning to look at Tavin.

"I'm sorry, I don't understand. What question?" Tavin
was most acutely aware of Emmalyne's father beside him
and had been waiting anxiously to hear what he wanted to
discuss. He looked to Knox and waited for him to answer.

The older man cast a sidelong glance at Tavin, then returned his gaze to the road ahead. "Ye know, the one I asked
a while ago. Do ye still love ma daughter?"

Tavin grew thoughtful. He could again refuse to answer
the man's question, but to what purpose? "I do, sir," Tavin
finally said in a barely audible voice.

Knox nodded and continued to stare at the landscape.

Tavin considered pressing the man for an explanation, but he held his tongue. He'd known Luthias Knox long enough to know the man wouldn't say anything before he was good and ready.

"Emmy still loves ye, as well." The statement was not said in anger or accusation. Knox cleared his throat and added, "She always has."

The breath caught in Tavin's chest. He didn't know what to say. He knew Mr. Knox was not a man to speak lightly about such things. His bringing the matter up would not have been done without a great deal of thought.

"It isnae easy for a man like me to admit his mistakes," Knox continued. His expression was still hard and fixed, but his voice had softened. "I did ye and Emmy wrong. I ken that now, but back then . . ." He sighed and rubbed his hands back and forth on his thighs.

"I cannae take back what's been done," the man finally said. "I've been the cause of a great deal of sufferin'. Emmy and the others, yerself included, have had to live with ma bad decisions." Knox fell silent then. His sigh seemed to indicate that the truth of his words was too much to bear.

Tavin felt awkward, wondering what he should say or do. The team handled well together and was easy to drive, so Tavin couldn't use that as an excuse to busy his mind. He thought to pray and started a silent request for understanding when Knox once again began to speak.

"Emmalyne is a guid lass. She keeps her word and isnae mindful of her own . . . heart. On the other hand, I hinnae had consideration for anyone save maself. I thought only to see to ma own needs and concerns." He finally looked at Tavin. "I've always been a willful and prideful man. I thought it served me well at times, but nae with ma family. They grew to despise me, jest as you must."

Tavin drew a deep breath, then slowly exhaled. "I don't despise you, Mr. Knox. And neither does your family. I used to, I have to admit, but no longer. My battle was more with myself . . . and God."

Mr. Knox nodded in a meaningful fashion. "Aye. It's been so with me, as well."

They were very nearly to town and to the railroad depot where they would off-load the stone. Tavin had a million questions running through his head—not the least of which was why Knox had chosen this moment to say something.

"A selfish man doesnae care about the pain he causes," Knox said before Tavin could pose his question. "He serves himself. 'Tis ashamed I am of the man I've become." He looked away, shaking his head. "I ken the truth, and it cuts me deep."

Turning the horses toward the tracks, Tavin noted a half dozen men standing around the loading platform. They carefully watched the approaching line of wagons and moved out to the road as Tavin drew closer. Two of the men held rifles.

"Hold up there, MacLachlan," one of the men called out.

Tavin reined back on the team and held up his hand as a signal to the wagon behind him. "What's the problem?" he asked the man. He noted that the other men had formed a line across the road.

"We know you folk aren't union men, and while we respect that," he said with a sneer, "this is a union loading dock. We can't allow you and your wagons to cross our lines."

"That makes no sense. We have a contract and have already arranged transport with the railroad," Tavin countered. He heard a rider approaching and knew it would be his father.

"What's going on?" Robert MacLachlan demanded.

"As I was telling your son," the sneering man began again, "this is a union loading dock. No one's allowed to off-load here unless they belong to the union." He crossed his arms against his chest and fixed them with a stern stare. "That's the rules."

"We have rock that's expected in St. Paul by the end of the week," Tavin's father stated. "I have already arranged for this load to go out today. These men are dependent upon this contract for their pay."

"We know that. That's why we're here," the man replied. "See, our union boss said we shouldn't go out of our way to force your hand in joining the union. Instead, he suggested we show you the merits of such an arrangement. See, we're not a bad bunch." He motioned to the men behind him. "We're hard workers, just like you and your men. But we know the power we can have if we join together in the union. With you running along all independent of our organization . . . well . . . it sends the wrong message to some."

"You mean others might not want to unionize?" Tavin asked, knowing the answer.

The man nodded. "See, I knew you fellas were smart. We're stronger together than separate. Even the Bible talks about how a house divided against itself can't stand. The union is looking out for everyone's best interest."

"Except ours," Robert MacLachlan said flatly.

"Even yours," the man countered. "It's you who don't seem to be concerned about what's best."

Tavin looked to his father. "What do you want to do?" he asked quietly. "I could go for the authorities and bring them back here."

Robert MacLachlan considered that a moment. He looked back to the man. "Look, our livelihood is at stake here. We need to honor our contract and get this granite to St. Paul. Why don't you let us ship our load, and then I promise to meet with my men. We'll put it to a vote. If the majority wants to join up, we'll comply."

The man stepped forward and took hold of the team's harness, shaking his head. "No, sir, I have my orders. By joining the union you'll have access to all that the union affords, including the loading platform and workers who will ensure your product reaches its proper destination." He gave a shrug and added, "I'd suggest you go home and have that meeting with your men. I'm sure if you give this a good think, you'll see things our way."

Tavin could see his father's jaw clench and unclench in anger. He started to speak again, then shook his head. Looking at Tavin, MacLachlan pulled back on his horse's reins. "Turn around. Head for the quarry," he growled.

His father took off before Tavin could question him. Luthias Knox muttered an oath, and for a moment Tavin thought the older man might well climb down from the wagon to take on the union man. Instead, he sat fast.

Tavin squinted at the man holding his team. "I can let the team run you over, if you'd like. Or you can let go and give us room to turn around," Tavin said in a measured manner.

The man released the harness. Joining his confederates where they blocked the road, he touched his finger to his hat in a mocking salute. Tavin yanked hard on the reins and called to the team. The horses strained against the weight of the rock, but in a few moments they had the load turned and headed back down the road.

They were more than a mile away from the rail lines when Tavin remembered that Mr. Knox had mentioned having business in town. He slowed the horses and turned to the older man. "I forgot that you had business in town."

"'Tis nocht that cannae wait."

Tavin nodded and kept the horses moving. Though he wanted to ask Knox about their earlier conversation, the problems that they'd met up with put a damper on further discussion. He couldn't say that he blamed the man for his silence. The union men's interference couldn't have come at a worse time: Every man at the quarry was awaiting his pay, Knox included. Not only that, but Knox was the man handling the bookkeeping. He would know full well just how grave the situation was. He would know that Robert MacLachlan's entire future depended on delivering this rock.

Back at the quarry, Tavin and the other men unharnessed the horses and cared for them before gathering back in the office as requested. Tavin could see the defeat in his father's expression.

"Men, you ken we've talked before about the quarry and whether to unionize." Robert MacLachlan paused and leaned back on his desk. "It would seem the time for decision making has been forced upon us. We can either join the union or we'll be forced to haul our granite to St. Paul on our own."

"We could take matters into our own hands," Tavin's brother interjected. "Maybe give back a little of what they've been giving us. They won't be expecting it, and we could catch them by surprise."

"And do what, Gillam?" Tavin asked, turning to face his brother. "Burn down the union office? Destroy the loading dock? Kill a few of them?" He paused a moment to let the words sink in and turned to face the other quarrymen. "I've belonged to the union, and I know it can be a powerful ally. My father has never been against the unions so much as he's been against being forced to join. He wanted each of you to have the freedom to decide for yourselves. So now we have to decide. That load of granite needs to be delivered to St. Paul. If we have to take it ourselves, it will be difficult at best and delayed. We'll lose money. You'll lose money."

"We're gonna lose money either way," one of the men declared. "I'll be payin' money to the union or havin' it taken out of this load's pay."

"I suppose that's one way to look at it," Tavin said. "However, I have another thought. We aren't going to change the minds of those men, and right now they hold all the cards. It would appear that even though the management of the union has come down against violent acts, they are not against illegal tactics that prove their strength."

"So what's your suggestion, lad?" Tavin's father asked.

"The union has some very good things to offer us," Tavin said. "I say we join and take advantage of those things."

"And just let them get away with bullying us?" Gillam spat out.

Tavin smiled. "Not exactly. It seems to me the best way to have some control over this union is to be an active part of it. We can better influence the way things are done from the inside, wouldn't you agree?"

There was a murmuring of comments around the room, but the general consensus seemed to agree with Tavin. His father nodded and came to stand beside him.

"I donnae wish to see any more damage done to you men or to the quarry. I cannae abide being forced into a thing . . ." He paused, shaking his head. "But I think Tavin is right. And . . . well, selfishly I need this contract fulfilled. I dinnae want to influence ye with ma own troubles, but truth is I put everythin' I had into this."

Tavin knew it had humbled his father to be so honest. He put his arm around the older man. "Each one of us needs this contract fulfilled."

The discussion continued for another half an hour, with Gillam raising the biggest protests. But in the end the men agreed to unionize. Tavin knew the decision came hard for his father. It wasn't all that easy for Tavin to swallow defeat, either. However, he had seen the way men with know-how could influence the union to better meet their needs. Tavin felt confident that, in time, they could find a way to make the union work for them rather than against them.

Once the crew had left, Robert MacLachlan turned to his sons. "I hope you donnae think less of me. When I consider the things we've suffered, Fenella's poor husband and the damaged equipment . . . well . . . I donnae have enough fight left in me."

"I don't think less of you, Father. I think you made the right decision. Like I said, the best way to make changes will come from using logic and reasoning from the inside."

"And you figure they'll just stop harassing us now?" Gillam asked, anger edging his tone.

Tavin gave him a pat on the back. "Gillam, you and I

are reasonably smart, are we not? And we know our father is wise. My thought is that God has brought us to this place and time for a reason. We must now trust Him for the answers."

Gillam seemed to lose some of his fire. "I . . . well . . . I'm like Father. I just don't like being forced into joining. It goes against my nature."

"And mine," Tavin agreed. "However, God is teaching me of late that my nature is rather self-centered and sinful and needs discipline." He looked to his father and grinned. "Who knows what else He will teach us in time?"

Tavin wasn't surprised to find Emmalyne at the house when he returned from the quarry. She and the little boys were in the backyard, where she was removing clothes from the line while the boys played nearby. He paused to watch her for a moment, her beauty causing his heart to pound. He longed to see her hair cascading down her back and remembered only too well the feel of it. Her tiny waist begged his touch, and her lips . . . He smiled, remembering their kiss.

"Uncle Tavin, come and see what we got," Gunnar called out.

Emmalyne looked up and met his gaze. Tavin let Gunnar take him by the hand and pull him to a wooden crate. Inside was a fuzzy ball of fur with a rather long pointed nose. The puppy yipped and whined at the sight of company.

"A man brought him today. Grandma said he's our new dog."

"Seems mighty small," Tavin said, reaching down to scratch the pup behind the ears.

"Grandma says he'll get pretty big. He's a Scottish collie dog."

"Aye. I can see that."

Lethan pounded on the top of the crate. "Goggie. Goggie."

Tavin laughed. "That's right. So what are you going to name him?"

Gunnar shook his head thoughtfully. "Don't know. I was thinkin' about that. Grandma says he needs a strong name."

"Maybe we could make a list tonight and figure that out." Tavin looked over his shoulder to where Emmalyne was folding the last of the laundry. "What do you think, Emmalyne?"

With a shy glance over her shoulder at his use of her name, Emmalyne said, "I used to have a dog named Duke. I thought that a rather nice name."

Tavin nodded and turned back to the boys. "That is a nice name. I used to have a dog named Laddie. That's another good one. Or maybe you could call him Scotty since he's Scottish."

Gunnar's eyes widened. "Scotty. I like that name." He reached into the box and lifted the puppy out. "Hey, Scotty." The animal licked at his face, and Gunnar giggled. "I think he likes it, too."

"Boys, it's time to get washed up for supper," Morna called from the back door.

Gunnar shoved the pup back into the crate and hurried toward the house. "Grandma, do you like the name Scotty?"

Lethan toddled off after his brother, jabbering about the pup in incoherent baby talk.

Tavin heard his mother discussing the puppy's name with her grandsons as they disappeared into the house. Emmalyne, meanwhile, hoisted the basket of folded clothes and started to move past him. Tavin stopped her and took the basket from her. "Let me," he said softly.

She nodded. "Thank you."

"Father and I will be coming over to help with the barn tonight."

Emmalyne smiled. "It's coming along well, especially since some of the other quarrymen came to help. Father was impressed with the kindness of everyone."

"Your father is . . . well . . . he seems to be changed."

"Does he?" Her voice was so soft, Tavin barely heard her comment.

He stopped and put the basket on the ground. Emmalyne looked at him in question. He couldn't help but smile.

"That isn't really what I want to talk about."

"It isn't?" She glanced at him, then away again, her face growing rosy.

"No." He reached out to touch her cheek. "You are more beautiful than ever, Emmalyne."

She blushed further and lowered her face. "Thank you," she murmured.

"Em, I'm sorry for the way I've acted."

She looked up again. "I'm sorry for so much."

He reached out and touched her cheek once more. "You did nothing wrong. You were an honorable daughter, and I faulted you for it. That was wrong. I was so angry—at God, at your father, at you even. . . . But after all that, after all the years that have gone by, I still can't imagine spending the rest of my life without you."

She nodded. "I know. Oh, Tavin . . . I . . . ."

He pulled her into his arms and hushed any further words with his lips. The kiss was slow and tender, but for Tavin it ended much too soon. Emmalyne pulled away and looked up into his face.

"I love you, Tavin," she said, as if the words needed to be spoken.

"I love you, Emmy. I always have. And I always will."

Chapter 26

Tavin reviewed his work on the new Knox barn. He'd spent almost all of his free time helping build the structure, and along with the help of several of the quarrymen and his father, the building was now nearly complete. Luthias Knox seemed quite satisfied with the results. Knox had even taken more opportunities to speak with Tavin and to assess the progress. Tavin was surprised to find the older man to be enjoyable company. Apparently Knox felt the same way, for this evening he asked Tavin to join his family for supper after the days' efforts were completed.

With the last of the evening light fading to the west, Tavin gathered his tools. The other men had already left for their homes, and even Tavin's father had departed. Glancing again at the barn, Tavin felt a sense of satisfaction. It wasn't a large structure, but it would suffice to house the Knoxes' horses and milk cow.

"It's looking good, don't you think?" Angus's voice sounded from behind Tavin.

Tavin turned. "I was just thinking that myself."

"It's smaller than the other, but I think it will serve us well."

"Aye," Tavin agreed. "And in time you can always add to it. It won't be hard to enlarge."

"No, I don't suppose so." Angus shoved his hands into his trouser pockets. "I have to admit, it surprises me that you were so willing to help with this."

Tavin shrugged. "It was the right thing to do." He looked at Angus. "I'm trying hard to do the right thing these days."

"I am, as well." He looked at Tavin for a moment as if he wanted to say something more, but just then Angus's mother called from the back door.

"Come on, lads. The bridies are getting cold."

"Well now, that would be a crime," Tavin declared and slapped Angus on the back. "We mustn't let that happen."

They laughed and made their way to the house, washed up, and joined the others in the dining room. The food smelled heavenly and reminded Tavin that he'd not eaten since lunch. It also reminded him of what a good cook Emmalyne was, even those many years ago. She passed by him with a platter of the meat pies, and Tavin gave pretense of reaching out to steal one. She quickly dodged his attack.

"You have to wait until everyone is seated," she reprimanded archly.

Tavin noted that Emmalyne was wearing a dark green gown that seemed to really draw out the red in her hair. She deposited the platter on the table, flashed him a smile, and then quickly turned back to her work in the kitchen.

"I'm glad ye could join us," Luthias Knox said. He motioned the men to the table. "Have a seat here," he said, looking directly at Tavin.

Tavin took the chair, and when the meal began he found himself directly opposite Mr. Knox and Angus while he was sandwiched in between Emmalyne and her mother. He couldn't have been more pleased. The sweet fragrance of Emmalyne's rose soap mingled with the scent of yeasty dough and onions. To Tavin it spoke of home.

"Leave us pray," Knox declared, bowing his head. "Emmalyne, would ye say grace for this bounty?"

Tavin noted her surprise, then gave her a quick wink before bowing his head. For a moment he thought she might refuse, but after a short silence, Emmalyne offered a prayer.

"Father, we thank you for this food and the provision you have given. We thank you for your mercy and protection. Bless us that we might bless others. Amen."

"Amen," Tavin whispered.

The meat pies were passed around, followed with a rich brown gravy. Tavin helped himself to two of the bridies at the insistence of Mrs. Knox and doused them in several spoonfuls of gravy. He wasted no time in getting the food to his mouth.

Closing his eyes for a moment, Tavin sighed. "This is wonderful, even better than my mother's." He looked to Mrs. Knox. "Just don't tell her I said so." Mrs. Knox and Angus laughed, and even Mr. Knox had a hint of a smile on his face.

"Emmalyne makes the best bridies in the state," Angus put in. "Maybe in the whole of the country."

Tavin laughed. "I seem to recall she was always a fair cook."

Emmalyne blushed at the praise but kept her gaze on her plate. Tavin couldn't help but steal a glance from time to time. Her beauty and grace, gentleness and sweet spirit were as evident as they were eleven years ago. If anything, she'd only grown lovelier, inside and out.

"The bern is nearly finished," Mr. Knox began. "I'm most pleased. Ye must thank yer faither for the lumber. I can pay—"

"He was glad to help," Tavin said quickly. "It seems like most in this community are. The problems with the union were . . . well, unfortunate to say the least. However, after Father talked with the union leader yesterday, it was implied that they would be replacing Father's lumber. I believe it's their way of making up for the loss of your barn."

"There's no need. I can do for ma family."

"It's a good thing no one was injured or killed," Emmalyne interjected, probably to distract her father from pressing his point. "There would be no making up for that loss."

"Aye," Tavin said, remembering Fenella and her deceased husband.

Emmalyne seemed to follow his train of thought. "Oh, I'm so sorry. I didn't mean to imply that . . . well . . . I know what your father believes about Fenella's husband."

"Aye. But as the authorities have said, there is no way to prove the truth. It could have been an accident. Sten might have been careless in his calculations. It happens when a man becomes overconfident."

"Has Dr. Williams informed you of when Fenella might move to the home in St. Paul?" Mrs. Knox wondered.

Tavin nodded. "He was at the house yesterday, Mother said. He plans to take my sister there next Tuesday. He will give her medicine that will keep her sedated for the trip. I thought I might go along with him to help."

"That's good of you, Tavin. I'm sure it will comfort your sister, as well as the rest of your family," Mrs. Knox said. She offered him a bowl of green beans. "These are from your mother's garden. She canned them in the summer. I believe they're some of the best I've ever tasted."

Tavin helped himself to the beans and passed the bowl

to Emmalyne. "I have to thank you for allowing Em—your daughter—to help out at the house. Mother is already looking better. She's not been nearly as weary, and I believe she's finally eating better."

"'Tis glad I am to hear it," Mr. Knox declared. "Yer guid mother has endured much."

"Aye," Tavin said, knowing he'd been the cause of some of her pain. "She has at that, but I intend to see it goes easier with her from now on."

They chatted on through the meal, sharing news of happenings in town and around the state. Mr. Knox commented on some new building projects that were going on in the capital, possible projects the quarry could bid on. Angus brought up a team of horses he was considering buying. The one who said very little was Emmalyne. Tavin wondered at her silence. She seemed well enough and ate her fill with the rest of them, but there was a reserve that he wasn't entirely sure he understood. Perhaps she was reflecting on their declaration of love. He certainly had done so. With a small grin he stuffed a forkful of the meat pie into his mouth lest he say something inappropriate. He wanted nothing more than to declare his love for her to the world.

Just when Tavin didn't think he could hold another bite, Mrs. Knox went to the kitchen and brought back a bowl of something steaming. Next she retrieved whipped cream and a stack of small bowls. She ladled dessert into each and topped them with cream. "This is a recipe my mother taught me," she declared. "It's rhubarb sponge, a sort of pudding cake. I've not made it in years."

"It smells wonderful, Mrs. Knox," Tavin said, eager to give it a try in spite of the large meal he had eaten.

Mrs. Knox beamed a smile and handed him the first bowlful. "I hope you like it."

"I'm sure he will. It's a right guid treat," Mr. Knox declared, taking the bowl his wife offered.

Tavin sampled the dessert as the rest of the bowls were passed around. The flavor was sweet and tart at the same time. "This is wonderful."

"And it goes even better with coffee," Mrs. Knox said, retrieving the pot. She refilled the men's cups and asked Emmalyne if she wanted more tea.

"No, Mother. I'm just fine. If I need more I can see to it. You should sit and enjoy the fruit of your labors."

They all ate the treat in relative silence. Comments about the flavor and other favorite desserts were passed back and forth, but little else. When the meal was complete, Mr. Knox got to his feet and asked for everyone's attention.

"I have somethin' to discuss," he announced, looking around the table.

All gazes turned toward the older man. He gave Tavin a rather serious look. "First I have a question for ye, Tavin MacLachlan."

Tavin nodded, but wondered uneasily if he'd somehow once more offended the man.

"I asked ye the other day whether or nae ye still loved ma daughter."

Tavin straightened and glanced at Emmalyne, who was staring wide-eyed at her father. "And I told you . . ." He paused, realizing some things he'd spoken then were best left unsaid. He smiled. "I do."

Mr. Knox nodded and looked to Emmalyne. "And, daughter, do ye still love this man?"

She licked her lips. "As I said that night in the barn, Father, I do love him."

"'Tis as I always believed," her father continued. "And because of that, I want to beg yer forgiveness."

"Forgiveness, Father?" Emmalyne asked.

Tavin could hear the surprise in her voice. He reached over and squeezed her hand. She looked at him, clearly puzzled by her father's declaration.

"Aye, forgiveness," Mr. Knox continued. "I've been a strounge of a man."

Tavin knew that it had taken great humility for Knox to admit his bitterness to his family. He could see tears in Mrs. Knox's eyes as her husband continued. "I've let anger and hate guide me instead of the guid Lord, and for that I'm heartily sorry." He looked from Tavin to Emmalyne. "I've wronged ye two more than a man has right. Ye were destined to marry, and even I knew that. But I took ye away from each other. . . ." He paused and swallowed. "And for that . . . I beg yer forgiveness."

Emmalyne began to cry softly, and Tavin tightened his hold on her hand. She entwined her fingers with his.

"It's a fearful man I've been. I've been a poor father and have wronged me guid wife." His voice cracked, and he drew a deep breath and fell silent once more. No one around the table said a word.

"Tavin, are ye still of a mind to marry ma guid lass?"

Tavin looked to Emmalyne and then back to Knox. "I am."

"And if ye were to do so, would ye take her away from her family?"

He met the older man's blue eyes and shook his head. "Never. You would become my family, as well."

Emmalyne's father nodded. "And would ye allow her to see to us in our auld age?"

"I would," he promised. "And I, too, would care for you . . . as if you were my own father and mother. I pledge to you now that you would never be alone or left to make your own way."

Knox again nodded, this time more slowly, as if each movement were an understanding between them. "Then I give ye leave to marry."

Emmalyne let go of Tavin's hand and drew the napkin to her face. Her shoulders trembled as she cried. Mrs. Knox, too, was weeping softly while Angus couldn't keep the grin from his face.

Tavin looked first at weeping Emmalyne, then back to her father. There didn't seem to be anything more to be said, at least in front of an audience. He wanted to thank Emmalyne's father for his blessing on their marriage, but he felt like he needed first to speak to Emmy and see if she was still of a mind to wed him.

Standing, Tavin said, "If you would allow us, Mr. Knox, I'd like to take Emmalyne for a little walk. If she's willing."

He agreed and Tavin reached down to take hold of Emmalyne's hand. "Come," he whispered.

She got to her feet, her tears still falling down her cheeks. He led her to the front door and out onto the porch. The chilled night air felt damp, but he doubted either of them would be cold. Pulling her along, Tavin led her in the darkness to a grove of trees that could offer them some seclusion from the rest of the world.

He drew her into his arms and held her tight. For a long while he said nothing. It was enough to hold her—to breathe the scent of her hair and to feel her soft skin against his neck.

He could hardly believe what had just occurred. He had given up hope for a future with Emmalyne long ago, certain that even God could not change the heart of Luthias Knox.

Tavin felt her begin to relax in his hold. The sobbing had passed. "Em," he whispered.

She lifted her head. Tavin couldn't see the details of her face, but he reached out to trace the line of her jaw. "I love you, Emmy. Will you marry me?"

"I will," she said without hesitation.

He lifted her chin just a bit and pressed his lips against hers. Tavin kept a tight rein on the passion that stirred within him. He wanted so very much to spend his life with this woman, and waiting even one more day to make her his wife seemed an eternity.

He pulled away just enough to ask, "When?"

"The sooner the better, lest Father change his mind again," she said, and they both chuckled.

"If that should happen . . . we'll elope," Tavin told her with another kiss.

"Aye," she promised. "We will do exactly that," she said when she next was able.

It felt wonderful to once more be in church without having to sneak away. Emmalyne looked at her family sitting beside her in the pew and wanted to weep all over again. She had always known that God was able to do anything, but her faith had been small and weak. To see her mother and father together in God's house was something Emmalyne wasn't sure she would ever see.

After a message that seemed to sparkle with insight and

application for the Knox family—for the entire congregation, actually, Emmalyne thought—Reverend Campbell stepped to the pulpit for the benediction. Emmalyne bowed her head. Peace washed over her as the pastor prayed.

"And, Father, we pray also for the upcoming marriage of Emmalyne Knox and Tavin MacLachlan. May your hand be upon them and your blessings pour forth on both their families."

Emmalyne heard little else. She found herself silently adding to the pastor's prayer, *God, make me a good wife to Tavin. Let me be the godly woman you've called me to be. Let me care for my parents with a tender and loving heart. And, God, thank you for what you've done for my father. I ask that you would continue to help him and draw him closer to Mother. Her joy has been lovely to see, her strength and energy so much improved. I want them to be even happier than they were when they first decided to marry.*

Angus nudged her with his elbow. "The service is over, Emmy."

She looked up, feeling a bit embarrassed. People all around them were departing. "I was caught up in my prayers," she whispered.

Angus grinned. "Praying about your wedding?"

She shook her head. "Oh, I did at first," she said, reconsidering. "But mostly I was praying for Mother and Father. Oh, Angus, they seem so happy now. Father isn't nearly so gruff and impatient. Mother is very nearly a new woman. I've never known her to be so content."

"I see it, too. God's blessing is finally upon our family."

"I don't think it really ever left us, Angus. I think we might have shunned it, might not have noticed the ways He was at work, but God never removed His blessing from us."

Angus escorted her from the church, where she was immediately joined by Tavin. "Sorry I was late. Fenella has been in quite a state. Mother needed my help, and Father also decided to remain at home with her and see to the boys."

Emmalyne shook her head. "I'm so sorry, Tavin. I know it cannot be easy to watch your sister suffer as she does. It grieves me deeply, knowing her to be only a shadow of her former self."

Dr. Williams joined them and extended his hand to Tavin. "Congratulations are in order." He looked at Emmalyne and offered his hand to her, also. "Although I cannot deny they are rather bittersweet in their delivery." He cocked his head to one side and looked back and forth between them.

Emmalyne shook her head. "Do not feel so, Dr. Williams. I have waited over eleven years for the world to be set right again." She smiled up at Tavin for a moment, and he squeezed her arm he was holding.

The man nodded and sobered. "I know you have. I am happy for you, Miss Knox. And for you, Mr. MacLachlan." Looking at Tavin, he continued. "I have the final papers prepared for your sister. Are you still of a mind to travel with us to St. Paul?" he asked Tavin.

"I am. I think it would give my mother comfort to know Fenella had a family member with her. It will be hard enough for Fenella to understand what is happening."

"That's true." The doctor's expression turned even more serious. "You know, it will probably be a difficult experience for you, as well."

"I have considered that," Tavin said with a nod. "Em and I have talked about it at length. I originally was against sending Fenella anywhere, but knowing there's a possibility she can be helped and understanding the impossible situation my mother has been facing . . . well, I've changed my mind on it. It will be difficult to see her leave us, but my prayers and hopes are that she might one day regain her sanity."

"There's only a slim chance, you realize," Dr. Williams cautioned. "I wouldn't want you to be unfairly hopeful. These doctors are doing good work with their patients. However, your sister has been in this state for a considerable length of time. She's grown progressively more violent, and in speaking with the doctors in St. Paul, I can't pretend that her condition will be easily resolved."

"But, Doctor, you sounded rather promising not so long ago," Emmalyne interjected.

"I know I did," he agreed, "perhaps too promising. And yet, I want to believe there is a possibility for healing." He shook his head. "The mind is such an unknown territory for science. We are learning more all the time, but it remains a mystery. As I told Mrs. MacLachlan, there is simply no possible way to know what the outcome will be for Fenella. But we will continue to have hope."

"She was quite a handful this morning," Tavin said. "I hope you have something stronger for the trip than the medicine you've been using. If we're going to put her on a train with civilized folks and not raise a terrible ruckus, it will need to be more powerful than what she has right now."

"I know. The doctor at the home sent a mixture of medicine for me to inject. It should cause her to sleep for the most part. I've spoken to the depot master about putting us in a car with few, if any, others. He has suggested maybe something in one of the baggage cars. Perhaps even set up a cot for your sister."

"That was smart thinking, Doc," Tavin said, nodding his approval. "That would definitely suit us better than having folks staring and asking questions."

"I agree." He looked again to Emmalyne. "And how has the horse worked out?"

"Quite well, although of course we will return him once we wed."

"No," he said with a nod, "I think I'll make it a wedding present." He turned to Tavin. "So long as your betrothed doesn't disagree."

Tavin smiled and put his arm around Emmalyne. "It suits me just fine, so long as Emmy is happy . . . and doesn't ride off too far away from me."

She couldn't help but laugh. For so long joy had been absent from her life, and now it seemed to overflow. "I am happy," she told the two men. "Happier than I've ever been."

The sound of a fast-approaching rider drew the attention of all the congregants still visiting after the service. Robert MacLachlan galloped onto the church grounds, reining the horse to an abrupt stop near Emmalyne and Tavin.

"Tavin, you must come home," his father called out. "Fenella is missing!"

Chapter 27

Emmalyne frantically looked between Tavin and Dr. Williams. "How did she get away? Where could she have gone?"

"We'd better go there immediately," the doctor said. "I'll get my bag and ride out."

Tavin nodded and touched Emmalyne's arm. "Come to the house and sit with Mother. She'll be beside herself, and the boys could use your attention."

"Yes, I'll do what I can to help. Father and Angus will also help look for Fenella, I'm sure." She gave Tavin's hand a squeeze. "I'll see you as soon as I can."

Emmalyne could already see her parents hurrying toward them, no doubt wondering what was happening.

"Fenella has gone missing, Father," she called to them. "The MacLachlans are frantic with worry."

"It wiltnae bode well for the lass out there alone," her father said. "Yer brother and I will help search. Let's leave quickly."

"I told Tavin I would go and help with the children."

Mother said, "And I'll sit with Morna, maybe offer some comfort. Let's just head right over there now."

Father didn't spare the horses, urging them onward at such

a rapid pace that Emmalyne had to hold tightly to the side of the wagon to steady herself. She prayed fervently over the miles.

Lord, please keep Fenella in your care. Let the men find her, she pleaded over and over.

Angus's expression was grave, and Emmalyne was certain it reflected his concerns about the dangers around a quarry. Emmalyne had heard accounts of loose, unstable ground, deep waters, and snakes the length of a man—only a few of the things that might cause problems for Fenella. Or she might have headed away from the quarry toward the river.

As they passed the Knox property, Emmalyne realized the thick forest of trees could easily hide someone as small as Fenella. "She might be out here somewhere," she told her brother. "We'd do well to keep our eyes open."

He nodded. "I'll keep watch in this direction. You look that way." But they saw nothing of the young woman.

After what seemed an eternity, they finally pulled up to the MacLachlan house. "Has she been found yet?" Emmalyne called to Tavin as he ran up to the wagon.

"No," he said, shaking his head. "I'm sure glad your father is here. He's the best tracker among us. If anyone can find her, my money is on him." He quickly helped Emmalyne and her mother out. "Father's trying to look for evidence of which direction she's gone, but he's so upset I fear he'll have little luck."

Morna appeared with the boys. Gunnar looked ashen. Emmalyne went to him immediately and lifted him in her arms. He clung to her while Lethan fussed in Morna's embrace.

"Oh, Emmy, I'm so glad you're here. I widnae ken what to do without you." Morna's words were a near whisper.

Mother joined them. "We'll do what we can to see you through this."

"It happened so quickly," Morna said, shaking her head as she held Lethan close. "Fenella had finally calmed down. I thought she'd fallen asleep. Gunnar had gone to feed the wee pup, and Lethan was playing in his crib. I decided to fetch some clean clothes for Fenella—she'd torn the others in a fit. I shouldnae have left her door open, but I was only gone a minute or two. I went to my room to get the clothes, and when I came back, she was gone. She'd been sleeping—from the medicine. I gave her a heavy dose. She shouldnae have been able to even walk. . . ."

"We understand, Morna," Mother assured her. "Let's go inside and rest a spell. The men will handle this well enough."

Emmalyne ran her fingers through Gunnar's hair, then led the boy back to the porch. "I'm going to go look for her, too." She touched Gunnar's cheek. "You stay here and keep the ladies safe. All right?"

"I wanna help look for my mama." His lower lip trembled.

"I'm sure you do, Gunnar, but you need to stay here with your little brother. My father is very good at this. He'll find your mama, and then we can spend some time playing. Would you like that?"

Gunnar nodded. "We can play with Scotty."

Emmalyne smiled. "Aye."

She headed out. Robert was beyond the barn, and it looked like he and her father were searching the ground for indications of tracks. Tavin looked up at her, then nodded his understanding.

"She has no shoes on," Robert was explaining. "The footprints will be hers, but I cannae seem to find any sign."

Emmalyne watched her father carefully scrutinize the area. He paced off several steps in half a dozen directions. From time to time he knelt to the ground and touched the brush or rocks.

"We looked for her on the road," Emmalyne told Tavin. "No sign of her there."

"I know. We did the same. Father had already searched it on the way to the church in case she might have headed that way."

"Here!" Father called out from a spot between two aspen trees. "There's a wee bit of fabric here." He held up a tiny piece of blue cloth. It wasn't much, but Emmalyne could see by the expression on Robert MacLachlan's face that it was Fenella's.

Father pressed farther into the brush. "Keep yer eyes open," he admonished them.

They set out through the forest, kicking through the first of newly fallen leaves. Emmalyne stared so hard and long at the ground around her that she lost track of the others. She could hear them just ahead of her or maybe just to her right.

"There are broken branches over here," Father called out. "She's gone this way."

They moved in the new direction, each following Luthias Knox at a reasonable distance so as not to complicate his tracking. He led them deeper and deeper into the woods. When they came to a boggy area, he frowned and raised his hand to halt the group.

"She walked through here. See the prints?"

Emmalyne craned her neck to see the footprints her father was pointing out.

"Then we go through here, too," Robert declared.

"Could be dangerous," Tavin remarked. "Maybe I should

go through the water and the rest of you could skirt around the worst of it and pick up the trail on the other side. It's not that far."

Tavin's father looked out across the wetlands. "I suppose you're right. That way if she dinnae make it . . ." Emmalyne shuddered as Robert's words faded away.

Tavin set out through the bog while the others hurried around the edges to the other side. Emmalyne watched as Tavin appeared to search the water. Her father and Mr. MacLachlan, in turn, studied the shoreline.

"She came out here," MacLachlan called out. Emmalyne could see from the marks in the wet ground that Fenella had fallen to her knees, then crawled a short distance before regaining her footing.

"This is going to take us around to the quarry," Tavin murmured under his breath.

Emmalyne looked at him. "The quarry? Oh no . . ." She couldn't even finish for the fear that gripped her.

Robert nodded. "Fenella used to come out to bring lunch to her husband from time to time. She would have taken the road back then, but in her current state of mind . . ." He fell silent.

Luthias was already well ahead of them, so they hurried through the woods to catch up. Just as Tavin had figured, they came through the brush and trees to find themselves on rocky terrain near the main area where the men had been cutting granite the previous year.

And across the open expanse on the opposite ledge was Fenella.

Emmalyne put her hands over her mouth. Tavin and the others had spotted her, too. "What do we do?" she whispered.

Fenella was sitting on the ground very near the edge. Very much in danger.

Then the sound of singing caught their attention. Emmalyne recognized the song. She'd heard the Scottish tune sung quite often by her mother when they were young.

"Dance to your daddy, my bonnie laddie, dance to your daddy, my bonnie lamb! And you'll get a fishie, in a little dishie. You'll get a fishie, when the boat comes home." The voice was weak, but the tune and words were unmistakable.

"She used to sing that to Gunnar when he was a wee lad," Tavin's father told them, his voice hushed. "I haven't heard her sing since Sten died."

"We have to get her away from the edge," Tavin said quietly, staring at the distant figure rocking slightly back and forth as she sang. "What do you think we should do?"

"When she was on the roof," Emmalyne said, "Dr. Williams had me talk to her while he came up from behind to grab her. Do you suppose that might work again?"

"It's worth trying," Mr. MacLachlan replied. "I have no better idea."

"If I walk in from Fenella's right side and call to her," she continued, "Tavin could go around behind and come in from the other way."

"First we have to get over there without upsetting her," Tavin said. "Father, why don't you and Mr. Knox go back and bring the wagon. We'll need it to bring her home. Angus, you and I will move around to the far side while Emmy goes to talk to her."

Her father looked at Emmalyne "Haste ye now, and God be with ye."

She drew a deep breath. "Haste ye back."

She walked slowly around the quarry, keeping to the trees and brush where she could. When only open rock was left to her, Emmalyne paused to consider how she should approach. Fenella was still singing and sat some fifty yards to the left— far enough away to give Fenella time to see Emmalyne and become agitated. The last thing Emmalyne wanted was for Fenella to get flustered and do something drastic.

"What do I do, Lord?" she whispered.

Fenella ended her song and began to sing another round. Emmalyne decided to join in. Perhaps if Fenella heard her singing, then saw her coming, it would pose no shock.

"Dance to your daddy, my bonnie laddie, dance to your daddy, my bonnie lamb," Emmalyne sang, slowly emerging from the bushes. "And you'll get a fishie, in a little dishie."

Fenella caught sight of her and smiled. She continued singing in perfect pace with Emmalyne. "You'll get a fishie, when the boat comes home."

Emmalyne's heart felt like it was in her throat, but she made herself finish the song.

Fenella waved. "Oh, Emmy. 'Tis you. I knew you'd come."

Emmalyne returned the wave, shocked at hearing Fenella speak. "I'm here, Fenella. I'm here." She picked up her skirts to better navigate the rock. For the most part the granite was fairly smooth, but it would be treacherous if she were to slip over the edge.

"You must come meet my husband. He's a wondrous man," Fenella announced, looking to her left as if Sten Edlund were sitting at her side. "I wanted you to come to the wedding."

"I would have liked that." Emmalyne continued walking toward her friend, her hand slightly outstretched.

Fenella seemed to change in the blink of an eye. She looked

back at Emmalyne and shook her head from side to side. Grabbing her head in her hands, Fenella moaned and muttered something. Emmalyne stopped moving immediately.

"What's wrong, Fenella? You can tell me. We're good friends, remember?"

The bedraggled, wild-looking woman paused her frantic movements and stared hard at Emmalyne. The slightest motion behind Fenella turned out to be Angus and Tavin splitting up to approach Fenella from different directions. Fearing the woman would hear or see them, Emmalyne took another step forward and called to her.

"Fenella. Fenella, aren't you going to come and embrace me? It's been ever so long since we've seen each other."

"The days," Fenella muttered. "The days are gone. The days." She slowly got to her feet and looked around.

Emmalyne shook her head. "We've plenty of days, Fenella. Plenty of time."

"No! No! No! No!" Fenella let out a scream that chilled Emmalyne to the bone.

Holding out her arms, Emmalyne begged, "Please come to me. Please, Fenella. I so long to see you."

Fenella seemed to calm for a moment. She surprised Emmalyne with a smile. "Sten is here to take me home. We have to go," she said.

"Oh, please wait," Emmalyne said, taking another step toward her. "We haven't had a chance to talk."

Fenella swayed. Her eyes seemed to roll back, and without warning, she collapsed in a heap over the quarry's edge.

Tavin ran to Fenella, grabbing for her as her form tumbled off the ridge.

Emmalyne screamed Tavin's name as he reached both

hands for his sister. She heard fabric ripping, and then a heartrending bellow escaped Tavin's lips. A moment later he pushed up and crouched at the edge, a piece of the blue cloth clutched in his hand.

Emmalyne stumbled to his side and wrapped her arms around his shoulders, shaking with sobs. "Tavin, we were so close," she wept into his ear. "And she was talking, Tavin. Did you hear her?"

"Aye. I heard." He pulled her close and held her tight against him.

"She said Sten had come to take her home. Then she fainted."

"I know," he said, stroking her back. "I heard."

Emmalyne moved out of his embrace to peer over the edge, but Tavin stopped her. "Don't. You don't want to see her that way."

"I'll go below," Angus said from behind them. His expression was full of sorrow and deep regret as the two looked up at him.

He turned to leave, but Tavin said, "Wait." He got to his feet and helped Emmalyne up, too.

Tavin drew Emmalyne away from the rock and led her to Angus's side. "Take your sister to the road. Our fathers will be here momentarily with the wagon. You need to break the news to them. I'll go to . . . Fenella."

Chapter 28

The chill of October meant frost on the ground and color in the trees. Because of Fenella's death, Emmalyne and Tavin had decided to delay their wedding, but now everyone was eager for the event to move forward. Even Morna, though deeply grieving the tragic loss of her daughter, wanted only for the couple to finally be joined.

"'Tis been a long time in coming," she told Tavin and Emmalyne. "Fenella wouldnae want you to put it off." She pressed her lips tight. "My poor lassie. If only I had locked the door . . ."

Emmalyne looped her arm through Morna's. "Now, hear me once more, my second mother to be: You cannot carry this burden any longer. You did what any of us might have done, considering the medicine she'd had." Morna looked over at her with a trembling smile and a nod.

Emmalyne had told Morna of Fenella's last words and of her singing. "We shall miss her," Emmalyne murmured. "But we know Fenella loved Jesus. Do you remember that she and I were baptized on the same Sunday?"

"I do remember. I was so proud of you both and so happy," Morna said, patting Emmalyne's hand. "And she did love the

Lord. I know I'll see her again." She paused and noticed her grandsons at play with their puppy. "She used to pray with Gunnar and tell him Bible stories."

At the sound of his name, Gunnar looked over and threw them a wide smile. "Watch, Grandma. I'm teaching Scotty to shake hands." He wrangled the dog away from his brother and pushed the animal into a seated position. Next he reached for the puppy's paw. "Shake, Scotty. Shake." The pup allowed the awkward interference, then did his best to get back to chewing on a stick that Lethan held.

"That's very good, Gunnar. You'll have him completely trained in no time." Morna turned back to Emmalyne. "I'm so grateful for all the time you've spent with the boys, Emmalyne," she said with another pat on her hand. "It's helped to have you here . . . just to talk."

"I'm glad," Emmalyne said. She looked over Morna's head to where Tavin stood. "It's been a blessing to me, as well. I've gotten to spend time getting to know your son again." They all chuckled and sat down on two wooden benches, Morna facing the couple.

Morna looked weary, but she smiled nevertheless. "Now we must talk about this wedding." She began listing things that needed to be done. "I must give your father's suit a good airing and brushing, and his boots will have to be polished. I still have to finish sewing the skirt I plan to wear." She smiled. "We want to look our best."

"You'll look fine, Mother, no matter what you wear." Tavin put his arm around Emmalyne's shoulder. "Besides, it's going to be a very short ceremony."

"But there's the reception, too," his mother reminded him. "That could go on all day and into the night."

"Well, it will have to go on without us." Tavin grinned and gave Emmalyne a squeeze. "I don't plan for the new Mrs. MacLachlan to spend her wedding day *and* night preoccupied with well-wishers. I want all her attention on me."

Emmalyne elbowed him lightly in the ribs. "My mother has been busy planning the reception festivities. Father has been very generous with his purse. He said it was only right that he make this wedding special since I had to wait so long for it."

"Will yer sisters be attendin'?" Morna asked.

Emmalyne shook her head. "No, the distance and expense are too great. I haven't seen them in such a long time, but I know they are happy for me. They were none too pleased when Father ended our betrothal."

"But now your father has let go of that tradition."

"Aye," Emmalyne replied.

"And I say good riddance," Tavin muttered. "Miserable, senseless tradition, if you ask me."

"Now, Tavin, I understand the fears of getting older and not knowing how you will manage," his mother said. She waggled a finger at him. "One day you will be old, and you'll wonder, too."

Tavin shook his head. "No, we'll have such a houseful of children that there will always be someone to care for us, married or not. And you needn't worry about your future, either. Emmalyne and I have decided we will simply build a very large house and have you and Father on one end and Em's parents on the other."

"That sounds quite interesting," Morna said, looking thoughtful. "And in between will be you and Emmalyne and your houseful of bairns."

"Exactly so," Tavin replied. "And all four of you grandparents will be begging for your turns to watch them while Em and I take long trips to Minneapolis and St. Paul. Now, *there's* a tradition!"

Morna laughed heartily at that, and Tavin and Emmalyne joined in.

"Tavin says you're to have a wee wedding trip." Morna looked at Emmalyne with a smile.

"Yes. We plan to take the train to Chicago. I've never been there, and Tavin says it's a sight to behold." Emmalyne lifted her shoulders in a little shrug and leaned back against her fiancé. "But like I told him, anywhere we can be together will suit me just fine."

"I hope she's always this easy to please," Tavin interjected.

Morna laughed at her son. "Just remember to love her, treat her kindly, and make time for conversation and laughter, and she'll be easy enough to please."

Tavin was glad when it was finally time for his mother to take the boys inside to take a nap. "Walk with me?" he asked Emmalyne.

Her face brightened. "Anywhere. Any time." She took his hand as he helped her up. She beheld him with such adoration that Tavin thought his heart might burst then and there.

"Keep looking at me like that, and we may yet elope."

She giggled. "Now, Mr. MacLachlan, you've waited eleven years to marry me, and you'll not be denying me a proper wedding."

Without warning he swung her into his arms and lifted her off the ground. "And if I insist?"

Emmalyne wrapped her arms around his neck. "Then I suppose I would yield." She sighed and looked quite content.

"Good. Yielding to me is likely a good idea. Don't forget." He captured her lips with his own and felt her fingers gently rubbing the hard muscles of his neck.

After a few minutes, Tavin reluctantly pulled away and put Emmalyne back on the ground. His mood turned serious. "I have eleven years of kisses to make up for."

She touched his cheek with her hand. "And I'm looking forward to each and every one."

Tavin momentarily closed his eyes. How he loved this woman! He silently prayed to be worthy of her love. He wanted to be a good and faithful husband—a man who would not allow joy to escape their household. Emmalyne had already endured enough years of sorrow, he thought. She deserved to be happy.

He opened his eyes to find her watching him still. "You said you had something to ask me," she reminded him.

"Aye. I do. I'm wondering about something. I've been thinking on this for . . . well, for some time now. What would you say to us adopting Fenella's boys?"

She stopped stock-still and turned to face him. "Tavin MacLachlan, I declare, you can read my mind. I was trying to think of a way to ask you the same thing. Do you think your mother would allow for it? She's awfully partial to them."

"That she is. However, she was just saying the other day that they needed to be around other children. To know the love of a mother and father. I think it might have been her way of putting the idea into my head."

"Well, it's a wonderful idea, Tavin. I love those little boys dearly." She drew her brows together. "I suppose, however, it would be best to ask them how they feel. At least Gunnar. Lethan will only babble at us for cookies and milk."

"And the 'goggie,'" Tavin added with a grin.

"Oh, to be sure." Emmalyne linked her arm with his and pulled him toward the house. "Why don't we talk to your mother first, and then we can speak with Gunnar when he wakes up."

Later Tavin and Emmalyne sat in the quiet of the front room with Gunnar. Morna and Robert had taken Lethan for a little walk so that they could speak, uninterrupted, with the boy. Emmalyne smiled, remembering Morna's delight and comment that she and Tavin were an answer to her prayers—only so long as they didn't take her grandbabies too far away.

"Gunnar, Emmy and I have been talking about something," Tavin began. "We were hoping you might let us share our idea with you."

"Is it something fun?" he asked.

"I think it is," Emmalyne replied. "I hope you will, too."

Tavin motioned him to come sit on his lap, and Gunnar quickly complied. Snuggling into his uncle's arms, he looked quite content. Tavin could only hope that the boy would be as happy once he heard their idea.

"I loved your mama, my sister, very much," Tavin began. "I'm sure I would have loved your father, too. But I never knew him."

"I don't 'member him much," Gunnar said, shaking his head.

"Well, that's all right. I'm sure your folks will always re-member you from up in heaven." Tavin gripped his hands together in front of the boy. "Emmalyne and I were talking about how sometimes when something or someone is taken away from you, God brings something else in its place. Now, with people you can't really take another person's place. Every person is special. Your mama was precious to me, and I know you loved her very much. Of course, she was very sick after your father died."

"Grandma said she hurt bad, in her head."

Emmalyne nodded and reached over to pat the boy's knee. "She did, Gunnar, and that pain made her do things she really didn't want to do."

"Like fall off the rock and die?" he asked innocently.

"Like that, yes, and the times she hurt you or Lethan," Tavin interjected. "She didn't know what she was doing because the pain and sickness made her not think right. Understand?" Gunnar nodded, and Tavin continued. "Like I was saying, nobody can take your mama's place. No one even wants to. We want you to remember her and always love her, but sometimes God sends other people to us . . . like a gift, a present to help ease our sadness. Emmalyne and I . . . well . . . we'd like to be a present to you from God."

The boy's eyes got big. "God is giving me a present?"

Emmalyne reached out to take hold of the boy's hand. "Yes. He is. You know Tavin and I will soon be married. And after that, we would love very much for you to live with us. You and Lethan."

"We want, in fact, to adopt you," Tavin explained. "That means we would become your new mama and papa. Would you like that?"

Gunnar frowned, his little brows knit together. "Will you go away like my other mama and papa?"

Tavin hadn't anticipated this question. He grew uneasy, wondering exactly how to help the boy understand. But before he could speak, Emmalyne was explaining.

"Gunnar, we don't know when or where, but every person on this earth will die one day. It's not something to worry about or be afraid of, because we love Jesus, and He's promised us that because we belong to Him, we will live forever with Him. Your mama and papa loved Jesus, and they will live forever. You will see them again someday."

"Will they be mad at me?"

Emmalyne looked at Tavin in confusion.

"Why would you think that?" Tavin asked. "Why would they be mad at you?"

"For havin' a new mama and papa."

Tavin shook his head. "No, Gunnar. They wouldn't be mad. They will be so happy that you have someone to love you—to love Lethan. They want you to be happy, Gunnar. They want you to have a new mama and papa."

The child smiled and the worry left his face. "Then I want God's present. I want you to be my papa, Uncle Tavin, and Emmy, you can be my mama. Lethan's too."

Only a few days remained until the wedding when Tavin's father appeared at the quarry and asked Tavin to join him back at the office. Since fulfilling the contract and joining the union, Robert had been very busy with a variety of further business deals. Tavin hadn't concerned himself with the details, since Gillam had always assisted their father.

"What's this about?" Tavin asked, matching his stride to his father's.

"I cannae say. I want to show you," he replied.

Tavin wiped granite dust from his face and rubbed his hands on his pants. "It's not like you to let a man neglect his work," he said with a grin. "Must be something mighty important."

"'Tis most important," Robert MacLachlan said, returning Tavin's smile. "Something that I hope you're going to like. Of course, I ken you and Emmalyne have been discussing all sorts of plans for after you're wed. This maynae be something you'll want, but I think it is."

Tavin shook his head. "Sounds kind of mysterious to me, Father."

They made their way to the office where Luthias Knox was hard at work. He glanced up when they entered but said nothing. Tavin couldn't help but note the sly smile on the older man's face. What were those two up to?

His father led him down the hall to his own office, Luthias following closely behind. To Tavin's surprise, Gillam was there, as well.

"Well, brother," Gillam said with a second sly smile, "are you ready to inspect your new shop?"

Tavin looked at his father. "I don't understand. Have I been fired? What new shop?"

"We had an agreement. You stayed on to help me with the contract, and I want to hold up my end of the bargain." Gillam began spreading out a large piece of paper while their father continued. "I had some plans drawn up, and I'm wondering what you think about them. We can make any needed changes."

Tavin looked at the paper and shook his head. "I still don't understand. I thought maybe you figured to add onto the offices here." What he was seeing on the drawing was a completely separate, free-standing building.

"I dinnae consider the dust. 'Tis hard enough already. I looked over the land and got to thinkin' that it would serve you well to be farther from the quarrying and closer to the road where folks could come and order their stones and monuments. We can always make it larger in the years to come."

Tavin looked a long time at the paper Gillam was holding open on the desk. "It's a lot more than I expected," he finally said. "What will this cost?"

"'Tis nae your concern. 'Tis our wedding gift to you and Emmalyne. Gillam and I have already discussed it. We only wanted your approval to get started."

Tavin thought of how he'd spent most of his adult life staying as far away from this place and its people as he could. Now he was on the threshold of becoming a permanent part of the community. He looked at his father and Gillam, who were both grinning from ear to ear.

"Well, seeing how you went to all this trouble," he said, unable to hide his own smile, "I suppose I'll need to approve."

"Aye," his father replied sagely. "You must, lest your mither give us both grief. 'Twas partly her idea."

Tavin laughed at this. He could well imagine his mother doing what she could to keep him and Emmalyne in the area, close at hand so she could be near her grandchildren. "Very well. You can assure Mother that the plans were well received. I think Emmalyne will be happy with this arrangement, as well, and I know her parents will, also."

Behind them Luthias cleared his throat and said, "That they will, ma boy."

After their laughter died away, Tavin said, "Now all I need do is find us a home."

His brother shook his head. "Didn't you tell him?" he asked their father.

"I dinnae. I couldnae find the words." Robert MacLachlan rubbed his chin. "You see, your guid mither had a hand in that, too. She wants you and Emmy to stay with us until we can build you a wee house close by."

Tavin looked at his father and then to his grinning brother. "I suppose Mother is of a mind to accompany us on the wedding trip, as well?"

Gillam broke into hearty laughter while their father patted Tavin on the back. "I told her we couldnae do that to you."

Tavin laughed along with his father and brother. He couldn't be exactly sure that his father was teasing, but it was good to share the humor of the moment. Life had taken so many unexpected turns. He'd thought so often that God had deserted him, forgotten him—when all the while He was making a way that Tavin couldn't discern. Now that way was becoming clear, and Tavin very much liked the look of the road ahead.

Chapter 29

With only their immediate families to stand witness to their marriage, Tavin and Emmalyne were wed. Reverend Campbell admonished them on the seriousness of the wedding sacrament first, and then added his thoughts on the joys.

"God has given you to each other," he told them. "God said it wasn't good for man to be alone, and I for one can vouch for this being true. Mrs. Campbell has been my mainstay, just as I'm sure Emmalyne will be for you, Tavin. And there will be times when he will serve in that role for you, Emmalyne.

"Take pleasure in your time together. Find delight in the simple things of life. Enjoy the quiet of morning in each other's arms. Make time for walks together. Cherish each other, and remember that God gave you back to each other after a very long separation. Rejoice in Him for that gift."

He paused and looked past Emmalyne and Tavin to where their families sat side by side. "Don't forget your part in this marriage, either. You, as godly parents, are charged to pray for your children. Set good examples for them and encourage their hearts when life's difficulties set in."

Emmalyne glanced over her shoulder to see Gunnar nudge his grandmother and whisper something in her ear. Morna

MacLachlan smiled and nodded. Whatever it was the boy had said, he looked quite content with her approval.

Emmalyne wrapped her fingers around Tavin's. The past was now nothing more than a hazy memory—a trial that had been endured. Emmalyne tried to focus on what Reverend Campbell was saying, but it was difficult. She had never thought this day would come, and the wonder of it was almost more than she could bear. God had changed her father's heart—a heart so hardened by life's disappointments and tragedies that Emmalyne had feared it to be an impossible task. *But nothing is impossible for God or with Him,* she reminded herself. She prayed that she would always keep that thought in mind when other problems in life arose.

"And now you may kiss your bride."

Emmalyne heard those words clearly enough. She looked to Tavin, who was grinning from ear to ear. He pulled her close in a secure embrace and pressed his lips to hers. Emmalyne wasn't sure that Tavin's kisses had thrilled her this much when she was seventeen, but now they left her breathless and longing for more. She didn't want the moment to end, but she knew they could hardly remain there at the altar of the church wrapped in each other's arms, with thoughts only for each other.

Tavin seemed to understand this, too. He released her but whispered against her ear, "I still have a lot of time to make up for."

She didn't dare look at him for fear of breaking out in laughter. Instead, she turned to her family and smiled. Her mother was the first on her feet. She walked to Emmalyne, her eyes bright with tears.

"I'm so happy," she declared, hugging first Emmalyne and then Tavin.

"But ye cannae tell it," her father interjected, shaking his head. "She sat here weeping the entire time."

"They were tears of joy," Morna MacLachlan corrected as she embraced the newlywed couple. "Just as mine are." She reached up to touch Tavin's face as tenderly as if he were a small child. "I'm so pleased."

He drew her hand to his lips, where he pressed a kiss to it. "As am I."

"And donnae you look lovely," Morna said, turning back to Emmalyne. "I've ne'er seen you more beautiful."

Emmalyne felt her face grow warm. "Thank you."

"Where did you get such a beautiful gown on such short notice?" Morna asked.

"Well, she says it isn't the latest fashion with its bustle and all—'tis the one she would have been married in eleven years past," Emmalyne's mother answered for her. "She tucked it away to dream on all this time."

Tavin touched Emmalyne's shoulders. "I hope they were good dreams."

"For so long," she admitted, "I didn't even dare to dream. I'm afraid I thought my life was forever altered—that I could never reclaim what was lost. I'm so glad to have been wrong." She pressed her gloved hand across the lace overlay of the cream-colored bodice. "So glad."

Just then Gunnar wrapped himself around Emmalyne's skirt. He had been greatly amused by the bustle, and even now he couldn't help but pat at the extra bulk in the back.

"Gunnar, stop that," his grandmother ordered. "You'll get Emmy's dress dirty."

"But it looks funny, Grandma."

Emmalyne laughed. "You wouldn't think it so funny if you had to wear it. It took forever to get into this dress."

"Bet it won't take long to get out of it," Gillam said, nudging Tavin.

"Gillam!" their mother declared, looking horrified and just a bit amused.

Gillam shrugged, Tavin laughed, and to Emmalyne's surprise, so did her mother and father.

"Grandma says I can pray for you just like the preacher said." Gunnar looked to his grandmother in confirmation.

"'Tis true, Gunnar. We must always remember to pray for one another," Morna declared.

"So that's what you were talking to her about," Emmalyne said, giving the boy's head a rub. "And here I thought you might be up to mischief."

The reception was held at the nearby home of one of the quarrymen. His wife, a good friend of Morna's, had quickly offered to host the party since both the Knox and MacLachlan houses were outside of town. Tavin had told her they would leave by train not long after the wedding. It would have taken precious time to come all the way into town to marry, then return home for a wedding party only to drive back to St. Cloud's train station.

Mingling among the guests at the reception, Emmalyne found herself face-to-face with Jason Williams. She pushed aside her mild unease and smiled her greeting. "Dr. Williams, I'm so glad you could be here."

"I wouldn't have missed it," he said, returning her warm smile. "You look beautiful."

"And maybe a bit outdated, perhaps?" she said, turning slightly to show off the gown's bustled back.

"You're a nice, old-fashioned girl, so it only seems fitting," he replied. "I'm sure it was a beautiful wedding."

"Small and simple, just like we wanted," she agreed.

"And very short," Tavin declared, coming up from behind her. "Just like we wanted. Even being October, the church was quite warm." He pulled at his stiff collar for emphasis.

"I wanted to express how happy I am for the two of you," Dr. Williams said. "Finding true love is hard enough, but finding it a second time is even more unlikely."

Tavin put his arm around her waist and nodded. "That's the marvel of our story. We didn't have to find love a second time because it was always there. We just had to find each other again. I have to admit, I feared Em had forgotten all about me."

"Forget about you?" Emmalyne looked up into Tavin's face, her eyes wide. "How could I ever forget you? Every thought I had was of you. Every moment of my day was spent longing to see you again. Every breath . . . every heartbeat . . . it was all for you."

Tavin bent his head so his forehead touched hers. "I suffered the same fate."

"Well . . ." Dr. Williams said, giving a slight cough, "hopefully the suffering is behind you."

"Aye." Emmalyne nodded her agreement.

"The suffering is certainly behind her," Tavin said, laughing. He turned Emmalyne around. "Have you seen this bustle?"

Emmalyne and Tavin were on board the eastbound train and settled into their places. Having changed from her wedding gown into a fashionably styled traveling suit—a store-bought one with a matching hat from the Sears and Roebuck catalog that fit her perfectly—Emmalyne couldn't help but feel that she had stepped into a dream.

"I never thought this day would come," she said, placing her hand in Tavin's. She shook her head in awe and glanced out the window of the train as it began to move through the evening shadows.

"Neither did I," Tavin replied, leaning over to follow her gaze. "What do you see out there?"

She looked back at him and smiled. "The past. I was just bidding it good-bye."

He nodded, and she knew he understood. Suppressing a yawn, Emmalyne unpinned her hat and leaned back wearily as she smoothed down the lines of her hunter green jacket. The black piping and buttons gave it a very elegant look, and she felt like a princess.

"Have I told you how beautiful you are?" Tavin asked, slipping an arm around her shoulders.

"You have, but I never tire of hearing your compliments." This time she couldn't stop her yawn. "It seems like this day has lasted a week." She laid her head against Tavin's shoulder and sighed in contentment.

"We'll no doubt cause a scandal," he whispered.

"No doubt. Do you think anyone will be able to tell we're just married?"

"Probably," he chuckled. "Pity we couldn't get a private car."

"Yes, it is. How long is this train ride to Chicago?" she asked.

"A lot longer than I wish," he murmured.

Emmalyne smiled and closed her eyes. "You're the one who wanted to go to Chicago."

"I know," he replied with a rueful chuckle. "It wasn't my best idea of late."

She giggled. "I agree." The train picked up speed after it rounded a turn, pressing Emmalyne even closer to her husband. She opened her eyes and pulled back just enough to see Tavin's face. "But I know what was."

He touched her cheek with his hand, and the warmth of it left Emmalyne with a sense of protection and surety. "And what would that be, Mrs. MacLachlan?"

"Marrying me," she said, cocking her head with an appealing smile.

He laughed and pulled her back into his arms to whisper a single word. "Aye."

Tracie Peterson is the author of more than ninety novels, both historical and contemporary. Her avid research resonates in her stories, as seen in her bestselling HEIRS OF MONTANA and STRIKING A MATCH series. Tracie and her family make their home in Montana.

Visit Tracie's Web site at *www.traciepeterson.com.*

More Adventure and Romance from Tracie Peterson

As the lives of three women are shaped by the untamed Alaskan frontier, they find it's a land of heartbreak and healing—and romance and adventure.

SONG OF ALASKA: *Dawn's Prelude, Morning's Refrain, Twilight's Serenade*

Romance and intrigue abound on beautiful Bridal Veil Island. Amidst times of change and disaster, three couples struggle to find hope. Will their love—and lives—survive the challenges they face?

BRIDAL VEIL ISLAND: *To Have and To Hold, To Love and Cherish, To Honor and Trust*
by Tracie Peterson and Judith Miller
judithmccoymiller.com

More Adventure and Romance from Tracie Peterson

To learn more about Tracie and her books, visit traciepeterson.com.

A family promise and a lack of ladylike qualities have kept Merrill Krause single. But newcomer Rurik Jorgenson isn't intimidated by her strength or her protective brothers. Can the two of them learn to trust God—and each other—and embrace a chance at true love?

LAND OF SHINING WATER: *The Icecutter's Daughter*

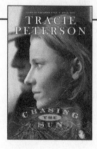

In the years following the Civil War, loyalties in the Lone Star State remain divided. Amidst the bitter prejudices and harsh landscape of the Texan plains, is there any hope that the first blush of love can survive?

LAND OF THE LONE STAR: *Chasing the Sun, Touching the Sky, Taming the Wind*